ELECTED
FOR DEATH

VALERIE WOLZIEN

FAWCETT GOLD MEDAL • NEW YORK

This book is dedicated to the staff at the Eastern Maine Medical Center in Bangor, Maine. In a crisis they were there and I thank them very much.

A Fawcett Gold Medal Book
Published by Ballantine Books
Copyright © 1996 by Valerie Wolzien

All rights reserved under International and Pan-American Copyright Conventions. Published in the United States by Ballantine Books, a division of Random House, Inc., New York, and simultaneously in Canada by Random House of Canada Limited, Toronto.

http://www.randomhouse.com

Library of Congress Catalog Card Number: 96-96499

ISBN 0-449-14959-9

Manufactured in the United States of America

First Edition: October 1996

10 9 8 7 6 5 4 3 2 1

Susan watched Jerry's departing back and sighed. Most of the crowd had departed, leaving only a few groups standing around chatting. She wondered if Jed would mind if she left, too. He hadn't said anything about wanting her to hang around. She looked down at her outfit. What a waste of time it had been to worry about what to wear. She didn't want to leave without letting Jed know, so she headed toward the rear of the building to look for him.

But the entire Hancock police department fleet was pulling up to the curb, lights flashing and sirens screaming. Uniformed men and women jumped from their vehicles and ran up to the front of the clubhouse. She noticed Brett Fortesque, the town's police chief and her friend, and jogged toward him.

"Susan Henshaw. I shouldn't be surprised to find you here. I don't suppose you've already figured out what happened to Ivan Deakin, have you?"

"Ivan Deakin? He's fine."

"Not unless you think being murdered is fine. . . ."

By Valerie Wolzien
Published by Fawcett Books:

MURDER AT THE PTA LUNCHEON
THE FORTIETH BIRTHDAY BODY
WE WISH YOU A MERRY MURDER
AN OLD FAITHFUL MURDER
ALL HALLOW'S EVIL
A STAR-SPANGLED MURDER
A GOOD YEAR FOR A CORPSE
'TIS THE SEASON TO BE MURDERED
REMODELED TO DEATH
SHORE TO DIE
ELECTED FOR DEATH

ONE

THERE ARE VARIOUS PERVERSE WAYS FOR MASOCHISTS to gain pleasure. Trying to get elected to town council in the suburbs may, perhaps, be kinkier than most, but any more obvious signs of sexual deviance were hidden by the well-groomed, conservative appearance of the seven candidates gathered around Susan Henshaw's dining-room table.

"They're really obsessive people, aren't they?" Kathleen Gordon asked Susan as voices floated out the open bay window above their heads. The two friends were enjoying a warm autumn day outside. Kathleen was helping her year-old daughter sort the brilliant-colored leaves that were falling from the trees as Susan gardened.

"That's one word for it," Susan agreed, continuing to cut back frost-damaged chrysanthemums in front of her white Colonial home.

"I suppose you'll be happy when all this is over," Kathleen suggested.

"Every day I wake up and the first thing I think of is how many more days until the election."

"How many?"

"Eleven," Susan answered. "But I keep thinking about the election results."

"You're afraid Jed might lose."

"Sure." Susan leaned back on her heels and frowned at

1

the garden. "First I worry about how badly he will feel if he loses—and then I worry about how our lives will change if he wins. Did you know that the Coopers had an extra phone line, two fax machines, and an expensive security system installed the week after Bob was elected to the school board? They even had sensors placed in their lawn and I think Margaret would have hired helicopters to circle overhead if she could have."

"But aren't people in town more involved in their children's education than in the town council?" Alex, Kathleen's son, had begun kindergarten last year, and she had been astounded by the passions seemingly innocuous topics evoked at school meetings she had attended. "No one even mentions the town council."

"Their children and their homes," Susan muttered, using more force than necessary to rip a mauve mum from the ground.

"Excuse me?" Kathleen removed a yellow Norway maple leaf from her daughter's mouth.

"Everyone cares about their children's education—and the other thing they care about passionately is their homes. That damn Landmark Commission has made everyone crazy. I can't believe Jed walked right into the middle of this one. He usually stays away from politics."

"He did talk over his decision to run with you, didn't he?" Kathleen asked, accepting the brown pin oak leaf that her daughter offered her.

"Well, sort of. He chose a warm spring day to take me to the Sign of the Dove in the city. We had kirs before dinner, a bottle of my favorite wine with the meal, then brandy afterward. . . ." She looked up at her friend with a scowl on her face. "Same old story—the man plied me with liquor and seduced me into saying yes." Then she laughed. "That's the trouble with being my age. Men still want me to say yes—just not in response to the same questions. Getting old is hard on the ego."

"Forty-seven isn't old," Kathleen protested like a good friend should.

Susan didn't answer. Kathleen might not be saying the same thing when she was Susan's age—ten years from now.

"Is there any way of knowing if Jed is going to win or lose? I suppose they don't do polls for town elections."

"I wouldn't bet on that. Hancock does everything in a big way, but this election is insane." Susan tossed the last of the dead flowers into the bushel basket she was using for trash and struggled to her feet. "I'm exhausted. Want some tea?"

"It's been a long few months for you, hasn't it?" Kathleen asked.

"Only the last month. I cannot tell you how glad I am that I spent so much of the summer in Maine. I should have stayed," she added, glancing up at the window.

"My own personal opinion is that citizens who live in contemporary homes should not be allowed to vote on this issue," an angry female voice insisted loudly from within the house.

"Listen. People who have so little taste that they would buy one of those ranch houses they built back in the fifties probably don't have the sense to get out and vote."

"My home was built in 1952 and it has been mentioned in numerous articles and books about design. It was even included in *The New York Times* listing of significant residences of the last half of the twentieth century. If you believe buying a home like mine displays less taste than buying one of the hundreds of Victorian clichés that line some streets around here, you're nuts!" These words were shouted in a deep male voice.

"They're angry again," Susan said, standing up. "You'd

never know they were running on the same ticket, would you?"

"Let's get out of here," Kathleen suggested. "I think Alice is too young to be exposed to so much anger. Might scar her delicate psyche and she'll never run for office."

"You're planning on raising the first female president of the United States?"

"Sure," Kathleen said, taking her daughter gently by the hand and leading her around the side of the house toward the brook at the end of Susan's backyard. "Who would have thought we'd be waiting until the next century for that one?"

Susan just shook her head and walked by her friend's side. "You'll never guess what I've been asked to do."

"Give the victory party on election night—Jed mentioned it to Jerry on the train on the way into the city the other day," Kathleen told her. "Are you going to do it?"

"I suppose so. I don't like turning Jed down and it has been a while since we gave a big party—but what if he loses? What sort of party will that be?"

"Good question. You won't even be able to hang up a banner saying 'Congratulations' in block letters, will you? Or serve champagne?"

"You can always serve champagne. It's just as good for drowning your sorrows as for celebrating a victory," Susan said. "Or maybe a celebration isn't exactly in order if Jed wins," she added, seeing her husband emerge from their back door. There was a scowl on his face. "He sure doesn't look happy about running. I can't imagine that he's going to enjoy spending time with these people if he's elected."

"Even Clue looks unhappy," Kathleen said as the Henshaws' large golden retriever followed Jed from the house.

"Anthony Martel is allergic to dogs, so she has to be put in the basement or the yard while he's here."

"You mean 'Call me Tony,' don't you?" **Kathleen** asked, referring to the button that Anthony Martel **had** been handing out all over town since collecting enough names to get on the ballot for mayor. A large circle, it displayed a photo of a smiling man with the words ANTHONY (CALL ME TONY) MARTEL FOR MAYOR OF HANCOCK, CONNECTICUT. PLEASE VOTE. The message was so long and the print so small that it was almost impossible to read.

"Look, he's not very original—or glib. But he's really bright and he's a hard worker. Jed says he'll make a good mayor—"

"As long as he doesn't bore all his constituents to death." Jed smiled at Kathleen as he joined them. "I thought I'd take Clue for a walk. Anyone want to come along?"

"It's time that Alice and I were heading home," Kathleen said.

"I didn't mean to run you off," Jed said immediately.

"You didn't. I have to get home and cook and clean for tomorrow afternoon." She gave Jed a pointed look.

"You and Jerry are wonderful to give a cottage party for me and my fellow candidates," he responded promptly. "And I'm sure Jerry will eventually figure out a way to apologize for the fact that he volunteered your home and your abilities as a hostess. I'll just start around the block with Clue," he added to Susan.

"Turn left at the end of the driveway and I'll walk in the other direction and meet you," she suggested. "As soon as I see Kathleen and Alice to their car."

Jed said good-bye to Kathleen and her daughter and started off.

"You're not too angry at Jerry for volunteering your services, are you?" Susan asked Kathleen as they returned to the front of the house.

"Not at all. And since my cleaning lady was there

yesterday and I'm having the whole thing catered, it hasn't been that big a deal. I was just kidding Jed. Although I must admit I was a little irritated when Jerry told me about it. I gather these cottage parties are common around election time in Hancock?"

"You're not telling me that you've lived here for six years and you've avoided going to election-time teas?"

"Yes. Have I been avoiding my civic duty?"

"You've been very lucky. You cannot imagine how boring these things are."

"Oh, thanks. I was hoping to give a really dull party," Kathleen said somewhat sarcastically.

"No one expects anything else," Susan assured her as they arrived at Kathleen's Jaguar. Kathleen fastened her daughter in the child safety seat as they continued to chat. "Most of the people who are coming are already supporters of the candidates who sponsor the party. Those people drag along willing neighbors and friends with the promise of food and a few drinks and hope that a decent repast in the middle of a fall Sunday will be a sufficient bribe to convince them to vote for the people they meet. The only problem usually is that one or two cranks try to corner the candidates and talk their ears off."

"That's not going to be the only problem unless I get home quickly," Kathleen said.

"Why? What's wrong?"

"When you said drinks, you meant alcoholic, didn't you?"

"Yes, but what . . ." A look of dawning understanding appeared on Susan's face. "You didn't think tea meant tea, did you?"

"How could I possibly have been so stupid?" Kathleen asked, slipping into her car and starting the engine. "I think I'd better get hold of the caterer—right away. Wave bye-bye to Auntie Susan, Alice," she suggested, and roared off down the drive before her child could comply with her request.

Susan chuckled and started walking around the block. She knew that Kathleen, having spent many years as a police officer before marrying a widower and moving to suburbia, was more than capable of producing the required libations tomorrow afternoon. It was time to find out why Jed had looked so serious when he left the house after his meeting.

Susan scuffed through the fragrant leaves drifting across the bluestone sidewalk that ringed the large block on which she lived, and thought about the election. Buck Logan, longtime mayor of Hancock, had left town suddenly last spring. There were those who blamed the move on his wife's drinking problem. There were those who said that his daughter, Cameo, had probably done things sober that were more likely to embarrass the family than anything her mother had done while drunk. The truth was that Buck had retired and moved himself and his family to North Carolina, but it wasn't a terribly interesting story, so the rumors persisted.

But Buck's departure had left a vacancy on the town council that, in past years, might have been difficult to fill. The real issue in town, as Susan and Kathleen had been discussing, was the schools, and every few years the battle to get elected to the Board of Education was fierce. But the mayor's job involved many hours of busywork and a commitment to making long, boring speeches at what were frequently long, boring events. Town council meetings, at which the mayor presided, rarely attracted many spectators, but to read the reports in the town's paper, they were nothing to write home about—unless you had a family fascinated by the minutiae of running a wealthy community in the last decade of the twentieth century.

Until recently, Susan reminded herself, walking around

a large pile of dog droppings in the center of the sidewalk. She forgot about the election long enough to wonder whether or not Jed had remembered to grab the pooper-scooper or a plastic bag on his way to the street.

Recently, she continued her ruminations, the office of mayor had become a hot property. Three people wanted the job and fourteen people were running for town council on one of the tickets. All because of houses like the one she was passing at the end of her block.

Susan stopped and stared at the humongous Victorian. Someone, she thought, had chosen the colors in the springtime. The muted blues and greens looked marvelous with the banks of rosy azaleas and rhododendrons that bloomed in May and June. Right now, surrounded by piles of yellow and orange leaves, it looked a little washed out. The house was large and ornate, built about thirty years before 1939—and that was the problem.

Last summer, the local Landmark Commission had decided that any homes or structures (churches, schools, even the old mill down by the river) built before 1939 were historical treasures—and were to be treated as such. Owners of these houses suddenly found that there were rules and regulations that prohibited them from what the commission referred to as "unwarranted change"—and that included remodeling and any number of things that owners felt entitled to do to their own homes.

Hancock was founded before the Revolutionary War. That many of its homes had been built before 1939 went without saying. Thus the outcry was enormous. Three separate people were running for mayor on three different platforms, all of which had to do with this issue. Town council meetings had become standing-room-only events. Letters to the editor threatened to become the fattest section of the local paper.

And Jed seemed to be taking an inordinate amount of

time getting around the block, Susan thought, smiling at the woman who was trotting down the brick pathway from the blue Victorian to the sidewalk. Susan didn't know this particular neighbor well, but she returned her wave, trying to remember the woman's first name. Something beginning with an *L*, she thought. Was it Lillian? Or Lillith? Or maybe . . .

"Susan Henshaw." Damn. Apparently her neighbor's memory was substantially better than hers. "You are just the person I wanted to talk to." The woman stopped at the end of her walkway. Her long blond hair was somewhat disheveled; she lost pins from her French twist every time she moved.

"What about?" Susan asked, hoping her cheerful demeanor would be a good cover for her poor memory.

"This election. I understand your husband . . . uh, Josh . . ."

Apparently her neighbor's memory was flawed, too, Susan thought, supplying the correct name. "Jed."

"Of course, isn't it terrible what getting old does to your memory? Jed. How could I have forgotten? Well, you must get him to vote against that absolutely absurd Landmark Commission thing."

"He's running on Anthony Martel's ticket. They want to alter the Landmark Commission's regulations," Susan began the prepared speech that she had been making in grocery stores, dry cleaners, aerobics classes, and every other place she had been for the past month. This woman, however, didn't want to hear it.

"There's absolutely no reason for this Landmark Commission to think they can tell me what to do with my own property. It was not a landmark when I bought it. It was a wreck. Now that we've remodeled every bathroom, the kitchen, and the laundry room—and have completely redecorated the interior, we can't extend the porch around the pool in the backyard because suddenly it has become a landmark. Ha! Tell Jeff I said that! Tell him ha!" Hair flying, she stormed back to her landmark.

Spying Jed walking around the corner, Susan hurried toward him. As they got closer she realized that the walk hadn't had a relaxing effect on him. Clue, in good retriever fashion, flung herself forward as if another moment without her mistress would be completely unbearable, pulling Jed along behind.

"Is something wrong?" Susan asked, when they were close enough not to have to shout. She noticed that he didn't have a pooper-scooper or bag in his hand.

"Everything is wrong. Do you have any idea how many of our neighbors have opinions about this election—opinions that they are only too willing to share with me!"

Susan was very aware of the almost universal need to badger the candidates—and the candidates' wives. "Maybe," she began in what she hoped was a soothing tone of voice.

But Jed wasn't any more interested in listening to her than she had been in listening to her neighbor. "Things have really gotten out of hand here, hon. Half of our neighbors have stopped to talk with me. And do you know what they're talking about?"

"I—"

"Apparently Bradley Chadwick was quoted in one of the local papers as saying he was afraid for his life."

"You're kidding," Susan said. "Why?"

"He claims threats have been made against him. Do you believe this? The man is running for mayor in one of the wealthiest suburbs on the eastern seaboard and he's afraid for his life! This election is insane!"

Well, she certainly couldn't argue with that.

TWO

Aᴛ ᴛʜᴇ ᴛᴇᴀ Kᴀᴛʜʟᴇᴇɴ ɢᴀᴠᴇ ᴛʜᴇ ꜰᴏʟʟᴏᴡɪɴɢ afternoon, everyone was talking about the death threats Bradley Chadwick had claimed to receive. "I can't believe it," Susan cried to Kathleen. "You give a party for Jed and the group he's running with, and everyone is talking about the man they're running against."

"Ivan Deakin?" Kathleen asked, looking anxiously at the buffet table. "Do you think I should ask the waiters to pick this up and start serving dessert?" she muttered without waiting for Susan to respond to her first question.

"Not Ivan Deakin! Bradley Chadwick—he's still claiming that he's gotten death threats. Kathleen, haven't you been listening to what people are talking about?"

"I've been too busy." Kathleen tucked her scarlet silk shirt more tightly into her slender black wool slacks. "Did you know that practically no one has had tea and the caterers are running out of gin? Who would have thought that so many people would be drinking hard liquor in the middle of Sunday afternoon? Jerry has had to go into our liquor cabinet."

"This election is enough to drive anyone to drink," Susan muttered. As a candidate's wife, she had been one of the minority that was sticking to the Earl Grey, but she was planning on a large goblet—or two—of chardonnay when she got home.

"Hmm." Kathleen was still staring at the ravaged buffet table.

"You're not listening to me, are you?" Susan asked.

"Yes, I am. You were talking about someone being driven to drink ... maybe someone like Theresa Martel?" Kathleen concluded, less sure of herself than she had been.

"Theresa Martel is drinking?" Susan asked.

"I'll say."

"That doesn't sound like Theresa," Susan muttered as Kathleen rearranged half-filled dishes on the table.

"Surprised me, too," Kathleen admitted, handing Susan a plate that held the rind of a wheel of Brie and a few broken water biscuits. "Will you take this to the kitchen for me? And will you ask whoever is in charge out there to start getting the desserts ready?"

"Sure," Susan muttered absentmindedly. She was puzzled by Kathleen's description of Theresa Martel. Until now Theresa had impressed Susan as being the perfect political wife: always neat, ineffably cheerful, and incapable of saying or doing anything controversial. The fact that Theresa was drinking so much that Kathleen commented on it came as a surprise.

Susan complied with Kathleen's request and then plunged back into the crowd to find Theresa. She had been wrong yesterday when she told Kathleen that these teas were always boring. If the noise level of the room was any indication of enthusiasm, then Kathleen's tea was in the running for the party of the year. But a more discerning listener would realize that, though the noise level was high, its tone was mainly angry.

Kathleen and Jerry lived in a large traditional home on a hilly, winding, tree-lined street in Hancock. Kathleen, not terribly domestic, had left the interior to a decorator and lived happily in someone else's dream of English country furnishings, accented with plastic creations from PlaySkool and Fisher-Price. Today the living room, dining room, den, hallway, and sunporch were filled with small groups of people who had come together in order to argue with their neighbors.

Susan squeezed through the crowd and smiled at Jed, who looked pretty uncomfortable penned in between a neighbor who believed that "the squeaky wheel gets the grease" and a man who explained his every thought with a reference to an event in his childhood. Under normal circumstances, Susan would have rescued Jed from such company, but during the first week of the campaign, he had explained to her that it was now his job to listen to people. So she left him to his fate.

Unfortunately there were a number of people, like the woman yesterday afternoon, who believed that listening to his future constituents was also the job of the candidate's wife. Susan had accommodated those people for a couple of weeks. Then she realized that she was going to have to choose between having a life and being a conduit to her husband. So she had perfected (she hoped) the art of looking like she was rushing off on an important errand no matter what she was actually doing. She frowned, knitted her brows, pursed her lips, and continued her search for Theresa Martel.

"Susan? Are you all right? You look like you have a toothache!"

"No. I'm fine. Just busy," Susan explained to a friend from the field club. "I'm looking for Theresa Martel."

"The last time I saw her, she was heading for the bathroom in the hallway—under the stairs. She didn't look very well," the other woman responded.

"Probably the seafood pâté," Susan suggested, hurrying toward the hall. Better, she thought, to trash the caterer than her husband's running mate's wife. After

Camilla Logan, no one wanted another mayor's wife with a drinking problem.

The downstairs bathroom was located under the stairway to the second floor. The door was locked, so Susan knocked politely and leaned back against the wooden wainscoting to wait for Theresa. Except for three women, resting on the stairs while trashing the elementary-school gym teacher, the hallway was empty. Susan thought about Theresa Martel as she waited.

She hadn't officially met the woman until the cocktail party the Martels had hosted the Friday of the week that Anthony—she must remember to call him Tony—had gotten his ticket together. She had seen her about town, of course. Theresa was an adjunct professor at a nearby community college. Susan wasn't sure what her field was, but she did know that Theresa was intensely involved in many organizations in town; the League of Women Voters, the PTA, and the local historical society had all benefited from her efforts. Dedicated and competent were words she had heard used in connection with Theresa. She hoped drunk wouldn't be added to the list.

Susan frowned and knocked on the door again.

"There are two other bathrooms upstairs," one of the women sitting on the steps called out.

"I know," Susan answered. "I was just looking for . . . for the person in this bathroom."

"Why? Are you going to have a baby?"

"I thought Theresa Martel was in there," Susan explained, bewildered.

"Nope. Dan Hallard is."

Susan immediately backed away from the doorway. Dan, her gynecologist as well as her next-door neighbor, had been cornering her ever since she returned from vacation. He had been buying older homes in town, having them remodeled, and then selling them at enormous profits; therefore he had very strong feelings about the historical-landmark issue—feelings that she was pretty sure she could recite in her sleep by now.

"I think I saw Theresa walking toward the kitchen," someone called out, and Susan started off toward the back of the house.

Only the caterers were in the kitchen, but one of them revealed that he had seen a tall, thin woman with a slash of white through her dark hair walking out the back door. Susan followed that path and discovered Theresa Martel throwing up into a patch of wilting Dusty Miller.

"Theresa? Are you all right?" Susan cried out, fumbling around in the pocket of her Anne Klein jacket for a clean handkerchief. "Here."

Theresa reached out to support herself on a nearby fence post. "Not really. I'm drunk for the first time since I was a sophomore in college."

"Well, everyone—" Susan started.

"Yeah, everyone gets drunk once in a while—everyone except in-control Theresa Martel," the other woman answered shortly.

"So maybe you deserve it more than other people do."

Theresa chuckled gently. "Yes. Maybe I do." She looked Susan straight in the eye. "I know Mrs. Gordon is a good friend of yours, but do you think she would mind if we abandoned this party for a few minutes and went to sit on that lovely bench I see by the bed of chrysanthemums?"

"Not at all," Susan assured her, starting toward the elegant benches that were placed near a large circle of dying flowers. The furniture was fashioned from wood that was supposed to last forever without having had even a passing acquaintance with endangered forests, rainy or dry. It was surprisingly comfortable. "Are you feeling better?"

"A little. A little better and a little embarrassed."

Susan didn't comment.

"You seem to be handling this campaign better than I am," Theresa suggested.

"I hate it so much that I abandoned my family and spent most of the summer in Maine," Susan confessed. "Actually, though, I knew I was going to hate this—just not how much. People are so involved in this election. It's like an obsession—and not the sexy thing from the perfume ads."

"I know what you mean," Theresa responded quickly. "This Landmark Commission issue is making perfectly sane people act like idiots. You would think they were talking about life and death instead of personal property! This is certainly not the way Anthony thought this election would go."

Susan noticed that Theresa did not call her husband Tony. "I know that Jed didn't even know about this Landmark Commission issue when he agreed to run."

"Neither did Anthony. Of course there's no way the same thing could be said about Bradley Chadwick." Theresa leaned back in her chair and took a deep breath.

"Are you all right?"

"Actually, throwing up helped." She grimaced. "That's truly disgusting, isn't it? I shouldn't be criticizing other people. This election isn't exactly bringing out the best in me. I thought that Anthony running for mayor would be an opportunity for me to make people aware of some of the things we can do for those less fortunate than ourselves—not just in Hancock but in the rest of the state."

Susan nodded. The alcohol was wearing off and Theresa's usual personality was returning.

"I thought I could convince people of the need to be less selfish, to look at how lucky most of the residents of Hancock are and share that wealth—and instead we have an election that seems to be entirely about property values! This is just not the type of election that Anthony and I should be involved in."

"More Bradley Chadwick's type of thing," Susan muttered.

"Definitely. I don't think Bradley has had an unselfish thought in his entire life."

"Well, what about Ivan Deakin?" Susan asked. "He didn't even enter the race until the Landmark Commission's decision was public knowledge and he isn't even campaigning on any other issues."

"True. But that's honest of him at least. Bradley claims to have been interested in . . . what does he call it? Leading Hancock into the twenty-first century? When all he's really interested in is keeping the price of housing so high that only the wealthy can afford to live in Hancock."

This was a new slant on the Landmark Commission's ruling and Susan didn't know exactly what to say. Like many wives, she didn't always listen to her husband's every word. (Although she did think that she was better than Jed was. She had even thought of having a T-shirt made with the statement I DON'T ASK RHETORICAL QUES-TIONS printed across the chest to wear when her husband was home.) But Susan had not heard this interpretation of the possibility of landmark status for some homes in town.

"I don't understand," Susan said slowly. "I thought the Landmark Commission wanted to keep houses built before 1939 from being altered in ways that were not in keeping with their history. Not that I understand exactly," she mused. "Most of those houses have been altered more than once—well, more than a dozen times, since they were built."

"That's the point," Theresa interrupted. "The point of this ballot isn't to preserve Hancock's history—if it were, the historical society would be supporting it. The point is to give immense power to Bradley Chadwick and his cronies."

"Why would Bradley Chadwick and his friends want to have anything to do with whether people in some parts of town paint their house in the original colors?" Susan said, completely confused.

"Because that's not at all what they want. They could care less about things like that. They want to keep some of the large estates up on the hill from being broken up into apartments. They're just rich people wanting to protect the value of their property." Theresa looked around the Gordons' large garden and bit her lip. "And Anthony and I are not going to let that happen."

Susan understood that a person of principle might feel that way, but why did she get the impression that the issue upsetting Theresa was more personal than she claimed?

THREE

IT WAS WONDERFUL OF YOU TO DO THIS FOR ME," JED said to Kathleen, flopping down on the couch after seeing the Martels to the Gordons' front door. "I know I owe you."

Kathleen was sprawled elegantly in one of the deep green leather-covered wing chairs that bracketed the living-room fireplace. She opened one eye and squinted across the room to where Jed and her husband sat. "You could become my on-call baby-sitter for the next twenty years," she mused. "That just might pay me back." She winked at Susan, who was sitting in the other wing chair. "Although I think it's Jerry who owes me. He was the one who volunteered us for this cottage party."

"I paid. I paid. I listened to half the cranks in town with an enthralled expression on my face." Jerry got up and headed over to the small bar set up in the corner of the room. "Would anyone like a drink? I think there's a bottle or two with a couple of inches of something left here."

"I'd love some soda," Jed answered. "With lots of ice, if there's any. I was so busy I didn't manage to get a cup of tea all afternoon. And I don't think I'd better have anything alcoholic. I have a lot to do when I get home."

"You have to work tonight?" Susan asked, adding, "I'd

love some" when Jerry waved a bottle of white wine in the air.

"The Haskell project?" Jerry asked Jed, referring to a campaign that was being developed at the advertising agency where he and Jed worked.

"That and a speech I have to write—I'm talking to the Elks Club tomorrow night."

"Can't you just repeat the speech you gave last week at—what was that group?" Susan asked, accepting the glass Jerry handed her.

"Church Men United or something like that." Susan knew that the groups were beginning to run together in Jed's mind. "And I don't think I can use the same speech. There are too many people who belong to both groups."

"Presidential candidates just have a basic speech that they repeat over and over," Kathleen commented. "There was an article about it in *The New York Times* last Friday."

"Presidential candidates campaign all over the country. I'm limited by Hancock's boundaries." Jed drained his glass and put it down on the coffee table. "I'm beginning to wonder how many ways I can think of to say that the Landmark Commission's ideas are bad for Hancock without offending anyone."

"Why?" Kathleen's question came out as a yawn.

"Why what?" Jed asked.

"Why is the Landmark Commission bad for Hancock?" Kathleen elaborated.

"Who is on this Landmark Commission, anyway?" Jerry asked, refilling Susan's glass. "I don't even remember hearing about them before last spring. Not that I'm all that involved in local politics."

"It's the commission's ideas that I object to," Jed said. "Not the commission itself."

"What *is* the commission?" Jerry repeated, resuming his seat.

"The Landmark Commission is a group that was set up just last year by the town council. They were supposed to investigate the question of whether or not the town of Hancock should declare landmark status on homes and buildings."

"This all happened after the Fromer mansion was torn down and those six hideous wooden houses put up on the property," Susan elaborated.

"I like those houses," Kathleen protested.

"They'd look wonderful in California, but there are people who think that they're out of place in Hancock," Susan said.

"In that part of Hancock," Jed added.

"Yeah. The rich part. Up there on the hill with all the historic mansions. And the mansions that are something less than historic," Jerry said. "There probably isn't an estate up there that would sell for less than two million— even these days."

"The destruction of the Fromer mansion really was a loss to the town," Jed explained. "It was built in the 1850s on land that had been settled by the Fromers in colonial times. There's reason to believe that the founding fathers of Hancock met on the property when they were setting the boundaries of the town back around the time of the Revolutionary War."

"You can tell he's running for office," Susan said to Kathleen. "Only candidates and characters in fifth-grade plays talk about our founding fathers."

"You're probably right," Jed agreed. "The idea of setting up a Landmark Commission was inspired by the loss of an irreplaceable bit of Hancock history. There was no intention of taking away the rights of home owners or prohibiting developers from making an honest living."

"But the people who live in the house behind us wanted to sell their home to a developer and then subdivide, and they weren't allowed to—and that was before there was any talk about the Landmark Commission," Kathleen protested. "And their house was built in the fifties anyway."

"They weren't allowed to subdivide that property because of the zoning rules around here. I don't think the Fromer mansion episode had anything to do with zoning," her husband explained.

"No, it didn't have anything to do with zoning. Although Hancock has pretty strict zoning laws, and that's one of the reasons given by opponents of the Landmark Commission for why things don't have to be changed. There are also sites already protected by state and federal landmark status."

"But they didn't protect the Fromer estate," Susan reminded him.

"Exactly. And in my opinion, that was a good reason to establish a Landmark Commission to set standards— so that Hancock doesn't lose another Fromer estate. Not," he added, "that I knew anything about any of this until I decided to run for town council. But the original intention seems to have been excellent."

"But you're against giving the Landmark Commission power now," Kathleen stated.

"No, I'm against this particular Landmark Commission claiming the power that they seem to think they should have."

"You are going to explain that, aren't you?" Kathleen asked. "I know you've been doing that all afternoon, but—"

"I don't mind. Especially not to a friendly audience." He glanced at his watch.

"You're sure you have time?" Susan asked anxiously.

She was sure that Jed was not getting enough sleep these days. And to think that he would start the week exhausted . . .

"I'll be fine," her husband insisted. "And my best friends should surely understand my position—or, to be more precise, the position of Anthony Martel and all of us running on his ticket.

"You see, there are three groups of people running Hancock. There are the citizens who are elected to the town council, there are the professionals who actually run things—like the police and firemen and the office staff down at the town hall—and then there are the people appointed to various boards and commissions. There's the Parks and Recreation Department, the Board of Health, the Inland Wetlands Commission, the Planning Board, the Zoning Board, the Conservation and Ecological Commission, and there are others as well."

"Sounds like it's a surprise that none of us has been on one," Susan quipped. A glance at the serious expression on Jed's face shut her up.

"Each board or commission has a different number of members and they all serve for different periods of time—these things were determined at the time the group was created," Jed continued. "The Landmark Commission is the newest commission and one of the smallest. There are only five members and a chairman. Or a chairperson, to be more exact."

"That's right," Kathleen said. "Penelope Thomas is chairperson, isn't she?"

"Yes."

"You don't like her?" Susan asked Kathleen. She noticed that Jed was looking as though he was interested in Kathleen's answer.

"I don't know her all that well, but she belongs to the garden club and comes to some meetings of the HEC.

She's very opinionated and very persuasive. I know we would never have agreed to participate in the Fall Festival if she hadn't convinced us to."

"By 'we' you mean the Hancock Ecological Committee, don't you?" Susan asked, seeing that Jed was mystified by this detour in the conversation.

"Yes."

"What's all this about the Fall Festival?" Jed asked. "I got the impression that it was a big success this year."

"That's because you were up on the dais speaking. The HEC was manning a booth in the back corner of the third tent from the entrance. You might have seen us and our display if you needed to use the Porta Pottis."

"But that wouldn't have been the fault of Penelope Thomas. The Fall Festival Committee must have put you there," her husband protested.

"They did. They put us there because we signed up late. And we signed up late because we let Penelope Thomas talk us into changing our minds about participating in the festival. She's the type of person who makes other people do things."

"HEC usually doesn't have a booth?" Susan asked.

"No. We do so much in the spring and summer and then we have our annual holiday wreath and tree sale. There really isn't much reason to get everyone together and plan something for the Fall Festival. Besides, our volunteers are so busy mulching and putting the gardens that we're responsible for in the parks to bed. And with the annual bulb planting—"

"We get the idea," Kathleen's husband stopped her.

"But why did the group let Penelope talk them into participating in the Fall Festival?" Susan asked.

"After all, you said she was persuasive, but it's not as though you all don't have perfectly good minds of your own," Jerry suggested.

"You don't know Penelope Thomas," Jed answered for Kathleen. "The woman could talk anyone into anything. She's a verbal bulldozer."

"Absolutely," Kathleen agreed, nodding vigorously.

"And that's why the Landmark Commission, the way it is now, is dangerous to Hancock," Jed added.

"You think that's an explanation?" Jerry asked.

"No, it's just that when I start explaining, it all sounds so petty."

"We know you," Susan said gently. "We know you're not petty. We know that you . . . have the best interests of Hancock at heart." She had better watch herself: she had almost said that he *thought* he had the best interests of Hancock at heart.

"Well then. As I was saying, the Landmark Commission was created to protect the houses and sites in town that have historical significance."

" 'Sites'?" Kathleen repeated.

"Well, there's the chapel at the hospital—it was an original ward and was actually used during the Civil War. And the old library—the building that is now being used as the headquarters of the historical society—it was the first Carnegie library in the state. Then there's the mill. That mill was there in the Revolutionary War and may have actually been used to hide local militiamen from the British."

"But the mill is part of a condo project down by the river. And everything else you're talking about has already been changed from its original form," Kathleen protested. "What is there to preserve? Or is the Landmark Commission demanding that these things be returned to their historical state? And what about 1939? If one other person had mentioned 1939 to me this afternoon, I think I would have screamed."

"Two separate issues," Jed insisted cryptically. "The

Landmark Commission exists because there was—and is—a perceived need to protect historical buildings. The group that now makes up the commission, however, decided to broaden their scope. Hancock was founded in 1725, but the official incorporation and acceptance of the boundaries as they are now happened in 1939. So the Landmark Commission decided that every building built before 1939 needed to be protected from 'unwarranted remodeling, reconstruction, and development.' Those are their words, not mine."

"And the group that decides what is or is not unwarranted is the Landmark Commission," Susan added.

"Wow. That sure gives them a lot of power," Jerry said.

"It's absurd," Susan said. "Why should things be preserved that aren't even a hundred years old? And why should the decisions to preserve them be left up to five people who aren't professional preservationists? Why—?"

"Why, in fact, would anyone want that power?" Jed interrupted his wife to ask gently. "That, I think, is the question."

"Yes. Why?" Jerry repeated the question.

"Money?" Susan suggested.

"Where is there money to be made in not doing something?" Jed asked.

"Then it doesn't make sense," Susan said.

"It doesn't to me. And it doesn't make sense to Anth—Tony Martel, and that's one of the reasons that I'm glad to be running on his ticket. The members of the Landmark Commission are only appointed to one-year terms. The next mayor and town council will be appointing new people and those people will be overseeing the adoption of the commission's final rulings on this matter. If we're elected, we'll have enough votes on the council to make sure that the Landmark Commission doesn't exceed its original mandate."

"But if Bradley Chadwick is elected—" Susan began.

"If Chadwick is elected, you'll be glad our house was built in the forties," her husband said. "And that a group of people you hardly know don't have a say over what you do with your own home."

"And what about Ivan Deakin?" Jerry asked. "He's running as a third-party candidate. According to the information he's been flooding our mailbox with for the last few weeks, he is convinced that both Martel and Chadwick are wrong about this issue. He apparently has some sort of idea about the Landmark Commission that is going to make everyone in town sit up and notice."

"And vote for him," Kathleen added.

"But he isn't even saying what it is," Susan explained. "All his literature says is that he will make an announcement at the Hancock Women's Club on Tuesday night. Who is going to show up for something like that?"

"Probably half the town," Jed answered, a rueful expression on his face.

FOUR

THE NEXT TWENTY-FOUR HOURS WERE TYPICAL OF Susan's life these days. By the time her son had dashed out the door, as perpetually late during his last year of high school as he had been during his first month of kindergarten, and she had poured herself a cup of coffee, the phone had begun to ring. Four phone calls later she had finished the pot (six cups), filled the dishwasher, wiped down all the counters, glanced through the local paper, *The New York Times*, and last week's *New Yorker*, and was thinking about the pile of laundry waiting for her in the basement. The phone rang again and she quickly reached out and punched a button on the answering machine. True, she didn't have to really listen to the callers these days, but it did get boring alternating "uh-huh" with "I'm sure Jed will be interested to hear what you think"—and anything else was risky. Arguing didn't win votes.

But she had to get some laundry done. The jeans Chad was wearing this morning were his favorites—full of holes. And she was going to be looking worse than her son if she didn't get a load or two into the washer. Also, there was dry cleaning to pick up ... grocery shopping ... Clue was almost out of food. ... She had an appointment to get her hair trimmed at noon. ... And everything would take twice as long as usual since, these days, she did many of her errands in a town almost fifteen miles away.

Okay, it was the coward's way out, she admitted it. Not to everyone, mind you, but she had spoken about it to Clue more than once. And being a golden retriever, Clue's sweet face was fixed permanently in an expression of love and understanding. Although Susan knew perfectly well that the dog's only real interest was food. She looked down at the animal, napping near the cupboard that contained her dog biscuits, and decided the laundry could wait.

"Want to go for a ride, Clue?"

"Ride" was the animal's fourth favorite word (after *dinner*, *cookie*, and *walk*) so Susan was sure of the response she'd get. Clue leaped up, pranced around, and generally made a nuisance of herself until Susan had confined her in the back of the Cherokee. Then the dog turned around a few times, lay down, and returned to her nap. Susan shrugged and backed out of the driveway. Four blocks from her house she stopped at a light and was signaled by a neighbor with strong views on the Landmark Commission. Susan feigned deafness and pressed on the accelerator rather harder than usual. The Jeep screeched off.

Susan's errands took even longer than she had expected and she was late arriving at the beauty parlor. "I'm really sorry," she began to say to the owner.

"Not to worry. We're backed up today. Everyone seems to be late. Go on back to Nadine's room. It'll be just a moment."

Susan grabbed last month's *Vogue* off the coffee table and headed down the narrow hallway to the familiar place where she got her hair done. Not actually a room, it was a booth with walls that didn't go all the way up to the ceiling. She sat down, glanced in the mirror, and once again considered the question of whether to cover the gray. A barely adolescent model stared off the cover of the magazine in her lap, an expression of unconcealed scorn on her face. Susan was fairly sure she knew what this particular young woman would have told her; she opened the magazine.

By the time Nadine arrived, she had decided to buy a new dress for the election-night party—a new dress in a color that would contrast nicely with her freshly dyed hair. "What do you think about a shade of red?" she asked Nadine after greeting her.

"Maybe a dark reddish ..." Nadine considered the question that the two of them had been discussing for the past couple of years as though it was new to her. "It would look nice. And you'd look special for the election. Not as splashy as that Mrs. Chadwick."

"You cut Cassandra Chadwick's hair?" Susan didn't admire the Chadwicks' politics, but she sure did envy Cassandra's good looks. Tall, thin, blond, with a classic profile and flawless skin ... Susan always felt frumpy standing beside her.

Nadine gave a ladylike snort. "You think she would trust someone who doesn't have a place on Madison Avenue? She gets her hair done in the city. We're only good enough to trim the girls' hair until they hit puberty. We're still allowed to cut Brittany's hair."

"She's the youngest?"

"Yup. Blake's the oldest, then comes Brooke, and then Brittany. Their son, Bradley Junior, is actually the oldest, of course."

"And they all have their mother's beautiful hair, don't they?" Susan could compete here; both Chad and Chrissy were exceptionally good-looking. The Chadwick youngsters may have inherited great hair, but their profiles were about as far from classic as it was possible to get and two of the girls had ears that stuck out.

"Yeah. They don't get their parents' faces until they're sixteen."

"Excuse me?"

"They don't get their parents' faces until they're sixteen."

"As they mature?"

"As they get old enough for their father to operate on them. You know, nose jobs, chin tucks. I don't suppose he would perform breast implants on them, but—"

"You're talking about plastic surgery," Susan said, finally catching on.

"You didn't know that Bradley Chadwick was a plastic surgeon?"

"I knew he was a doctor. . . . But surely he wouldn't operate on his own children!"

"Why not? He operated on his wife, didn't he?" Nadine always had the last word. Susan's head was tipped back into a deep sink and she felt a rush of warm water on her brow. Nadine chattered on, but she had already given Susan a lot to think about.

One of life's small mysteries had been solved for her: she had always wondered how two such attractive people had created four homely children. She had even speculated on the possibility of adoption. Now that she knew the answer, her speculating took a personal turn. Just what would plastic surgery do for her? After all, if she was going to have her hair dyed . . .

"So what color have you decided on?" Nadine asked, flipping off the water and deftly swaddling her hair in a large pink towel.

"Well, maybe not this time," Susan began, squinting into the mirror. "You can't see the gray all that well yet."

"Okeydokey." Nadine flipped the towel off and began

to comb out Susan's medium-brown hair. There was a knowing smile on her face.

"Why don't we cut off an inch—or two," Susan suggested courageously.

"Well, it didn't help Hillary Clinton, but we can give it a shot."

The next hour was spent creating a "new look." By the time she left the salon, Susan was relaxed and convinced that her new bob was modern and attractive. Glancing in the window of the bakery next door to the beauty parlor, she decided she looked at least five years younger.

Despite the transformation, Clue recognized her when she returned to the Jeep. As did three women walking down the street.

"Susan Henshaw, just the person I was hoping to see. I've been leaving messages on your answering machine, but it must not be working or something," one of the three called out so loudly that Susan couldn't possibly pretend not to hear.

"Chad sometimes doesn't give us the messages," Susan said. It was true, but not in this case. She felt guilty about casting aspersions on her son's sense of responsibility, but these days it was anything to get votes. Besides, she paid for it. The next hour was spent listening to the women with an interested expression on her face. If Clue hadn't started barking at a chocolate Lab walking down the street and given Susan an excuse to leave, she might have been on that street corner until election day.

"And no one even noticed my new hairdo," Susan commented, glancing at Clue in the rearview mirror. Clue turned around a few times and resumed her nap. Susan pressed on the accelerator. She was driving to the Martels' house to help address envelopes for the last preelection mailing. Someone had decided that the personal touch was needed and that this particular mailing shouldn't be handled by computer. Besides, Susan thought, a hand-written address made it a little more likely that the envelope would actually be opened. She dropped Clue off at home and sped to her destination.

Susan pulled into the Martels' driveway and wondered where everyone else was. Her watch indicated she was only an hour late. Maybe they were already finished. The thought disappointed her. Not that she had wanted to spend the afternoon doing drudge work, but she had hoped to get to know Theresa a bit better—as well as get a peek at the Martel home. Well, maybe she would be offered a cup of tea or something, she thought, knocking on the door of the huge home. From a distance the house had a certain elegance, white pillars holding up the large front porch. Many-paned double-hung windows lined the porch and three bay windows jutted out from the second floor. Close up, it became apparent that the windows needed washing and the paint was peeling. The ornate wooden railing around the porch hid piles of papers and plastic garbage bags; from the dust on them, it was clear that they had been sitting there for quite a while.

The door opened and Theresa Martel appeared. She looked, at two in the afternoon, like she was still hungover. Susan put a perky smile on her face. "Am I too late?"

Theresa crinkled her lips into an imitation smile. "I gather you think we're finished for the day? That a horde of enthusiastic supporters has come, written their little hearts out, and gone home to continue to spread the word to vote for Anthony Martel and his ticket?"

"But no one's here," Susan protested, feeling like an idiot when she realized what must have happened. "No one showed up."

"Bingo."

Susan sighed. "Well, let's get going," she said.

"Come on in. I had everything spread out in the dining room. I was expecting a crowd, after all," Theresa added ruefully.

Susan glanced from side to side as she was led through the large square entryway. The inside of the house was messier than the exterior. Towers of newspapers were toppling onto the floor and the stairs leading to the second floor were cluttered with things ready to be carried up, including a half-dozen library books and more than a few piles of laundry, folded and unfolded. Theresa didn't apologize for the mess. Susan wondered if this was because she was so accustomed to her house looking like this.

It was a long afternoon. Susan and Theresa worked without a break. Susan would have been happy to chat, but Theresa had gently explained that she couldn't work and talk at the same time, so instead of launching a monologue, Susan shut up and wrote. And wrote. And wrote. At the end of two hours, her hand was cramped, her back ached, and she could feel a headache gathering behind her eyeballs. "I have to get home and start dinner for my son. I think I'll take the rest of these with me and finish them tonight." It wasn't actually true. Chad was going to be at a soccer game until heaven knew when and then he'd probably stop and get a pizza, but why have children if you can't use them for an excuse—twice in one afternoon?

"Fine." It was the first word Theresa had said in over an hour.

"Would you mind if I used the bathroom before I left?"

"The one on this floor isn't working properly—the tank leaks. Try the one at the top of the stairs. First door on your left."

Susan maneuvered around the messy piles and mounted

the stairs. The door to the bathroom was ajar, revealing that the neglect extended into the personal areas of the house. Inadequate shelving was jammed with bottles and jars, some uncapped, some looking as though they had been around years beyond their shelf life. Susan shut the door firmly behind her, realizing the latch was broken. The place was so dirty that normally she would have hurried to finish, but a stack of books on the floor attracted her attention.

She left the room fifteen minutes later and confronted Theresa, standing outside the door with a worried expression on her face.

"You were in there a long time. I . . . wondered if you were feeling well . . . if you needed something," Theresa explained.

"Just a little indigestion," Susan lied. "Probably something I ate yesterday."

"Some of the food at the cottage party *was* very rich," Theresa agreed. Susan got the impression that her hostess was trying to peer over her shoulder into the room.

"Yes. Kathleen probably should have hired a different caterer," Susan agreed, wondering if she was going to end up blaming everyone she knew for something they had or hadn't done before election day came around. Since she was anxious to get home, she refused Theresa's surprising offer of refreshments, grabbed her coat and bag of envelopes, and headed for the door.

"I'll mail these when I finish," she added, smiling a little insincerely. The expression remained on her face until she had left the driveway and was sure Theresa could see only the back of her head. Then it was replaced by one of puzzlement. Why, for heaven's sake, was there a large pile of books on poison on the floor next to the toilet in the Martels' bathroom?

FIVE

SUSAN KNEW IT WAS FRIVOLOUS OF HER, BUT SHE forgot all about the unusual reading material in the Martels' bathroom while worrying about what to wear to the announcement Ivan Deakin was scheduled to make the evening of the next day. She was so frazzled about her decision that she had called Kathleen while she was cooking dinner.

The announcement was to take place at the Hancock Women's Club clubhouse, a large Tudor building a few blocks from the municipal offices downtown. While not a member, Susan had been there many times, as it was a popular spot to hold receptions. Since the kind of reception dictated the attire and this event was unique in her experience, Susan was in a quandary about what to wear.

"But everyone is going to be there to see Ivan Deakin," Kathleen told her.

"I know, but I want to present the right image—to help Jed. If it were up to me I wouldn't go, but Jed insisted. Not only did every single one of the candidates in both parties receive a personal invitation to attend, but we both got separate notes from Ivan." She peered into the pot of chili that she was stirring. Maybe a bit more chili powder . . . ?

"So what are you so concerned about?"

"Feeling like a fool. I don't mind going. I just wish I

could sit with Jed." She reached for the chili powder on a nearby countertop.

"Why can't you?"

"Jed is going to be there with Tony Martel—in hiding."

"Where, for heaven's sake? Behind the curtains?"

"No. Upstairs." Susan chuckled as she added the spice. "You've been to the Women's Club, haven't you?"

"That's where the Guttmans held their fiftieth anniversary party, wasn't it?"

"Right. Did you happen to notice the large glassed-in balconies on either side of the reception room?"

"Is that the room with the fireplace or the one with the stage?"

"The one with the fireplace."

"I don't think so."

"There's an outside entrance and he and the other candidates are going to enter that way and listen together."

"Isn't that sort of strange?"

"Very. But no one asked my opinion. The official line is that this is Ivan Deakin's night and their presence would be a distraction." Susan's voice was muffled as she had just burned her tongue on a steaming kidney bean. "They were scheduled to meet with a group from the Board of Education. But that was canceled right after Ivan announced this date. I think Jed was a little upset until Ivan Deakin suggested they could respond to his speech on TV—"

"Susan! Jed is going to be on TV! Will you be at his side? No wonder you're so worried about what to wear."

"It's going to be on Channel 46."

Kathleen paused before answering. "I don't think we get that on our TV. . . ."

"You do. Everyone does. It's a public-access channel. The cable companies are required to carry it. But no one watches. So should I wear the Anne Klein outfit or—"

8 Valerie Wolzien

"Yes. The Anne Klein. Susan, I have to run. One of the kids is crying." Kathleen hung up without waiting for an answer.

Susan, knowing that most tears at five o'clock in the afternoon were the result of hunger and fatigue rather than injury, tossed a little more chili powder in the pot, turned down the heat on her stove, and headed upstairs to search through her closet.

Chad was going to be home late, due to an out-of-town soccer game. Jed, busy at work, was going to go straight to the Women's Club. So she had a lot of time to spare. After all, how long could it take to pick out clothing?

Over an hour and about a thousand calories later, she was sitting in the kitchen dressed in the outfit she had discussed with Kathleen. She didn't have to leave for a few minutes, so she grabbed the Mint Milano bag (being a firm believer in finishing what she had started) and went to Jed's study to watch the network news. She was, she realized, flopping down on the couch and picking up the remote, becoming very narrow. There was a presidential election taking place and here she was merely concerned about what was happening in her neighborhood. She flicked through the channels, briefly considering the women who were campaigning to be first lady. After these last few months, she felt only empathy for them.

Fifteen minutes in front of the television convinced her that she was hopelessly behind in current events. However, she reminded herself on the way to the Women's Club, it was unlikely that anyone would mention anything other than the Landmark Commission to her until after the election.

As Jed had predicted, the event was extremely popular. The parking lot was full and she had to circle a couple of blocks to find a space on the street. The evening was becoming chilly and Susan pulled her jacket closer to her neck as she joined the crowd hurrying toward the building. She recognized many of her friends and neighbors, and a few of them, spying her, made jokes about her interest in Ivan Deakin's speech. She smiled, waved, and hurried on. She wanted to be sure to get a seat in the back of the room so she could leave as soon as the speech ended.

As she was walking through the door, she realized she was going to be lucky to get any seat at all. After a small foyer, one entered a large meeting room dominated by a gigantic stone fireplace on the far wall. A podium stood before the fireplace, facing hundreds of tiny gold chairs that had been set up in rows, filling the room. Susan spied an empty seat and she hurried toward it.

The women on either side of her smiled politely and then ignored her. Susan pulled her coat off, draped it over the back of her chair, and looked around. The room was mobbed. She frowned, realizing that these people were here hoping Ivan Deakin was offering a sane solution to the Landmark Commission muddle—something that would make everyone on every side of the issue happy. If he did so, both Anthony Martel and Bradley Chadwick would lose. On the other hand, if Jed lost maybe they could go on a second honeymoon in Bermuda for a week or so. It was a nice idea and she was so involved in thoughts of rum punch and moonlight walks on the beach that she didn't at first realize Ivan Deakin had appeared at the podium.

"Good evening, ladies and gentlemen . . ."

An earsplitting screech filled the air, causing many in the audience to cover their ears. Ivan stepped back from the podium as though denying any responsibility for the sound. Three women, who Susan assumed were the club members in charge of the evening, dashed to the podium, waving their arms and calling to someone high above their heads. Susan wondered if the public-address system was in the balcony with her husband. She swiveled around and peered upward but couldn't see anyone.

As she had explained to Kathleen, the room was flanked on either side by room-size balconies. Underneath the balcony on the right were two rest rooms and a large kitchen. The balcony on the left hung over open space, presently filled with spectators. Susan had been told that balcony was the caretaker's studio apartment. At the back of the room, over the foyer was a glassed-in passage between the two spaces. (Both balconies were glass above waist level.) The caretaker had his curtains pulled. The other side, although lit, was darker than the main room and she could barely make out a few shadowy shapes up there. But the sound system appeared to be fixed and Ivan Deakin was beginning his speech again.

"Good evening, ladies and gentlemen . . ."

This time the loud noise was accompanied by a brilliant flash and Ivan Deakin disappeared behind the podium, crouching on the floor. The thought occurred to Susan that he had been killed, but if so, his resurrection was immediate. Leaping to his feet, Ivan grabbed the microphone and began all over again.

Only differently. "Ladies and gentlemen. They are trying to stop me from giving my speech. But they won't. I am going to explain to you exactly what I think should be done about the Landmark Commission and why you should vote for me."

And then the lights went out. Two or three people screamed, but almost immediately the room was reilluminated. Taking a deep breath, Ivan Deakin started again. "La—"

"I'm sorry." A very large woman in a mannish-looking navy suit commandeered the podium. "The Women's Club has been informed by officials in the fire department that the room must be cleared. This is an unsafe situation. We apologize to Mr. Deakin for the electrical problems that make it necessary to call off this event. I'd like to ask everyone to move to the center aisle and leave the building immediately. Thank you."

A wave of disappointment swept through the room, but it was a tribute to the woman's personality that the room was cleared in moments. Susan, wanting to find her husband, hung behind, hoping he would appear, but when no such thing happened, she glanced up at the podium and started after the crowd. She had been wondering about the electrical problems until she saw the look on Ivan Deakin's face. Then she began to wonder why a man who had just had his big moment interrupted by technical problems would be smiling happily.

"Sue! Susan!" She recognized her husband's voice as soon as she left the building.

"Jed?" She peered into the crowd milling around on the sidewalk and the leaf-covered lawn.

"Over here!"

Susan ran toward the voice, tripped over a tree root, and almost fell into her husband's arms.

"Hey, hon. Are you okay?" He propped her up.

"Yes, I'm—"

"What did you think about that mess just now?" he asked before she could assure him of her health. "I don't think it's going to help Ivan get elected." Susan could see his frown in the lights from the building. "I just wish we knew who he was going to be pulling votes from."

"Maybe no one," she suggested, annoyed. Jed wasn't usually this self-centered. In her humble opinion, this election wasn't good for him. And what did that mean if he actually won? she asked herself.

But the Martels had joined them. "Jed, we have to get to the back of the building," Anthony announced. "The

TV crew is still set up and they want to talk with opposition candidates right away! It's a wonderful opportunity. Have you seen—oh, there he is!" And Anthony was off.

"I'd better get going," Jed muttered, following him without waiting for his wife's response. She smiled, noticing that he was rubbing his chin to see if he needed a shave.

"Guess there's no reason for us to hang around anymore." Susan turned and discovered that Theresa Martel had joined her. "I can give you a ride home if you and Jed came together," Theresa offered.

"Jed came here straight from the city. I have my own car, but maybe we could go someplace for a cup of coffee?" Susan suggested, trying to be friendly.

"I don't have time for things like that. But thank you." Apparently Theresa was completely disinterested in small talk. "I suppose we'll be seeing each other again soon."

"Probably," Susan admitted as Theresa turned and walked away.

Jerry Gordon appeared at her side. "Hi! Where's your husband? I was going to see if he needed a ride home, but if you're here, then—"

"The Mercedes is here, too," Susan said. "But thanks. Did Kathleen come with you?"

"No. She said you told her the speech was going to be on TV, so she decided to stay home and watch—if the kids leave her alone. Otherwise she'll tape it."

"I hadn't even thought of that. I hope she keeps the tape running even though Ivan's speech was canceled. Jed just took off to be interviewed. Originally the candidates were going to respond to the speech. I guess now they're just going to have a chance to repeat their campaign promises."

"Maybe I can catch him if I rush home," Jerry said, buttoning his top coat.

"Good idea. Tell Kath I'll call her in the morning and she can give me a complete report on the interview," Susan said. She watched Jerry's departing back and sighed. Most of the crowd had departed, leaving only a few groups standing around chatting. She wondered if Jed would mind if she left, too. He hadn't said anything about wanting her to hang around. She looked down at her outfit. What a waste of time it had been to worry about what to wear. She didn't want to leave without letting Jed know, so she headed toward the rear of the building to look for him.

But the entire Hancock Police Department fleet was pulling up to the curb, lights flashing and sirens screaming. The hospital had contributed an ambulance and an emergency response van to the bedlam. Uniformed men and women jumped from their vehicles and ran up to the front door of the clubhouse. Susan assumed they had been called earlier by the fire department and no one had headed them off when the speech was canceled. She noticed Brett Fortesque, the town's police chief and her friend, and jogged toward him.

"Brett! Everyone is gone. The Women's Club canceled the event."

"Susan Henshaw. I shouldn't be surprised to find you here. I don't suppose you've already figured out what happened to Ivan Deakin, have you?"

"Ivan Deakin? He's fine."

"Not unless you think being murdered is fine."

SIX

IVAN DEAKIN HAD BEEN POISONED. IT WAS AS OBVIOUS to Susan now as it had been to the women standing nearby when he picked up his water glass, took a large gulp, and then, gagging and choking, dropped to the floor. He was dead within minutes. Susan, who had followed Brett back into the Women's Club, took one look at Ivan's scarlet face and frothy mouth and moved away.

The rows of gilt chairs were in disarray due to the audience's hasty exodus. Susan found one at the back of the room and sat down to await Jed. She knew he would see all the cars with flashing lights and come inside to investigate.

The body was still on the floor behind the podium, a few rescue workers gathered around it. Brett, she noticed, had moved over to one side of the room and was dialing his cellular phone, a grim expression on his face. Susan watched for a few moments before her attention was drawn to noises coming from outside the building. Had the audience heard about the murder and returned? Were there even more police cars arriving? There were certainly lights. . . . Susan got up to peer out the windows when the front doors slammed open and a young man entered the room. He was, Susan thought, quite a sight.

Tall, thin, his thick brown hair desperately in need of a barber . . . Susan guessed he was in his early twenties. He wore jeans, boots, a plaid flannel shirt, and a down vest and he carried a video camera and two bright lights in one hand. In the other he held a sponge-covered microphone. A bulky belt with large pockets was draped around his waist. Eyes flashing behind thick horn-rim glasses, he stomped down the main aisle toward the front of the room.

Brett, who had returned to the body and had knelt on the floor, got up quickly and addressed the intruder. "No one is saying anything to the press at this time, Tom."

"So why don't I just look around and see what conclusions I can draw on my own," the younger man replied, a personable smile cutting across his pale face.

"Why don't you just wait right there and I'll talk to you myself as soon as I have a free moment," Brett countered.

"You're offering us an exclusive?" the young man asked quickly.

"You're the only journalist in sight," Brett answered, turning back to his task.

At that moment the young man seemed to notice Susan for the first time. He smiled at her and, after glancing back at the podium, made his way to her side. "Interesting, isn't it?" he asked so quietly that she could hardly make out his words.

"I don't know what you mean," she said, thinking that interesting was one of the last words she would use to describe a murder.

"Well, no matter how personal a tragedy it is, a political assassination is always big news."

"A what?" Calling Ivan Deakin's death a political assassination was a completely new idea to her.

"What exactly would you call it when a man is killed for his political beliefs?" He looped his leg over the back of a chair and plopped down, apparently oblivious to the chair's creaking protest.

"Why do you think that's why he was killed? People are killed for all sort of reasons, personal as well as professional."

He frowned, crinkling up his light blue eyes, and Susan realized that he was, like a messy and overenthusiastic puppy, terribly appealing. "Of course, that's true," he admitted slowly. "Was there anything in his personal life that would cause someone to want to kill him? His bio said he was divorced."

"His bio?"

"There was a brief bio included in his press packet."

"What else did it say?" Susan asked. She didn't think Jed had made up a biography to give to the press.

"Just the normal stuff. Schools attended, professional experience, volunteer positions. You know the type of thing."

"Sure." Susan paused. "So you're a member of the press." Who else, after all, would be dragging all this equipment around?

"Want to see my press pass?" he asked proudly. "I'll probably have to get it out to show the police." He was fumbling around, trying to remove his wallet from a pocket underneath his well-weighted belt.

Susan sensed that he wanted to show it to her, so she carefully examined the piece of paper he held out.

"It's not the best picture in the world," he began.

Susan, who had noticed that he wore the same clothing in the photograph as he was wearing now, was checking out the date. The identification had been issued just a few weeks ago. "It's almost new," she said.

"I just graduated from college in August," the young man answered. "Not that this is my first job. I worked while I was going to school—at the college TV station— and I did some freelance work. And I held a summer internship at a public station in Boston, too."

"You're very well qualified," Susan said. "And it's wonderful that you got a job right out of college. These days—"

"It's in the contacts you make along the way. One thing leads to another," he said earnestly, his hair falling into his eyes as he leaned toward her. "Like I had this internship, and one of the men on the staff there knew about this station, so, when I began looking for work, I called him. Three months later I had moved to Hancock and had this job." He took back his card and held out his hand. "I'm Tom Davidson, by the way."

"Susan Henshaw." She shook hands, noticing that he was employed by the public-access channel.

"How do you do? Hey, you're the woman who is always involved in murders here in town, aren't you?" he asked, obviously excited by her name.

"Yes. But if you don't come from around here, how do you know about me?" She felt a little thrill, wondering if her fame had spread all the way to Boston.

"I've read the back issues of the *Hancock Herald* for the last ten years since I've been working."

Since he had only been working for a few weeks, Susan was impressed.

"So how did you know about this before I did?" Tom Davidson asked.

"I was in the audience tonight. And I was waiting around afterward for my husband when all the police cars showed up—"

"Your husband wasn't with you? Say, is he the Jed Henshaw who is running on Tony Martel's ticket?"

Susan just nodded.

"Son of a gun. So you have a personal connection to this murder."

"Well, not really," Susan insisted.

"But you'd admit that it's more than likely that politics

is involved, wouldn't you?" He was fumbling around with his belt as he spoke.

"What are you doing?"

"I just want to make sure my tape recorder is going. And you wouldn't mind if I turned on the video camera, would you?"

"But I would. I don't have anything to say about this," Susan insisted.

"She certainly does not."

Relieved to hear her husband's familiar voice, Susan smiled. "Jed. I was waiting for you," she explained, turning around.

"What's going on? Why are all the police cars out front? It looks like someone died in here." He looked closely at his wife. "Susan? What happened?"

"Ivan Deakin died," she said quietly.

"Would you like to make a statement, sir?" Tom offered the microphone that he held in his hand. "It will only take me a minute to change the battery on the camera. This will affect the election and—"

"I certainly do not want to make a statement. And I think right now we should be considering the personal loss involved when someone dies unexpectedly rather than any political question—"

"He was murdered, Jed." Susan didn't want to tell him like this, but she was sure he should know immediately.

"Murdered? How? How do you know?" He glanced at the podium, obviously stunned by her words.

"He was poisoned. I saw him," she added, nodding.

"You saw him die?" Tom Davidson jumped in.

"No, but—" Susan began.

"Would you mind leaving my wife alone?" Jed said, suddenly angry. "She's just had a shock. She shouldn't be asked any questions right now. Especially not by the press."

"Fine. Is Tony Martel still around?" Tom stood up.

"I don't think so," Jed answered. "He left right after you interviewed us. I imagine he was planning on going home. Which is what we should be doing," he added to his wife. "Chad will be home and I want to talk with him about the college recommendations he needs to get."

Susan suspected this was an excuse to leave, but it sounded like a good one, so she stood up. She could give Brett a call tomorrow and he would tell her about Ivan's murder. Or at least she could ask. "It was very nice talking with you," she said to Tom Davidson. She might not be running for first lady, but she knew it was smart to be nice to the press—no matter how lowly the office or small the newspaper. "Have a good evening and good luck with your new job."

"Good night," the young man had just enough time to say before Jed tugged her through the door.

"Why are we in such a rush? I thought we agreed to let Chad handle these things by himself," she said, trotting by her husband's side into the dark.

"That was just an excuse to get out of there. I have to call Anthony. He should hear about this from me and not some young reporter." He strode off in the opposite direction of Susan's car.

"Where are you going?" she called out.

"To make a call on the car phone. You don't need me to walk you to your Cherokee, do you?"

"Of course not," Susan said rather sarcastically, watching her husband's departing back. "Especially since I might as well hang around here if I'm not needed at home."

And she turned and walked back into the Women's Club.

Tom was obviously not a young man who let the grass grow under his feet. He was back at the podium talking earnestly to Brett. Susan noticed Brett was looking worried. Since everyone was occupied, she decided to do a little investigating on her own. Somewhere around here there was a way to get up to the balcony. . . .

There was, she discovered, a stairway on the far right of the foyer. She climbed up quickly and found herself in a small vestibule. Directly in front of her was a large room furnished with a massive mahogany refectory table and a couple of dozen leather and mahogany chairs. A faded watercolor of the building she was in hung on the wall opposite her. On either side of the painting hung commemorative plaques with tiny brass plates on their surfaces. A long sideboard stood along one wall and the other was glass from the waist up. Susan walked over and looked down upon the scene below. More people were arriving, trying to walk to the podium without being accosted by Tom Davidson on the way.

Susan continued to explore. She left the room where Jed had listened to the speech—through, she assumed, the square speakers hanging in the corners—and reentered the vestibule. A door led to the long hallway that crossed the back of the building over the vestibule. Like the room she had just left, it was glass from the waist up. She walked across quickly, wondering how she would explain her presence if she ran into the caretaker toward whose apartment she assumed she was heading. There was a door at the end of the hallway. A brass plaque, larger than those on the wall of the room she had just left, explained that the apartment belonged to the caretaker of the Hancock Women's Club. It suggested that she knock if his presence was required. She didn't.

She returned to the hallway and headed for the stairs. She was halfway down when she heard someone call out, "Who's there?"

Assuming the question was directed at her, she ran

down quickly and stuck her head back into the room. "It's me. I—" She realized where she was standing. "I was just using the ladies' room."

She wondered if her lie had been so obvious; Brett was walking over to her with a frown on his handsome face. "Susan, did you see Mr. Deakin die? Or drink from his glass? Or anything like that?"

"No," she answered, shaking her head.

"Then why are you here? The only people who have any business being here are those who are material witnesses to Mr. Deakin's death."

"I was waiting for Jed."

"Jed's still here?"

"I was looking for him. I guess he's gone home," she said. After all, she didn't actually have proof that he hadn't.

"It's late. Maybe you should join him."

Susan didn't even bother to say good night. She had helped Brett solve murders in the past, so why should he be acting like her presence was only an irritant? She noticed Tom Davidson standing in the back of the room, where, she imagined, Brett had banished him. She pulled gloves from her coat pocket and headed for the street. She was so angry that she didn't hear the footsteps behind her until she was almost to her car.

"Wow! Are you a runner or something? I was afraid I wasn't going to catch up with you," Tom Davidson said, panting.

"Are you all right?" Susan was amazed by this lack of stamina in such a young person.

"Yes. I have asthma. This time of year is always difficult for me. Don't worry, I have an inhaler if it gets too bad."

"But why were you trying to catch up with me? I told

you that I wouldn't make a statement and I haven't changed my mind in the last fifteen minutes."

"No, that's not it. This is off the record," Tom replied, still breathing heavily. "I did want to ask you a question, though."

"You can ask, but I don't know that I will answer."

"Did you see who was up there when you were on the second floor of the Women's Club? Did you see who was walking around?"

SEVEN

WHY WAS HE SO SURE THERE WAS ANOTHER PERSON up there?" Kathleen asked, pressing the fast-forward button on her television's remote control. A very blurry Barney zipped around the screen. Susan, whose children were almost grown up, thought the purple dinosaur was adorable. Kathleen, who had lived through every episode of the Barney show at least a dozen times with her son, Alex, hoped the animal would be found politically incorrect before her younger child became interested in watching television.

The two women were sitting in Kathleen's family room, watching the tape Kathleen had made of the previous night's events. Kathleen had dozed off before the show last night and had no idea that Ivan Deakin had been killed until Susan appeared on her doorstep a few minutes earlier. Now she was hearing about Tom Davidson's last meeting with Susan.

"He claims he saw the shadow of someone walking across the hallway between the apartment and the large room at the top of the stairs."

"How did he know it wasn't you?"

"I asked the same question. Apparently he had no trouble recognizing me when I walked across the passageway. He only saw this other person's shadow. He claims this other person was following me."

"Male or female?"

"The other person? I don't know. In fact, I don't think anyone could tell. He just referred to it—or him—as another person."

"Oh. And you didn't see anyone else?"

"No one. I thought maybe the caretaker was up there, but Tom had asked the club women who were on hand and they said the caretaker's out of town this week."

"And why does he think this has anything to do with the murder? Couldn't it be that someone was curious and wandering around just like you were? Isn't he jumping to conclusions?"

"Probably. He's young and enthusiastic and he's driving Jed nuts. We were talking about it when Jed finally got home last night. He says this Tom Davidson follows the candidates around looking for a scoop like a newspaper reporter in the old movies."

"That would drive anyone crazy."

"I think he's sort of charming."

Kathleen grinned. "He's a little young for you, isn't he?"

"I was thinking about Chrissy!" Susan protested.

"Since when has she asked you to find boyfriends for her?"

"You're right. Since never. Wait! That's Bradley Chadwick!" Susan pointed at the screen.

Kathleen pressed the pause button and then rewound to the beginning of the program. The two women leaned forward and peered at the television. The scene changed to behind the building and Tom Davidson appeared, hair as unruly as ever.

"We'd like to thank our viewers for their kind attention and we will reschedule this program as soon as Mr. Deakin notifies us of the new time for his announcement. Our coverage will continue with interviews with the other two mayoral candidates and some members of their tickets. First, Dr. Chadwick." He turned his back on the camera and Bradley Chadwick walked into view.

"I'd like to make a statement, Tom," Bradley began, probably unaware of the fact that the camera had dipped south, cutting off the top of his head and centering the picture on his tie's knot. "Ivan Deakin called this meeting to announce what he claimed to be a solution to the problems the Landmark Commission has caused in our lovely village of Hancock. You can see exactly how disorganized his event was, how poorly planned—so poorly planned, in fact, that he was unable to even make his announcement. I think this bodes ill for his plan, his abilities, his very candidacy. I think we can all agree that any ideas put forward by Mr. Deakin can be counted on to be incompetent at the very least. We used to say that a man who cannot run his family should not be allowed to try to run the country. That is all I have to say." He ended abruptly, turned, and walked out of camera range.

"Thank you very much, Dr. Chadwick," Tom jumped in. "And now we have asked Mr. Martel to make a short statement. If he would like to."

The camera swung around to the left and Anthony Martel was seen, clearing his throat.

"This should be good," Susan muttered.

"Hmmm." Kathleen realized that she might be being unfair. The only time she had gone to hear Anthony Martel speak, she had fallen asleep.

"Well, I think the first thing I would like to say, initially, is that I'm very sorry we didn't get a chance to hear Ivan Deakin's plan. It behooves each and every one of us in Hancock, citizen and candidate alike, to listen to all opinions and suggestions about the Landmark Commission conflict. A solution will come only when everyone's ideas and feelings have been considered. However . . ."

"Does he always go on like this?" Kathleen asked, putting down her empty coffee cup.

Susan shrugged. "Terrible, isn't it? He's fine when someone has prepared a script; otherwise he runs on and on during public statements. Jed thinks it's just nerves. It's too bad, because he really alienates people who probably agree with his viewpoint."

"So now that Ivan Deakin is dead, the voters of Hancock have a choice between a pompous bore and a verbose one?"

"Don't forget. The verbose bore doesn't want every house in town built before 1939 to be under the jurisdiction of the Landmark Commission."

"I wasn't suggesting that there wasn't a real difference between the two—"

"Only that the candidates are among the most boring people in town," Susan finished for her. "Wait!" she interrupted herself. "There's Jed! He's going to say something." She bit her lip and leaned forward, intent on listening to her husband express his sadness over Ivan Deakin's inability to make his announcement and recap the platform on which he and the other candidates on Anthony Martel's ticket were running. The whole thing took less than a minute.

"Susan!" Kathleen cried when the camera had moved on to someone else. "He's wonderful on TV!"

"He is, isn't he?" Susan was pleased and more than a little surprised. After almost twenty-five years of marriage, she couldn't remember having seen her husband speak publicly more than a half-dozen times, and never on television. "I guess we should listen to the other candidates."

"I think that's the end," Kathleen stated as Barney returned to the screen in all his purple glory. "The VCR is new and I don't think I set it correctly. I would have gotten the whole thing if I hadn't fallen asleep again, of course."

"It doesn't matter," Susan said. "Jed was the most important part—to me at least."

"Do you want to take the tape home with you? Maybe Jed would like to see it."

"I'm sure he would. Thanks. I suppose I'd better get going. I promised Jed that I would check on the organization of the calling chain for election eve. We have less than a week to go, after all. I have to contact almost three dozen people and make sure they got their information in the mail and answer any questions they have."

"Isn't an awful lot of this falling on your shoulders? Don't the other candidates have families?"

"I'm the only spouse without a full-time job. And that doesn't mean the other spouses aren't busy—they're probably talking to divorce lawyers at this very moment."

"What about loyal volunteers? If so many people have such strong feelings about this election, why aren't they working on it?"

"Excellent question." Susan stood up and stretched. "If you find an answer to it, be sure to let me know."

"If you need any help . . ."

Susan could hear the reluctance in Kathleen's voice. "You're a great friend—and you were wonderful to give Jed that party—so I'm not going to take advantage of your offer. Women with small children should enjoy what little free time they have. However," she added, moving toward the door, "I won't be so nice when Alice and Alex are in high school."

Alice, perhaps hearing her name, became bored with her playpen, and Susan said good-bye and saw herself to the door as Kathleen picked up her daughter. Since the women lived only a few minutes apart, she was soon letting herself into her own home. Clue, a typical golden retriever, jumped around joyfully until realizing that her owner had the poor sense to prefer hanging out in the house to taking a nice long walk. With a loud snort, the dog settled down in the corner of the kitchen. Susan sighed, looked longingly at her empty coffeepot, told herself that too much caffeine was bad for her, picked up the list of people who had volunteered to spend the evening before the election calling two dozen people who were thought to be loyal to Anthony Martel. She intended to spend a couple of hours doing this, leaving messages on answering machines if necessary and then getting back to the people she had missed after dinner.

Dialing the first phone number on the list, she decided that herb tea not only had no caffeine but might actually be good for her, and filled a pot with water and put it on the stove. She was settling back to wait for it to boil, when the first name on her list answered.

"Hi, Connie. It's Susan Henshaw. I'm calling about—"

"Susan! I was just talking about you. What do you know about Ivan Deakin's murder? Who do you think did it? Do the police think Jed is in any danger?"

"Jed? Why would Jed be in danger?" Susan focused on the only question that had compelling interest for her.

"If someone is killing all the people who are running for office . . . But maybe it's just the candidates for mayor. I was just talking with Miffy Cahill—you know she and her husband are good friends with the Chadwicks—and she said that Cassandra was on the phone practically all night long trying to hire a bodyguard for Bradley."

"You're kidding." Susan was amazed. She had always thought that Bradley took himself too seriously, but this was a little extreme. "Bradley has been talking about someone trying to murder him for days. Surely no one thinks that someone is out to kill all the mayoral candidates?" she asked, making herself a cup of tea.

"Why would you assume that isn't true?"

Susan took a deep breath. She couldn't answer that question. "What about Ivan Deakin's personal life?"

"Well, there's his ex-wife, of course. I understand it was a very messy divorce."

"Really?" Susan told herself that she was only interested because of the election.

"Well, I don't know all the details, but I understand Ivan had a reputation of being quite a ladies' man, that he was involved with other women the entire time he was married. Younger women is what I heard."

"He wasn't that old when he died—"

"And Erika doesn't strike me as someone who would take insults like that lying down."

"Erika is his ex-wife?"

"Yes. You don't know her?"

"Erika Deakin? I don't think so. I know they didn't have any kids in the school system, otherwise I would have run across them before this. Is she a member of the Field Club?"

"I don't think so. They didn't have any children and she works full-time. She owns that chic little garden shop downtown. Stems and Twigs. You must have been in there."

Susan had. But she didn't remember any of the healthy-looking saleswomen being old enough to be married to Ivan Deakin. "How long were they married?"

"Not all that long. I think Erika said just a couple of years once when I was talking with her."

"When did they get divorced?"

"Quite a while ago—years, I think."

"And she waited for all this time to poison her husband in a very public place?"

"Doesn't make much sense, does it? That's probably why everyone is saying that it was a political assassination."

Susan doubted that everyone was saying this, so she decided it was time to get back to the task at hand. "Did you get the list in the mail?" she asked, abruptly changing the subject.

"What list?"

"The one the Martel campaign sent out," Susan explained, realizing that she wasn't being very clear. "You agreed to call the people who have committed themselves to voting for Anthony. On the night before the election, remember?"

"Oh, yes." Connie seemed to hesitate.

"I can send you a copy of the information if you've lost it," Susan added quickly. "It was sent out over a week ago in a manila envelope. There's a sheet of names and phone numbers as well as an instruction sheet. The people on your list live in your neighborhood, so you probably know some of them. I can send out another list," Susan repeated when Connie didn't say anything. "Or I could drive over and drop it off at your house."

"Susan, I was talking with some people down at the club. . . ."

"And?" Susan prompted, curious about what was to come. It was highly unlike Connie to be at a loss for words.

"I'm not sure I'm going to vote for Tony Martel. I mean, I like him. And you know that I like you and Jed. And certainly I'll vote for Jed. You don't have to worry about that for even one second. But . . ."

"But you're not sure you can call twenty-four people the night before the election and urge them to get out there and vote for Anthony Martel."

"Tony Martel. He wants you to call him Tony, remember."

"I remember," Susan said a little grimly. "I guess I'll just turn your list over to someone else," she added, as though there were legions of people just waiting to volunteer for the job.

"That would be lovely."

Susan could hear the relief in Connie's voice now that this dilemma was resolved for her.

"And don't forget to call me when you find out who killed Ivan Deakin," Connie trilled before hanging up.

Susan hung the phone up with more force than was necessary. "Sure," she muttered. "I'll just fit in a little investigation in my spare time—right after I find someone to make your phone calls." She reached out for her own calling list and made a slash through Connie's name. Then she got up, prepared a large pot of coffee, and when she had finished her first steaming mug, got to work and dialed the next name on the list.

By the time the pot was empty, she had contacted almost half the names on her list. Happily, no one else had changed their political convictions and one woman, home with a broken ankle, offered to call another list as well as her own. That was the good news.

The bad news was that every single person to whom she spoke had heard about Ivan Deakin's death and those who had heard it was a murder were wondering whether the killer was killing off the candidates one by one. She spent a long time on the phone, and by the time she got off, it occurred to her that if Bradley Chadwick was murdered next, Anthony Martel would win the election and, presumably, Jed, too.

"And that wouldn't be such a bad thing, would it, Clue?" she asked the dog, still lying in the corner.

Clue's tail thumped on the floor.

Susan stood up and stretched. "How about a walk?" she asked, although she knew the response she would get.

Minutes later Susan was closing the front door behind herself and her dog when a police car pulled into her driveway.

EIGHT

THE CAR STOPPED AND BRETT FORTESQUE GOT OUT. Susan dropped the leash and Clue ran down the drive and threw herself shamelessly at the chief of police.

The tense look on Brett's face melted into a smile and he knelt down and scratched Clue's stomach. Susan joined them and retrieved the retriever's leash.

"Hi. I was going to take Clue for a walk. Do you want to go with us?"

"Sure."

"But I have to warn you that as a candidate's wife, people are forever stopping me and offering their opinions about the election."

"Sounds good to me," Brett said, his grin fading. "As the chief of police, people are forever stopping me and offering their opinions about Hancock's latest murder."

"According to everyone I've talked with this morning, the two are inextricably related."

"Who have you been talking with?" Brett asked.

Susan explained her morning's phone calls as they walked down the street. Brett listened silently, occasionally asking a question; when she finished, he walked silently by her side. "So most people think the murder was politically motivated," was all he said.

Susan didn't think he was interested in a response and

she just scuffed through the leaves knowing that he would explain his visit when he wanted to.

And maybe he would have if the walkie-talkie in his back pocket hadn't demanded his attention.

"I'll be right there," Brett said to the person who had called. "Guess I've got to go," he said to Susan.

"I'll walk you back to your car."

"Don't bother. Go ahead and enjoy this beautiful day. I just have to head back to the station." He turned around and left Susan standing with her dog near a large pile of brilliant maple leaves.

"Well, what do you think of that, Clue?" she asked the dog. Clue was more interested in a chipmunk that had inopportunely appeared nearby than anything Susan said. After a lot of tugging they continued their walk.

Brett's car had been replaced by a rather beat-up Volvo station wagon when Susan had finally convinced Clue to return home. Theresa Martel was leaning against the car, smoking a cigarette, which she tossed on the ground and crushed with her heel as Susan approached.

"Disgusting habit," Theresa said, bending down to pick up the butt.

"Just toss it in the bushes. If you leave it there, Clue might eat it. She loves paper. We have to keep tissues and paper towels away from her or she just chews them up." Susan jerked Clue away from Theresa, who obviously didn't find the dog enchanting. "Would you like to come in and have a cup of coffee—or maybe some lunch," she offered. "I'm hungry, aren't you?"

"I guess so. But I don't want to be any trouble."

"No trouble at all." Susan didn't know what was in the refrigerator, but she knew her house could live up to the neatness standards of the Martels. "You don't mind being in the kitchen, do you?"

"I suppose your dog will be there, too?"

"No, Clue likes to go out in her run in the backyard when she's done with a walk," Susan lied. "She's digging a huge hole—reminds me of when Chad was little and he was always trying to find China. You just go in through there"—she pointed the way—"and I'll take her out."

When Susan returned to the kitchen, she found Theresa sitting at the kitchen table, looking over the lists of volunteer callers and smoking another cigarette. As an ashtray, she had appropriated a small Italian fish plate that Susan treasured. The size of the purse sitting in front of her on the table gave Susan an idea that maybe she would need a larger ashtray soon.

"Do you mind?" Theresa asked, glancing at the cigarette.

"No." Why was this woman making her lie so much? "I didn't notice you smoking yesterday," she added.

"I wasn't. I stopped and bought my first pack of Marlboros in seven years last night on the way home." Theresa sighed and stared down at the gleaming cigarette. "It was hell to stop."

Susan started opening cupboards and thinking about what to have for lunch. "There's lots of soup. And maybe a salad, cheese, and crackers?"

"Sounds good," Theresa said in a less-than-enthusiastic-sounding voice.

Susan opened a can of black-bean soup and dumped it into a pot. After turning up the heat, she pulled a box of water crackers from the cabinet, then turned to the cheese drawer in her refrigerator. Brie, Port Salut, and a nice chunk of Gorgonzola were sitting beside a crock of duck-liver pâté. A lot of people had been dropping in recently and she was well prepared. She set the table and arranged the food in the center of it, added a generous dash of sherry to the bubbling soup, and turned off the heat. She pulled two pottery bowls from the cupboard and filled them with steaming soup, placing a dollop of sour cream on each before setting them on the table and sitting down herself. During all this time Theresa smoked silently.

Susan picked up her spoon and then put it down. "I forgot to get something to drink. What would you like? Tea?"

"Tea sounds good," Theresa said.

Susan got up, boiled the water, heated the pot, made the tea, and put it and two mugs down on the table. Then she decided to throw good manners to the wind and blurted, "Why are you here?"

"You must be thinking I'm the rudest person in the world."

Susan frowned. "You didn't answer my question," she reminded her gently. She picked up her spoon again and began to eat, thinking that Theresa would answer eventually.

But Theresa seemed to be making up for lost time. She sat and lit one cigarette off the butt of another. Once in a while she sighed. Susan had finished her soup and was starting in on the cheese and crackers when Theresa sighed extra loudly and began to talk. She started off with a small bombshell.

"I'm afraid Anthony might have murdered Ivan Deakin." She inhaled deeply.

"Why?" What else was there to ask?

"He hated him. He wanted to win. I don't actually know." Smoke swirled around Theresa's head as she spoke.

"I meant, why do you think that? What makes you think it? Did he say something? Or maybe you saw something?"

"Maybe I should begin at the beginning."

"Yes. I think that's a good idea."

"Well, I left the Women's Club last night and I was on

my way home when I heard the announcement of Ivan's death on the radio. They didn't say it was murder in the first report. They didn't actually say much of anything, but I knew something terrible had happened. I stopped at that bar down by the railroad tracks." She paused for a moment, seeming to remember. "I bought a pack of cigarettes there and then went home to listen to the radio. I was there when your husband came over."

Susan remembered that Jed had gone to the Martel home to alert his running mate to the facts of Ivan's death. But Theresa implied that she had been alone when he arrived. She asked the other woman about that.

"Anthony didn't get home until almost four this morning. I . . . I didn't ask where he had been and he didn't offer to tell me."

Susan thought that was strange, but let it pass for the moment. "But when Jed told you that the death hadn't been accidental . . ." she prompted.

"Poison. He said Ivan had been poisoned. And all I could think of was that Anthony had done it." She stopped to light another cigarette.

"Because of the books on your bathroom floor?"

Theresa looked surprised. "How do you know what is in my bathroom?"

"I was at your house, remember? Addressing envelopes."

"Oh, that's right. It seems like such a long time ago."

She paused and Susan realized that she had heard that comment made after murders before—usually by someone closely connected to the victim. "So because your husband was reading books about poisons"—did people actually just *read* books about poisons?—"and then Ivan Deakin was poisoned, you believe that your husband killed him?"

"No. Those books have nothing to do with it. They're

mine, not his. I was doing research. I want to write mystery novels. I've actually started a manuscript. But I needed a way to kill off my primary suspect, and I was looking for something quick, odorless, and tasteless, something that has never been used before." She grimaced. "Needless to say, I didn't find it."

"Probably doesn't exist." Brett had once regaled her with a detailed critique of a best-selling mystery novel and its tenuous relationship to reality. Susan had ignored him; the reason she read mysteries was because they were not real life. "But Anthony could have looked over your books while he . . . while he was in the bathroom," she ended primly.

"Possibly. But that isn't why I think he did it. You see, I think my husband is having some sort of breakdown. Normally, of course, he wouldn't even think of killing anyone. My husband is a very gentle man, but this election has driven him over the edge."

"Surely—" Susan began to protest.

"Really, he's become obsessed with winning. When he started talking about running, we thought he would just walk in to the mayor's seat. After all, how many people really want to be mayor? We thought we could do so much good." She inhaled and exhaled a few times before continuing. "And then this Landmark Commission thing came up and Bradley Chadwick decided to run. But we probably could have beaten him, and Anthony just did what he always does when he wants something—he worked harder. And then Ivan Deakin threw his hat into the ring and Anthony began to think that with the vote split three ways, he might lose. He couldn't bear it. He started coming up with all sorts of foolish plans. . . ." She began to cough and took a sip of her untouched, and by now lukewarm, tea.

"Like what?" Susan asked when Theresa had regained control.

"The first one was that we would hire someone to look into Ivan's background and see what sort of scandals might be there."

"Blackmail?"

"Sort of. I don't think Anthony got that far with his thinking."

"And did he hire anyone?"

"Not that I know of. I don't think Anthony would even know how to go about finding someone to delve into a person's past."

"You said that was just the first thing," Susan said, wondering if Anthony could simultaneously be as helpless as his wife implied and as brilliant as her husband believed.

"It was. His second idea—or was it his third? I keep getting confused. Well, I think the next idea was that I should become friends with the ex–Mrs. Ivan Deakin and discover the details about their divorce."

"Isn't this just a variation on the first theme?"

"Not exactly. You see, Anthony had decided that Ivan must have some sort of financial interest in those houses up on the hill that spurred him to get involved in this election. The ex-wife was supposed to know all about that sort of thing because of the financial terms of her settlement."

This was sounding less crazy by the second. If Ivan Deakin was going to benefit financially from the election, certainly the voters had a right to know. "And the next plan?"

"Oh, I don't remember!" Theresa said, growing impatient. "He just keeps brainstorming about all this. He wakes me up in the middle of the night with these crazy ideas for getting elected. And then last night . . ."

"What happened last night?" Susan asked when Theresa seemed to run out of steam.

"When he came in last night . . . or early this morning . . . when he came in, he seemed so relaxed. Almost happy."

"Happy that Ivan was dead?"

Theresa nodded slowly. "He was happy like a man who had accomplished what he set out to accomplish. I haven't seen him like that since the day he received his doctorate. Or in the operating room right after Terry was born."

"Terry is your daughter?"

"Our son."

"I didn't know you had children."

"He's away. At school."

Susan was interested in other things. "Did you and Anthony talk about the murder? Or did either of you know that Ivan had been murdered at that point?"

"We both knew. I had turned on the radio as soon as I got home and it was announced sometime after midnight. That's actually why I was still awake when Anthony got home. And Anthony said he had heard it on the radio, too."

"In his car?"

"That's just it! I don't know. I was sitting up in bed when he got home and he came right upstairs and told me that Ivan Deakin had been poisoned. And then, of course, I told him I knew that from the radio and I asked him if he knew anything else. He said he didn't. And then I asked him where he had been for the past four hours and he . . . he said he had been driving around, thinking."

"And you don't think that's possible?"

"He didn't come home to talk with me." Theresa looked stunned by the very memory. "It's not like Anthony to stay away from me when something is bothering him. We've been married for almost thirty years. We're very close."

"Maybe he thought he was protecting you from something by not telling you what he had been doing," Susan suggested.

"That's it exactly," Theresa said, a sad look on her face. "That's the real reason why I think Anthony killed Ivan Deakin. That's why he won't talk to me. He's protecting me. He doesn't want to involve me in the cover-up."

"But that's not the only explanation for his behavior, not by a long shot," Susan insisted. "There are dozens of things that might be going on that you know nothing about. Jed and I are close, but I certainly don't believe I know everything about his life. Maybe you should try talking to him again."

Theresa frowned and pushed herself back from the table. "Maybe you're right. But there's something else you should know. It's the reason I'm here."

What else? Susan wondered. Certainly nothing could be worse than thinking that your husband was a murderer.

"Anthony told me this morning that he was thinking of withdrawing from the race. He doesn't want to be mayor anymore. And he's going to propose that Jed lead the ticket."

"Lead the ticket?" Could that possibly mean what she thought it did?

"Run for mayor," Theresa explained.

NINE

Theresa's announcement stunned Susan so much that she walked her to the door, said good-bye, returned to the kitchen, and ate every bit of cheese on the table without a second thought. She was starting on the crackers when the phone rang. She answered it without thinking.

"I understand Theresa Martel has been at your house," Brett began without any preamble.

"Yes, but—how do you know?" Susan interrupted herself to ask.

"Susan, surely you know that we keep certain people under surveillance after a murder."

"Does that mean she's a suspect? Or do you subscribe to the notion that someone is killing off all the candidates for office?" Susan asked, realizing that she was talking about her husband.

"Neither. We're just keeping track, like I said," he answered.

Susan noticed that he wasn't saying very much—or explaining anything. "So . . . ?"

"So I was wondering what she said to you about last night."

"Does this mean you're asking me to help you investigate the murder? Is that why you were here earlier?"

"I'm asking for your help during this part of the investigation. Yes." He ignored her second question.

Susan wasn't used to Brett acting like this, but she was interested in what he knew. "What sort of poison was used?" she asked, thinking of Theresa's search for an unknown, untraceable, fast-acting poison.

"Nothing unusual. Cyanide. Killed him before he realized that the water didn't taste as usual, probably."

"So it was in his water glass?"

"And in the pitcher of water on the lectern."

Susan thought for a moment. "So it's a good thing no one else took a drink."

"There was only one glass. Certainly no one would borrow the speaker's only glass. And what else would anyone do? Lift the pitcher to their lips and take a drink?"

"Oh. No, I guess not." She paused and thought for a minute. "Brett, is there something different about this murder? Something more upsetting?"

"Are you asking me who is mourning Ivan Deakin's death?"

"Not really," she answered hesitantly. How could she explain that she was asking about his attitude? If being abrupt and oblique meant anything, he certainly was acting differently than she had seen him act before.

"Well, I don't think we need to look for a murderer in the midst of his family circle," Brett insisted. "We have enough suspects if we look into the election. And don't forget that he was killed in a public place before he could make a political statement."

"I—"

"Susan, I have to go. Just keep anything Theresa Martel said under your hat until we've had a chance to talk, will you?"

"I—"

But he was off the line before she could utter the sentence.

Susan frowned and hung up the phone. Her hand was still on the receiver when it rang. She sighed and picked it up. Jed greeted her.

"Susan, I'm going to be late tonight. Anthony just called and he wants to meet for a short time. He thinks we should make a public statement about Ivan's death."

"Good idea. You could meet here if you want to," she suggested, looking at her kitchen table and wondering what she might offer any guests to eat.

"No. We're going to meet at the Martels'. Anthony doesn't want to leave his wife alone. He said this murder has upset her terribly."

Susan decided she would wait until Jed got home to tell him about Theresa's visit this morning. But there was something else on her mind. "Jed, do you have a minute?"

"Just about that. What's up?"

Susan told him briefly about Brett's phone call.

The policeman's behavior didn't seem to be a mystery to Jed. "Susan, technically Brett works for the town council. Not that I think that the next mayor, no matter who wins this election, is going to fire Brett. Nevertheless, in this investigation he's looking into the life of his potential employer."

"I'd never thought of it like that," Susan said slowly. "And that goes for all the police in town, doesn't it?" She heard a voice in the background at the other end of the line.

"Guess so. Listen, hon, I've got to run. Sorry about tonight. After this is over, why don't we go away for a long weekend? Maybe someplace warm."

Promises, promises, Susan thought. If he won, wouldn't he be even busier, what with town council meetings and all? But her husband had given her something to think about as she went to the backyard to collect poor Clue.

The dog, instead of wasting her time, had dug another huge hole in her dog run. Susan decided that she would fill it in another day and led the dog back into the house. It was occurring to her that she had to help Brett with this investigation even if he didn't come right out and ask. After all, she wasn't working for the town government. She had more freedom to act and nothing to lose if she made a few enemies along the way. And she knew exactly where to start her investigation, she decided, heading straight for Jed's study. What she needed was the names and addresses of the members of the Landmark Commission.

Jed's study was one of her favorite rooms in the house. Bookshelves lined the walls, and a built-in bar, stereo system, and comfortable chairs surrounded the large desk. It was used by everyone in the family looking for a comfortable place to nest. Usually, of course, it was neater than it was at present. No one was going to be lounging here now, Susan thought, looking around. Papers had flowed from the desk onto each and every horizontal surface. Susan only hoped that what she was looking for was still around. She shuffled through piles of papers, some printed, others in her husband's spiky writing. A stack of notebooks fell to the floor, revealing a small booklet printed on bright yellow paper. Eureka!

The local League of Women Voters published a yearly directory of the elected and appointed officers in Hancock, as well as various other publications that Jed had been studying for the last few months.

Susan picked up a pile of newspapers from a chair and tossed it on the floor before sitting down. She flipped through the pages of the pamphlet before she found what she wanted. Then, grabbing a piece of paper that was only half-filled with what looked like a draft of a speech Jed was composing, she copied out the five names and four addresses of the members of the Landmark Commission. Except for the commission chair, Penelope Thomas, the names were unfamiliar. Erika Eden, Rosemary Nearing, Lyman Nearing, and Foster Wade. Rosemary and Lymen lived at the same address, so Susan assumed they were married. The booklet didn't provide phone numbers, so she reached for the phone book.

On the other hand . . . The element of surprise was not to be sneezed at, she decided, stuffing the paper in her pocket and leaving the room. She'd change her clothing and drop in on the members of the Landmark Commission.

As she was about to back the car out of the driveway, Susan glanced through the list and noticed that Foster Wade lived on a street she recognized, so she decided to start with him. She drove over to Caldwell Avenue, a long street of small Victorian homes that eventually merged with Hancock's shopping area. Easily finding Foster Wade's number, she parked her car in front of his peeling, white three-story home. The sidewalk had been upended by the roots of a large maple nearby and she barely escaped falling. The porch looked like it had been screened in years ago and was now being maintained by someone who either didn't like to work or loved bugs, or so Susan concluded from the long rips in the screen.

She climbed the leaf-strewn steps and pressed the doorbell. Nothing happened. No one appeared. Probably, she guessed, because the bell wasn't working. She peered through the screen at the dark porch and noticed the Halloween decorations that hung around the door. The Wades must use the same decorations year after year: they looked very worn. The skeleton, in fact, did not have its legbone connected to its hipbone. . . . She must be getting punchy. She pulled herself together and knocked firmly on the screen door—and a foot or so of molding fell on her foot.

"Are you looking for someone?" A young man who seemed to be in his early thirties stood in the doorway of the house. He was wearing holey gray sweatpants and a Disneyland sweatshirt.

"I'm Susan Henshaw. And I'm looking for Mr. Foster Wade."

"I'm Foster Wade."

He stood there, apparently expecting her to make the next comment. "I'm Susan Henshaw," she repeated, feeling like a fool. "I understand you're a member of the Landmark Commission."

She paused and he nodded.

"Well, my husband is running for a seat on the town council."

"And you wanted to talk to me about the Landmark Commission's work," he said genially, opening the door for her.

Surprised, Susan walked into the house. She was even more surprised by what she found there.

About twenty-five years earlier, she had attended her first and last fraternity party. Except for the noticeable lack of empty beer bottles, the Wade home looked a lot like that fraternity house in the late sixties. Clothing wasn't so much left behind as strewn like seeds onto the fertile ground—where they had sprouted. There was no other explanation for the mess. From the banister in the hallway to the mahogany sideboard to the knickknack shelf in front of the window, each and every surface had been used as an impromptu hanger. Susan guessed that all the clothing belonged to Foster. Certainly all of it was casual, dirty, and full of holes, like his attire today.

But the other surprising thing was the furniture beneath the clothes. Susan had seen it before, too. And not at the fraternity house (which had tended toward broken-down Danish Modern) either. Her grandmother would have felt right at home underneath the layer of laundry. The room into which he had led her was furnished in the fussy style of the late twenties and early thirties. Whatnot shelves hung on walls, and underneath the clothing, tatted antimacassars were pinned to all chair and sofa backs.

"This is very nice," Susan said, seeing that her staring was being observed.

"It's my parents' home. In fact, it looked a lot like this right before they died."

So it was possible to die from the shock of seeing what a slob your child had become. She must mention that to Chad the next time she was forced to spend any time in his bedroom. "How nice," is all she said.

"You wanted to talk with me about the Landmark Commission," he reminded her, not even bothering to pick up the clothing on the couch before he sat down.

Susan sat, too, but not before moving a particularly dirty sweater from the velvet chair. "Yes, how did you get involved?" And did you have any reason to murder Ivan Deakin? she thought.

"Oh, I was asked to serve," Foster replied airily. "My family has been in Hancock for years and we've always believed in doing our civic duty."

"Someone on the town council asked you to ... to serve?"

"No, it was Mrs. Thomas. Penelope Thomas. She's the chairwoman of the commission. She was always a dear friend of my parents and she's a very important person in town. Perhaps you've met her?"

Now, Susan had changed into her very best conservative Talbot's suburban casual outfit to speak with these people today, and she didn't intend to be talked down to by a man who chose not to dress properly and didn't even bother to pick up his clothing at all. But her better self kicked in and she reminded herself that after all, Foster Wade was an orphan. "Penelope and I have met a few times," was her answer.

"Well, I imagine that I was her first choice for the commission. I have a great interest in preserving older homes."

Susan hoped the expression on her face didn't reveal her thoughts. The man hadn't even learned to pick up his underwear! And those holes in his screen didn't indicate an interest in preserving anything!

But Foster Wade had gotten up and was pacing the floor, removing books from a nearby shelf and shuffling through the pages. "I've read all these books," he continued. "Studied them, in fact. And I feel a deep personal need to take part in preserving the very best of what our forefathers left us."

"Of course," Susan agreed. But Foster gave her no chance to continue. He sat down on the arm of her chair and thrust a book underneath her nose.

"Look at these photographs! Look!" he insisted as though she had a choice, with anything held so close to her face. "All of those buildings were destroyed to make way for skyscrapers. All those beautiful details smashed to smithereens just so huge impersonal hunks of stainless steel could climb up to the sky! It's a crime! A real crime!"

Susan managed to glance at the caption underneath one of the black-and-white photos. "But that's New York City," she said. "And there aren't any skyscrapers in Hancock!" She twisted around so she could see Foster's face. Was he putting her on?

But the only thing on Foster's face was the gleam of fanaticism.

And that was just the beginning. Susan sat for over an hour listening to a tirade that seemed to go nowhere. His one and only point, repeated over and over, was that it was important to preserve historical buildings. Every time she tried to change the subject, to ask him questions about the Landmark Commission, to ask him questions about anything, he just returned to his main theme.

Finally, rude or not, she stood up and said good-bye. "Thank you for talking with me," she continued. "I appreciate your time, but I do have to run. As you can imagine, everything is at sixes and sevens since Ivan Deakin's death last night."

That stopped Foster Wade. He dropped his books into his lap, leaned forward, and stared into Susan's face. "What did you say?"

"I—I'm sorry. I guess you didn't know. I shouldn't have broken the news to you like that. Ivan Deakin was killed last night."

Foster blanched to the roots of his thinning hair. "He was killed? You mean someone killed him? Or was it an automobile accident or something?"

"It was poison. Someone put poison in the water that was provided for him at the podium."

"The podium?"

"At the Women's Club. He was scheduled to speak at the Women's Club last night. You know, he was going to make an announcement of his plan to solve this . . . all the problems over the election," Susan ended, not wanting to mention the Landmark Commission specifically.

"What did he say?" Foster spoke slowly.

"He didn't say anything. He died. I mean," Susan continued, "that he died before he had a chance to make his speech." She decided there was no reason to go into all the details about the lights and the public address system.

"That's horrible," the man said. "Just horrible." He looked down at the floor and stopped speaking.

"Are you all right?" Susan asked. "Maybe I shouldn't leave just now," she added, although she was anxious to go.

"No, I'll be okay. I . . . there are some people I should call." He stood up and looked around as though he couldn't remember where he had placed the telephone.

"Then I'll say good-bye," Susan said, edging toward the door.

He didn't even answer, just wandered out of the living room.

Susan let herself out of the house, wondering what to make of Foster Wade.

TEN

After leaving Foster Wade's, Susan returned to her own home and spent the evening on the phone. Chad arrived around seven, grabbed some dinner, and headed off to his room, promising to work on the pile of college applications on his desk just as soon as he made "a few calls." Susan was yelling up the stairs at him when her husband walked in the front door, a frown on his face. It was, she decided, not the time to mention Anthony Martel's idea that Jed move up on the ticket.

Jed refused her offer of dinner and headed straight to his study. Susan reminded herself that nagging accomplished nothing and picked up the phone to continue her calling. She found her husband asleep at his desk a little before eleven. Chad was still talking on his phone line when she urged her husband upstairs to bed.

Both of the men in the family dashed out the door early the next morning—without breakfast. Susan took the time to shower, admire her new hairstyle, and clean up her house (not that the kitchen needed much straightening) before starting out to talk with the other members of the Landmark Commission.

The Nearing couple were the next names on Susan's list and their street, named after a hardwood tree, was almost certainly somewhere around Elm Drive, the only elm left in town after the invasion of Dutch elm disease years ago. Susan headed over to that section of Hancock and found the Nearings' home after driving up and down Dogwood, Maple, Beech, and Birch.

Appropriately enough for a family with two members on the Landmark Commission, the Nearings lived in one of the few stone Colonials left in this part of Connecticut. Though there were lots of copies of these homes around, mostly in the wealthier parts of town, the originals could be distinguished by the fact that they were always set right next to the road, our forefathers apparently feeling a need to be as close to the lines of communication as possible in times when danger lurked in the trees and company was a welcome relief rather than an interruption.

Susan pulled her car into the gravel drive by the side of the house and stopped beside the navy Volvo parked there. Massive golden chrysanthemums lined the drive and the tiny path to the Dutch door. Beige homespun curtains hung in all the windows and little brass candles were centered on each and every windowsill. Susan mounted the steps, trying not to knock over either of the large crocks displaying bunches of dried cattails.

She could hear footsteps before her hand was off the heavy wrought-iron door knocker. She peeked through the tied-back curtains and saw a heavyset woman trodding toward the door.

The door was opened.

"Hi, I'm Susan Henshaw," Susan said, a polite smile on her face.

"I know who you are. You try to solve murders—and your husband is running on Anthony Martel's ticket." The voice was completely lacking in interest.

"Yes." What else could she say? "I was wondering if I could talk to you—just for a few minutes."

"I didn't think you were here to look at the flowers," the other woman said, holding the door open so that

Susan could enter. There was no sign of welcome in her manner, but Susan figured she shouldn't quibble and she entered the doorway.

"Shoes."

"I . . . Excuse me?"

"Shoes." The woman indicated the little pine bench running along one side of the hallway. Almost a dozen pairs of shoes were lined up underneath. Susan saw that her hostess was wearing red felt moccasins.

"You'd like me to take off my shoes?"

"These floors are over two hundred years old. Chestnut."

Susan sat down and took off her shoes. After tucking them under the bench in what seemed to be the required manner, she stood up. And almost fell back down. "Slippery," she commented, reaching out to the wall for support.

"Those walls aren't painted. The plaster is dyed and then applied in infinitesimally thin coats. Two men came here from Sweden just to do it—took them almost a month."

Susan pulled her hand back and, stepping gingerly, followed her hostess down the narrow hallway that seemed to mark the center of the house. They entered a small dark room dominated by a massive brick fireplace, and Susan was allowed to sit on a painted wooden bench, its hardness unrelieved by anything like a pillow or a slab of foam rubber. The fireplace, unlike the ones in Susan's home, didn't smell faintly of wood smoke and charcoal, but reeked of Lysol, or possibly its colonial equivalent. Certainly it didn't look like anyone had burned anything in it for years and years; the only thing blackening the brick was paint.

Susan had plenty of time to consider her hostess, as Rosemary Nearing no sooner sat down than she got up and began to straighten the curtains in the three windows that ran across the front of the room. Rosemary was built like and dressed like an old-fashioned German hausfrau. Her graying hair hung down her back in two lanky braids. Her bulky width was encased in a forest-green drindel with rows of rick-rack running around the hem. A ruffled white blouse emphasized her massive chest, and matching cotton tights made her plump calves resemble floury sausages. So intent was Rosemary upon making the drapes of the curtains exactly equal that Susan felt it would have been rude to interrupt with a comment. She tried to find a sitting position that would be less uncomfortable than the one she was in and, folding her hands in her lap, waited quietly.

Finally Rosemary sat down on a bench across from her guest and peered at her as if noticing her presence for the first time. "Does your husband leave everything a mess?" she surprised Susan by asking, and then looking back over her shoulder at the curtains as though expecting to see a disembodied hand pulling them out of alignment.

Susan thought about the bathroom after Jed had showered. The man didn't seem to realize that bath mats weren't meant to stay on the floor. And his attitude toward socks . . . "Yes."

"Lyman is a slob."

"Well, men . . ." Susan began.

"Some men are very neat. Penelope Thomas says that her late husband couldn't sleep at night unless he knew every little thing in the house was in the correct place."

Susan, who had begun to remember how many times her bra kept Jed's socks company on the floor overnight, thought that sounded pretty terrible, so she just smiled.

"But you are not here to talk about the noble art of housekeeping. You are here to talk about the murder. I think Tony Martel did it."

"Oh, well, I ... You do?" The words Susan was thinking made their way out of her mouth.

"Who else?" Rosemary Nearing leaned back in her bench and crossed her hands across her ample chest.

"Bradley Chadwick? I mean, I don't think he did it, but isn't he as logical a choice as Anthony?"

"Not at all. Tony Martel only has a chance of winning now that Ivan is dead. Once Ivan had entered the race, it was between him and Bradley."

"Tony Martel has some very good ideas, he's a hard worker, and would make an excellent mayor," Susan insisted.

Rosemary Nearing shrugged her massive shoulders. "So what? He has no sex appeal and it's sex appeal that wins elections."

Susan didn't see much evidence of that. She watched her share of C-SPAN and would have absolutely no trouble distinguishing the United States Congress from the line at Chippendale's. "You think Ivan Deakin had sex appeal?"

"Everyone knows that the man was a satyr."

"Really?"

"Just because Erika doesn't talk about it doesn't mean it didn't bother her."

"I don't think I've ever met Erika."

Rosemary didn't seem to have anything to say to that, so Susan changed the subject. "The Landmark Commission must be very important to you. . . . You obviously care so much about your house." Susan couldn't bring herself to call it a home. It seemed more like a museum where only the very neatest tourists were allowed to enter.

"I will tell you what I told Penelope Thomas when she asked me to work on the commission: I was honored to help such a fine cause. Honored."

Susan was impressed; it was short, but still a paragraph. "Then you think that all the buildings built before 1939 should be under the jurisdiction of the Landmark Commission?"

"We must preserve our heritage."

"Yes, but—"

"Some people might be surprised by how little other people care about our heritage."

Susan had the feeling that Rosemary Nearing would put her in both categories. "Did Ivan Deakin support the Landmark Commission's ideas?"

"That's why Lyman attended the meeting last night. We thought it was imperative to discover the answer to that question."

"And you stayed home?"

"Last night was ironing night."

"You do all your ironing at one time?" Susan did, too—usually when she found an old Fred Astaire movie on TV.

"Every Tuesday night."

"So your husband isn't home?"

"Is the house neat? If the house is neat, he's not here." She looked around proudly and then back at Susan, as though daring her to find a speck of dust.

"Your house is beautiful. But I'd like to talk to your husband, if it's possible." Susan certainly wasn't going to get the information she was looking for from Rosemary Nearing.

"You might find him at his job."

"Where does he work?"

"He runs his family's business." Rosemary had gotten up and was peering at the top of the mantel.

"Which is?" Susan was getting the urge to grab the dust cloth from Rosemary's hand and smack her with it.

"They make things." Rosemary peered suspiciously at

a candlestick. "Have you noticed how brass seems to attract dust?"

"Possibly a sticky residue from the polish you use," Susan suggested rather maliciously. "Is his company located in town?"

"Stamford." She went so far as to give Susan the address. "Just look for Nearing Rings, Incorporated. The sign is blue."

"Thank you. I'll just go get my shoes, unless . . ."

"Yes?" Rosemary asked with a loud sigh.

"I don't mean to be rude, but I wonder if . . . I would love to see the rest of your house."

"This house is not a museum."

"I—"

"And I am not a docent."

"Of course . . ." Susan could feel her cheeks getting pink. She had only made the request to be polite.

"Do you usually ask people if you can see their homes, Mrs. Henshaw?"

"I—I think I'd better just get my shoes and be on my way." She could barely force the last few words out of her mouth. "I didn't mean to offend you. . . . It's just that this house is so unusual and . . ."

The change of mind was startling. "I will give you a quick tour." Rosemary stood up more quickly than Susan would have supposed her bulk allowed. "This, of course, is the original keeping room. . . ." she began in her best docent voice.

The "quick tour" took over an hour, and during it Susan discovered two things. The house, in fact, *was* a museum. The building itself had been restored to pristine historical accuracy, and except for modern appliances and cleaning products, it was being run like it had been two hundred years ago. All fabrics were handwoven. Each and every pot was hand-thrown. The windowpanes were made by a company in England that still made glass "the old-fashioned way"—impossible to see through. The furniture was spare and uncomfortable, but authentic. Susan suspected, although she was not completely sure, that the mattresses were actually stuffed with cornhusks. She was, however, positive that the beds were shorter and narrower than anything anyone she knew slept in. Apparently dust and dirt were unknown two hundred years ago, because the entire place was spotless.

By the time Susan was returned to her shoes, she was dying to leave. The house was like an elegant prison. She thanked Rosemary as sincerely as possible and fled to her car. With the address of Nearing Rings, Inc., tucked into her jacket pocket, she decided to proceed with visits to the commission members and drive to Stamford. Besides, she realized, starting her car, she would rather visit Lyman Nearing at his workplace than return to his house.

The drive to Stamford was anything but wasted. It gave her time to sort out her thoughts and try to figure out what, if anything, she had learned from Foster Wade and Rosemary Nearing. The only conclusion she reached was that both of them were living rather strange lives in rather strange houses. Rosemary was convinced that Anthony Martel had murdered Ivan Deakin, but her ideas were based on nothing and she had not been at the Women's Club last night. Foster Wade claimed to know nothing about the murder, but could have been lying. She wondered whom he had called after she left him alone.

Susan flicked around the radio dial, and discovering an oldies station that was in the middle of a Beatles day (she wondered if George, Paul, or Ringo was celebrating a birthday), she stopped worrying and sang along. The drive passed quickly and she was looking for Nearing

Rings long before the first half of the *White Album* ended. She found it almost immediately. It would have been hard to miss, occupying as it did the largest building in a very large industrial park down by Long Island Sound. The sign out front was, indeed, blue. But no one had warned her about the concertina wire wound around the top of the chain-link fence that surrounded the building.

Susan had assumed Lyman Nearing's company made rings, possibly the little silver things that were so popular among teens, or even expensive wedding bands and engagement rings, but this factory looked capable of out-fitting every finger of every American alive while still doing its bit to keep up the trade balance. Nearing Rings must be a different type of ring, she decided, slowly driving up to the woman in the guard box at the entrance gate.

"Uh, Lyman Nearing," Susan said hesitantly. "His wife . . ." she began to explain her presence.

"Oh." The guard straightened up and pressed a button that opened the gate. "Just head straight ahead and park in the empty spot by the main entrance. Someone will be out to escort you inside immediately."

"Thanks," Susan said, and did as she was told. A quick glance in her rearview mirror left her puzzled by the expression of interest on the guard's face as her car passed down the road.

As promised, someone was ready and waiting to escort her into the building. Susan was thankful for the friendly-looking man who waited by the empty parking spot. The building was huge; she would never find her way around without guidance. But the smile on the young man's face turned into a frown as she drove up.

"You are not Mrs. Nearing," he announced as she got out of her car.

"Of course not . . ." Then Susan realized what had happened. "Oh, that must be what the young woman at the gate thought. I didn't mean to confuse her. I was trying to tell her that Rosemary Nearing had sent me. To talk with her husband," she continued when the welcoming smile refused to reappear.

The man's frown deepened. "Then I guess you'd better see Mr. Nearing."

And he led her into the factory.

ELEVEN

LARGE COLOR PHOTOGRAPHS LINED THE HALLWAY and Susan quickly realized that the rings the Nearing company produced were anything but the kind that encircled a finger. Many of the photographs featured military equipment as well as actual battlefield scenes, but she decided this wasn't the time to ask questions. The stern look on her escort's face was making her nervous about meeting Lyman Nearing—very nervous.

The door at the end of the hall had MR. LYMAN NEARING printed on it in large black block letters. It swung open at their approach and a short man in a conservative gray suit appeared. He was beaming.

"Mrs. Henshaw. I was watching the security monitors and thought I recognized you. I've always wanted to meet you. I'm Lyman Nearing." He extended his hand and shook hers energetically. "Come into my office. I suppose you're here about the murder the other night. Shocking, wasn't it? But you must be more accustomed to this type of thing than I am. Florence, would you please get us some coffee and some of those wonderful orange-apple muffins?" he asked the lovely blond secretary sitting at a desk in the outer office.

"Of course, Mr. Nearing." She sprang up as Susan was led through the door into the farther office.

"Have a seat, Mrs. Henshaw."

"Please call me Susan," she responded, sitting down in one of the plush corduroy-upholstered Lawson chairs that ringed a glass coffee table on one side of the comfortable office.

"Well, Susan, how can I help you? I suppose you're looking at all the members of the Landmark Commission, hoping to find Ivan Deakin's murderer."

The secretary's return forestalled any response Susan might have made. Coffee and three types of muffins were passed around the table. Susan piled a plate high, suddenly realizing how hungry she was.

Lyman Nearing chuckled at the sight. "I gather you've been to see my wife." Susan must have looked puzzled because he continued: "Everyone leaves her house hungry."

"I'm always hungry," Susan confessed. "I spoke with your wife." She paused to take another bit of muffin and swallow it. "Why do you call it *her* house?"

"Well, my house, too—technically. But my wife and I are separated and I haven't lived there for years. Of course, I grew up there."

"You did?" Susan was surprised.

Lyman peered at her through his heavy horn-rim glasses with interest. "I guess you have to find background information about everyone you investigate, don't you? And you don't take notes? I would have thought you did."

"Not usually," Susan admitted.

"I'm impressed. Have a memory like a sieve myself," he admitted cheerfully. "Well, let's see, where should I start? With the Nearing family, I guess. I inherited this business—along with the house I grew up in—when I was barely twenty-one years old. My mother died when I was in my early teens. I don't remember her very well, but everyone has always told me that she was a very sensible woman. If she had been alive, I suspect she would never have let my father draw up a will giving me so much money and power at such a young age. Of course, he probably thought he would live forever. We all do, I find." He stopped to take a large bite from his muffin.

"Well, my father died in a plane crash and I discovered myself with a company to run and a house. And to make a long story short, a wife, very soon afterward."

"Things changed pretty quickly," Susan commented.

"Well, that happens frequently when a person who doesn't know what he wants meets someone who knows exactly what she wants."

"You mean your wife."

"Exactly. Rosemary has always known what she wanted—and how to get it." For the first time in their conversation a frown replaced the cheerful expression on his face. "Of course, it's not so difficult to get what you want if all your wants are simply material."

"Like the house," Susan guessed.

"The house. Period."

"It's some house."

"It is now. I grew up there. Well, I told you that already. It was a simple family home then. Old, of course, in fact a little scruffy—sort of worn at the edges, if you know what I mean." He raised his eyebrows at her.

"Comfortable," was the word Susan suggested.

"Exactly." He looked at her as though she had just said something profound. "Rosemary saw the house's potential and she married me for it. Not," he added quickly, "that I'm accusing her of not loving me. But you know the old saying that it's just as easy to fall in love with a rich man as a poor one? Well, I think Rosemary knew that instinctively. And when she met me, she thought she had fallen in love." He chuckled and reached for another muffin. "And she had, in fact. She had fallen in love with my money, my house, and what the two of them offered."

"Remodeling, you mean," Susan said, knowing all too well how much money it cost to redo older homes.

"I think of it as unremodeling. It costs a lot to modernize an older space. But you would not believe what it costs to return a building to historical accuracy. Amazing."

"You said you don't live there," Susan probed gently.

"Wouldn't be caught dead spending the night in that place. Uncomfortably authentic and uncomfortably clean. You know, that's not historically accurate. Things used to be much dirtier than they are in modern times. But try telling that to my wife."

"You're still married, then?" Susan wondered if their separation was just a step on the road to a divorce.

"Sure are. Don't be embarrassed. Everyone is shocked. But, you see, Rosemary brought something to our marriage that's worth a lot more than that damn house. She had a son by another man—she wasn't married to him. It happened back in her teens. Her son's name is Josh and he's a man now. A good man. I adopted him and raised him and was thrilled when he decided to become a mechanical engineer. He's going to inherit Nearing Rings someday. I wouldn't do anything to jeopardize our relationship. So I stay married. I have an apartment near here, and Rosemary and I don't see much of each other—"

"Except that you're on the Landmark Commission together," Susan said.

"True. That was probably a mistake, but Rosemary can be very persuasive."

"She's the one who asked you to join?" As far as Susan knew, Penelope Thomas had asked all the other members.

"Yes. Penny . . . Penny Thomas asked Rosemary. She

is a logical choice since Rosemary loves that house and it is going to be left to the local historical society when we're both dead. I guess Rosemary asked me to join since the house is actually still in my name." He took a sip of his coffee before continuing. "I went to a few meetings, but it's not my thing. I tell Rosemary to go ahead and vote for me."

That was interesting. "How do you feel about the decision of the Landmark Commission to grant landmark status to every building built before 1939?"

"Most ridiculous thing I've ever heard, but I didn't think it would ever happen. I thought this election would take care of all that. I had put my faith in Anthony Martel and his ticket. I was sure they were going to win the election. Until recently, that is."

"What happened recently?"

"Ivan Deakin."

"You think he would have won the election?"

Lyman frowned. "I don't know. But I think he could have taken votes away from Martel and caused Brad to win. Don't you?"

Susan remained silent.

"So what do you think? Do you have any clues yet?"

"I'm still asking questions. You know, gathering facts." Susan hesitated and then plunged in. She hated to risk insulting this nice man, but he was the only person she had spoken with so far who had actually been at the Women's Club last night. "What did you think when you saw Ivan Deakin hide behind the podium the other night?"

"I didn't think anything. I didn't see anything. And I wasn't there when he died."

"You weren't? But your wife told me . . ."

Lyman began to chuckle. "Rosemary told you that I went to the meeting, didn't she? I guess this is one of those examples of 'what a tangled web we weave,' etcetera, etcetera."

"You lied to her about going," Susan guessed.

"True. I'm ashamed to admit it, but telling little white lies is something of a habit with me. Only to my wife, mind you. But it makes it much easier to get along with her if I claim to be doing things that she approves of."

"Like going to the meeting at the Women's Club."

"Exactly."

"Or accepting a spot on the Landmark Commission and voting in accordance with your wife's wishes."

"Don't misunderstand me about that. I agreed to be on the commission before I had any idea that they were going to do anything serious. I thought it had been created for the sole purpose of getting historical fanatics like my wife off the necks of the members of the town council. Who would have thought that anyone would actually give them any serious control over the lives of about half the people in town?"

"But the other commissions . . ." Susan began her protest.

"The other commissions were set up with very stringent guidelines and their members haven't violated them. Believe me, I know."

"How?"

"Nearing Rings encourages its employees to work in their communities. They're allowed to use the facilities here to do volunteer work. They can leave early to go to meetings. I've never heard of something like this 1939 thing being done before."

"But a lot of communities have dates that they consider important and they declare landmark status based on them—at least that's what my husband, Jed, said."

"But they don't make laws that affect the present owners—just people who buy after the law is passed.

Otherwise the Ecological Commission could decide that all the backyards on Long Island Sound should be returned to their wetland status. And that's not saying anything about how ridiculous the date 1939 is in a community where the earliest homes were built almost two centuries earlier."

"Does your wife agree with you?"

"Not on your life. She'll agree with anything that Penny Thomas says. She ignores me."

"You must know Penelope very well," Susan said.

Lyman chuckled. "Because I call her Penny and no one else in town would dare? Yes, I know her. We grew up together. I remember when she was the terror of the Hancock Episcopalian Church Sunday School—and that was in first grade, before she had properly developed her dictatorial skills. Of course, I also remember when she wet her pants on a kindergarten class trip to the Bronx Zoo. That type of knowledge gives a person a certain amount of power."

"So she doesn't mind that you call her Penny?"

"She hates it. That's the main reason I do it. It's so easy to irritate her."

Susan was impressed. "I didn't think she would let people, uh, treat her like you do."

"She wants my house. It is the last remaining Colonial home in absolutely pristine condition in Hancock. It's in my will that it will go to the historical society, but I could change all that at any time. So she puts up with my little foibles."

"And the Landmark Commission . . ."

"Is going to be the controlling influence over the historical society. That is, at least, if Brad Chadwick wins the election."

"Which he has a better chance of doing today than he had before Ivan was murdered."

She paused while munching on another muffin. "You know, there is something else."

"What?"

"This whole thing depends on what Ivan Deakin was going to say, doesn't it?"

"Good point. I wonder what happened to his speech."

Susan looked at Lyman curiously. "He didn't get a chance to make it," she explained. "He died before he could say anything."

"But he probably wrote it down, didn't he? At least I don't know many speakers who talk without some notes. . . . What are you thinking about?"

"I was just wondering if I saw him take some papers out of his pocket and put them on the podium—or if I could be imagining it now that you mention it." She frowned. "You know, I think I did see it."

"Then all you have to do is find out who picked them up after the murder. Right?"

Susan nodded. She wondered if it could possibly be so easy.

TWELVE

SUSAN DROVE OVER TO POLICE HEADQUARTERS thinking about the Nearings. She had, of course, liked Lyman and disliked Rosemary almost immediately upon meeting them. On the other hand, she was well aware of the fact that she had, more than once, liked a murderer before knowing everything there was to know about the case. It was interesting that neither Lyman nor Rosemary admitted to being at the Women's Club the night Ivan Deakin was murdered. Not that murderers told the truth, but smart murderers didn't tell lies that could be checked out easily, and in that crowd it should be easy to discover someone who might have seen Lyman or his wife. So, if either of them was lying, it was a pretty stupid lie. Susan was beginning to feel an idea forming in the back of her mind as she arrived at the municipal center.

But it would have to wait. Brett was standing by the police cruiser in the parking lot next to the police-department building. Susan steered over to him, stopped her car, and got out, a smile on her face.

A smile that wasn't returned.

"Susan. What are you doing here?"

"Looking for you," she answered. "I was wondering what happened to the speech last night."

"You were there. You know Deakin was killed before he could deliver it," he answered irritably.

Susan remembered what Jed had said and reminded herself that Brett had a right to be cranky. After all, his job was on the line here. "I was talking about the sheet of paper that Ivan had written his speech on. I've thought about it and thought about it. I'm almost sure I saw him take a folded page—or pages—from his jacket pocket and place them on the podium. I was just wondering who picked them up after he was murdered."

Brett seemed to perk up at the thought. "Good thinking. Good question." He nodded to himself a few times. "Really good thinking," he repeated.

"You don't have to sound quite so surprised."

"I'll get right on that," Brett said, ignoring her and hurrying up the sidewalk toward the building.

Susan fled after him, barely avoiding getting smacked in the face by the building's heavy door as it closed behind him. "Brett! I—"

"I can't talk now, Susan. I have to check up on that script," he told her as swinging glass doors closed behind him, leaving her standing in the small lobby.

Susan smacked her hand against the door, stunned when it didn't budge. She heard a sound and turned around to see a uniformed police officer sitting at the reception desk. He pointed over her head. She glanced up. A large sign read OFFICIAL POLICE BUSINESS ONLY: SPEAK TO OFFICER BEHIND DESK FOR ADMISSION.

Susan smiled and approached the said officer. "I need to see Brett, please," she explained politely.

"It looked to me like Chief Fortesque was busy," he answered. "But I'll check. What name shall I give?"

"Susan Henshaw."

Everyone else today had recognized her name, but apparently not this young officer. "Mrs. or Miss?"

"Mrs." She decided it was foolish to be flattered. He certainly wasn't interested in asking her for a date.

He snapped the glass panel shut and spoke into a small microphone on the desk before him. After waiting for a reply, he looked up at her. "Chief Fortesque is busy," he said, an implied "I told you so" in his voice.

Susan began to reminisce mentally about the friendly dispatcher who was usually here. "What happened to—" she began.

"Budget cuts," he interrupted.

"You didn't even know what I was going to ask," she protested.

"No matter what the question, the answer is the same. Lots of rich people live in Hancock, but they don't like paying taxes any more than the rest of us. The last election required lots of budget cuts and now everyone wants to know why things aren't the same."

Susan decided not to pursue the subject. "I'd like to leave a message for Brett."

"Fine." He picked up a yellow pencil and a scrap of paper. "Your name again?"

Susan repeated the information, asked Brett to call her at home as soon as possible, and left. She still had two members of the Landmark Commission to see, and while the muffins she had eaten would suffice for lunch, she was going to have to shop for dinner if her family was to eat tonight.

She got back in her car and picked up the list of Landmark Commission members. Erika Eden was the only remaining name other than the chairperson. Susan knew she was avoiding the unavoidable, but she decided to visit this Erika first. The address was unfamiliar to her, but when a police officer who knew her drove up, she was able to obtain complete directions to Erika's home. The broad smile on his face as she left was a marked contrast to the reception Brett had given her. If she hadn't had such a difficult time finding the street number she was searching for, she might have given it more thought.

Erika Eden, she discovered eventually, was living in a converted carriage house behind a large Victorian in the hillier part of town. The carriage house, a tiny white board-and-batten two-story affair with a minuscule deck across the front of the ground floor, intrigued Susan, but no one answered her knock and she had to be content to peek through the French doors. The interior seemed as interesting as the outside, but a more thorough inspection would have to wait. She walked back down the long driveway and got in her car. She couldn't put it off any longer. It was time to talk with Penelope Thomas.

Of the three people on the commission she had spoken with, only Lyman Nearing seemed to have shared her feelings for Penelope Thomas. He didn't seem to like her very much. But he wasn't afraid of her.

Well, Susan chided herself, it wasn't that she herself was actually afraid of Penelope Thomas. After all, what could the woman actually do to her? she asked herself, driving between the two raven-topped pillars that bracketed the entrance to the Thomas driveway. Weren't ravens, she wondered, glancing back into her rearview mirror, scavengers?

Trying not to imagine herself as well-dressed carrion, she parked her Jeep behind the Mercedes 250 coupe that bore a license plate proclaiming it an antique—if anyone was unsophisticated enough to miss that particular fact.

Penelope Thomas's house was as distinguished as her automobile. The Thomases didn't have to wait for a local Landmark Commission to validate the significance of their abode. It was already listed in the National Registry of Historic Places. It deserved to be. It was a castle.

Built in Victorian times, this castle didn't have moats or drawbridges, but it made up for the loss of these picturesque features with enough towers, turrets, and pinnacles to satisfy any king. Susan had been told that there even was a rampart encircling the roof, but she had never been allowed above the first floor. The castle had been built by an eccentric millionaire who claimed to be a direct descendant of Henry VIII. While his marrying habits imitated those of his more famous alleged ancestor, laws had changed over the years, and after building his castle, all his income was required for alimony and child support. He died penniless. Susan thought it served him right. His heirs had sold the castle to the first available buyer. Fortunately for Penelope Thomas, that buyer had been her husband's father.

Susan pressed the small cross that she knew, from experience, was the doorbell and waited. She knew that Penelope Thomas, who, in her own words, "despised the ordinary," rarely traveled without her Mercedes (except for time spent crossing the ocean on the Concorde or "gallivanting up to Martha's Vineyard" in her husband's World War I biplane. It was typical of Penelope that she managed to speak of the popular island as though she knew Martha personally.).

As she expected, Penelope herself opened the door. From the expression on her face, it was fairly obvious that she had been expecting someone other than Susan Henshaw.

"Susan." Well, at least she remembered her name. "What on earth are you doing here?"

"I'd like to talk with you about Ivan Deakin's murder," she explained.

And was surprised when the door was held open for her.

"I forgot for a moment," Penelope explained, "that you are a close friend of Chief Fortesque, aren't you?"

"I guess you could say that," Susan admitted, tossing

her coat upon a tall gilded rack and following her hostess across the marble foyer, through a pair of carved wooden doors, and into the surprisingly comfortable living room. Oriental carpets lay on the floor, a pair of plaid couches stood before a blazing Adams fireplace, and on a side table, full decanters and tiny glasses waited on a gleaming silver tray.

Apparently they were going to keep waiting. Penelope sat down and motioned for Susan to follow suit. "So what do you want to know?" she asked abruptly.

"Were you at the Women's Club on Tuesday night?" Susan asked, taken aback by the blunt question.

"Are you hoping that I saw someone put poison in Ivan's water pitcher?"

"How did you know there was poison in the pitcher?" Susan asked quickly.

"It's in the evening paper," Penelope answered, nudging the *Hancock Herald* that lay on the coffee table with the toe of her well-polished, handmade shoe. "I read it every single evening. As well as *The Wall Street Journal* and *The New York Times* in the morning. I never understand people who don't insist on being well informed. Do you?"

Susan thought guiltily of the papers that were lying unfurled on the kitchen counter. She always meant to read them daily. She gave herself a mental shake. "So were you at the Women's Club?"

"Certainly. I believe I have an obligation to be at important events in town—no matter how silly."

"You thought it was silly?"

"Not the murder, certainly. But the idea of Ivan Deakin running for office was ludicrous. Absolutely ludicrous."

"Why? I . . . I didn't know him at all," Susan added quickly when Penelope granted her a haughty stare.

"Then, of course, you won't understand," Penelope

admitted begrudgingly. "The man is a cad. Was a cad, I suppose I should say."

"I've heard that he was involved with a lot of women," Susan muttered. In fact, she hadn't really heard anything else about him.

"A lot! Ha! I think I am the only woman he ever met that he didn't make a pass at."

Susan couldn't imagine anyone making a pass at Penelope—although certainly Mr. Thomas, one assumed, whoever he might be, had done just that at one time or another. Susan glanced over at the tray of drinks. They were waiting for someone. Perhaps for Penelope's husband?

"I thought you were here to ask me questions?"

The question startled Susan from her reverie. Why was she acting like a foolish child? She remembered the story Lyman Nearing had told and the image of Penelope wetting her pants (though many years ago) gave her courage. "How a man treats women frequently has little to do with how electable he is," Susan reminded her.

"Well, I won't argue with you there," Penelope agreed while implying that it was practically the only thing she wouldn't argue about.

"So are there any other reasons you don't think Ivan would have made a good mayor?"

"You mean besides this foolishness about the Landmark Commission?"

"What foolishness? I thought you agreed that all the homes built before 1939 should be regulated by the commission—"

"Protected by the Landmark Commission. Not regulated, protected! Do you have any idea what has happened to much of Hancock's heritage in the past few decades?"

"I—"

Apparently excited by this subject, Penelope began to

wave her arms in the air. "The old mill on the river—turned into a restaurant. A Japanese restaurant! The old wooden bridge that spanned the same river, the very bridge that possibly Washington and his troops marched across, torn down and a new cement-and-metal thing built in its place. The traffic on that road has increased at least twofold, making it a danger to people who walk there. The old elementary school converted into expensive condominiums. There are rich people with absolutely no taste bathing in the corner of my first-grade classroom!"

"Well—" Susan began.

"And that's not the worst of it. Look what people have been allowed to do to their homes. Old Victorians with graceful wraparound porches have added modern wings with hideous square lines. Nice, sensible fifties ranches have second, third, and even fourth floors added. Hancock was a charming residential community before all these new people came in with all their money and poor taste. The Landmark Commission is going to stop all that!"

"But we have zoning laws—" Susan began.

"They are not enough! These people are good at using the law to their own advantage. If Bradley Chadwick is elected, the Landmark Commission will prevent these desecrations from happening."

"I—"

"I know that your husband is running on Tony Martel's ticket, but believe me, Susan, Bradley is the only opportunity we have to keep Hancock the charming village it has always been."

She might have continued, except at that moment the doorbell pealed. Penelope leaped up to answer it, smoothing down her hair as she went. Susan sat back on the sofa and thought about what she'd just heard. She had barely begun to process the information when Penelope returned, Bradley Chadwick at her side.

"I'm sorry, Susan, but you will have to excuse us. Bradley and I have a lot to discuss. Maybe we could talk some other time."

Susan said hello to Bradley and agreed that another time would be better. "I can let myself out the door," she offered after Bradley's perfunctory if charming greeting.

"Fine." Penelope had turned to the drinks tray and managed only a vague wave at Susan's departing back.

Susan collected her coat and let herself out the door. She would be back to talk with Penelope. There was something else to be discovered here—she just didn't know what it was.

THIRTEEN

Susan DECIDED TO GO SEE ERIKA EDEN AFTER dinner, so she headed for the grocery store, trying to think of a meal she could make quickly that would keep until Jed and Chad appeared—and that she hadn't made a half-dozen times in the past two months. Chad would be going off to college next year—if he ever got around to filling out those application forms—and Susan was looking forward to having to provide only one late meal each evening. Of course, if Jed lost the election, he might actually have his evenings free to spend with her. Maybe they could even sign up for a class at the New School and she could meet him in the city. She could do a little shopping, meet him for dinner before class. It would be like twenty-five years ago when they were in college. . . . What was she thinking? she asked herself, parking in front of the grocery store. It almost sounded like she wanted her husband to lose the election!

Once inside the store, she quickly realized she was dreaming if she thought she was going to come up with an unusual entrée for dinner. Salmon was on sale, but Chad didn't eat salmon. She headed for the butcher. Chicken again. Without skin or cream sauce for Jed, who was always talking about cholesterol. Without vegetables no matter what the sauce for Chad. Susan spent almost half an hour in the store and ended up standing in line at the checkout counter with the same items that she put in her cart each week. Oh, well, it would be Thanksgiving in a few weeks—and she loved having turkey with all the fixings. Except, she realized, and paused in placing her groceries on the checkout counter, that Chrissy had recently called and talked about bringing home a young man she had met—and casually mentioned that he was a vegetarian.

Susan was so busy imagining a tofu turkey that she didn't realize Kathleen was trying to get her attention until she grabbed her sleeve. "What the . . ."

"Susan, it's me. What in heaven's name are you thinking about?"

"Thanksgiving," Susan muttered.

"So that's why your meals are so inventive. You're always thinking about food," Kathleen said, pulling her cart in line behind Susan.

"That's why my thighs are so fat. I'm always *eating* food," Susan muttered, grabbing the latest *Vogue* from a metal rack and dropping it on the moving belt. Maybe the models' bodies would inspire her. Although, actually, she'd only had those muffins today. "Do you have time to stop over at the house? I've been talking to all the members of the Landmark Commission—except for Erika Eden—and I need someone to help me sort through what I've heard."

"Everyone except Erika Eden?" Kathleen mused. "Sounds interesting, but you'll have to come to my place. I have a new girl staying with the kids and I want to see how things are going."

Susan thought for a moment. It was cold enough for the frozen groceries to wait in the car. . . .

"Jerry went to the liquor store yesterday. We can have some wine and cheese and relax," Kathleen suggested.

"Sold! I need to make one more stop and I'll meet you

there," Susan said, offering the young man at the cash register her credit card. She had considered charging groceries to be an insane financial decision until she and Jed got a credit card that awarded frequent-flier miles for dollars spent. She now thought of it as eating her way to Italy. She packed up her food while Kathleen unloaded her cart, and then, with a wave and a promise to see her friend shortly, she hurried back to her car.

Susan had meant to stop quickly in a nearby drugstore and pick up a notebook to keep track of her investigation but a rack of toys near the door caught her eye. She loved all these little plastic things now that she wasn't constantly picking them up off her own floors. A windup turkey caught her eye; she thought it would impress baby Alice. And Alex was always thrilled to receive another Matchbox car for his collection—there was a hideous purple Ferrari that she knew he would love. Susan added the toys to the bright red notebook she had picked out and went to the counter to pay for her purchases. She got in line, admiring the swirling French twist of the blonde in front of her for a few minutes before she realized that it belonged to the head of Cassandra Chadwick.

"Cassandra?" Susan hesitated over the name, unsure whether or not a nickname would be more appropriate. Cassy? Or maybe Cass? She was glad she had chosen the more formal route when the woman turned and looked down on her. And it was down, since Cassandra Chadwick was a half dozen inches taller than Susan.

"Oh, Susan. I didn't see you."

Or the other slugs, was what Susan heard. "Oh, well, I didn't notice you for quite a while either," she answered. "I always get a little frazzled waiting in line—I worry if I've forgotten something," she added, thinking that the first statement sounded terribly rude.

"I find that a list helps." Cassandra made the suggestion as though it was an original idea.

"Of course, but at the last minute . . ."

"I keep two lists on the refrigerator—one for groceries and one for other essentials. And then I don't go out of the house without one or the other in my purse. I find that it saves a tremendous amount of time."

"I'm sure it does. I just can't seem to get organized—"

"Of course. With the election, it is more difficult." Cassandra surprised Susan by agreeing with her. "I've been asked to make so many speeches, and the public appearances have been truly onerous."

Susan had been about to make a comment about cottage parties and teas but decided to change the topic and discuss the murder. After all, Cassandra's husband might be running for mayor, but her own relationship with the chief of police was unique. "How does your husband think Ivan's death will affect the election?" she asked. They had time for a long conversation; it was becoming obvious that the woman in front of them had managed to pick out several unmarked items with bar codes that did not scan.

"Bradley is, of course, heartbroken," Cassandra began.

"I'm sorry. I didn't know they were good friends."

"They weren't. Ivan Deakin and the Chadwicks do not travel in the same circles. I was speaking of the election. Ivan added a lot to the race."

"Well, of course, I believe that Tony Martel is an excellent opponent," Susan said.

"Naturally, I would expect you to say that. He is not exactly a charismatic personality. And his programs are so far out—almost libertarian, wouldn't you say?"

"A libertine!" Susan gasped. "Nothing could be further from the truth! He and his wife have been happily married for—"

"I said libertarian. Not libertine," Cassandra said, a large smile on her face.

Susan assumed the teeth were capped. "I certainly wouldn't say libertarian either. Anthony is very well informed and his ideas are"—she searched for a word—"very mainstream. He's a hard worker, dedicated to the town, and—"

"Heavens, Susan, no one asked you to stump for the man. He can at least do that himself, can't he?"

Susan wanted to punch Cassandra in her perfect little pug nose. What sort of adult *chose* to have a nose like that? But that wasn't exactly what they were talking about. "I've been talking to a lot of people today and some of them think that Ivan's candidacy was going to hurt your husband's chances of becoming mayor," she said.

"Susan, how can you say that? Ivan Deakin was a flake. The citizens of Hancock are well educated and naturally conservative. They weren't going to vote for Ivan."

"But you said that Bradley wanted him to run!" Susan reminded her.

"Just to keep the voters from getting bored," Cassandra said, her smile becoming a smirk. "Just to make things interesting."

"When is the debate?" Susan asked quickly, seeing that the checker was starting on Cassandra's order.

"On Friday night. Why?"

"You don't think it will be canceled because of Ivan's death, do you?" Susan asked, ignoring Cassandra's question.

"I shouldn't think so. It's the last opportunity for the public to hear the two candidates before the election next week. Why?"

"Because I think you'll see something then that will

make this election just as interesting as you and Bradley think it should be," Susan announced loudly.

"A surprise? Will you give me a hint or will my viewers have to wait until Friday night?"

Susan realized that they had been joined by Tom Davidson. The young man was standing by her side, a long thin notebook in one hand, a pencil poised above it in the other. "Any statement?" he asked again.

"Yes, Susan. Give Mr. Davidson a statement," Cassandra urged, picking up the bag of toiletries she had just paid for.

"But then . . ." Susan began, thinking fast, "it wouldn't be a surprise, would it?"

"Can't argue with that," Tom agreed, writing something down.

"I think I'd better pay for my things," Susan muttered, moving up to replace Cassandra at the counter.

"And I guess I'll see you Friday night—if not before," Cassandra said, managing to include both of them in her good-bye.

Susan noticed that Tom was blushing at the attention he had received from the attractive woman. She resisted the admittedly bitchy urge to tell him how little of Cassandra was natural. "I—" she began.

"I'd be happy to make a statement to the press if you'll accompany me to my car," Cassandra said.

And the two of them left Susan to her purchases. It made her nervous, and she was glad that the transaction took little time. Nevertheless, she was surprised to see Tom Davidson and Cassandra still talking seriously when she left the store and headed back to her car. She would have loved to have known what they were talking about, and was still thinking about it when Kathleen opened the front door of her house a very few minutes later.

"You will not believe what just happened," Susan announced, stepping inside and putting the package from the drugstore on the side table in the hallway.

"Probably not, and you're going to have to come upstairs to tell me about it. Alice is in her crib and I have to give her a bath right away." Kathleen started up the stairway without waiting for a response from her friend.

Susan trotted up the stairs, stopping for a moment on the top landing to try to decipher a strange noise coming from one of the nearby bedrooms.

"That's Alex. He's crying," Kathleen explained. "Don't worry, he hasn't been hurt. He has to stay in his room to think about what he's done for another few minutes."

"What has he done?" Susan asked.

"He painted his sister's face with Magic Markers."

"He what?"

"Look!" Kathleen said dramatically as Susan followed her into her daughter's bedroom.

Alice was sitting in the middle of her crib, happily smacking a stuffed clown on the head. The toy responded with inane phrases. The little girl's face was streaked with fluorescent lines and swirls. There was even a third eye drawn rather inexpertly in the middle of her forehead.

"Alex did that?"

"Yes. He went to a birthday party Saturday afternoon with a carnival theme. A clown painted some cute flowers and hearts on the kids' faces. Then the baby-sitter let him watch an old sci-fi movie on TV this afternoon. So while the sitter was fixing the kids a snack, he painted his sister's face. He said he wanted to make Alice into a Cyclepop. I think he meant Cyclops," Kathleen explained, picking up her daughter.

"He didn't mean to do anything wrong," Susan said. "Probably no one told him not to draw on his sister. And what with Halloween so recent . . ."

"I know. I may have over reacted. Alice does need a bath." She looked at Susan with a silent appeal on her face.

"Why don't I do that and you can have a little chat with your son. It's been years since I washed anyone's face but my own."

"Thanks." Kathleen handed her daughter over. "This will only take a moment. I'll probably be in before you have everything scrubbed off."

It turned out to be an easy promise to keep. Susan was still scrubbing the chubby child's face when Kathleen entered the bathroom, her sniffling son at her side. "I think these may be permanent markers," Susan said gently.

Kathleen took a deep breath and looked down at Alex. "Honey, where did you get the markers you used to do this?"

"Cathy gave them to me," he answered.

"Do you know if she got them from the box of your art supplies?" his mother asked, taking the washcloth from Susan's hand and looking at its clean surface.

Tears began to form again in the corners of the six-year-old boy's eyes. "I don't know where she got them. I thought they were ones that I was allowed to use," he sobbed. "I didn't mean to hurt Alice. She liked it," he added, his sobs increasing to wails.

Seeing her older brother crying, Alice decided to join in, and soon both children were sobbing in Kathleen's arms.

"It's okay, guys. I know you didn't mean to do this," she told her son. "And Cathy is a new sitter. I should have told her about the art box. And Alice doesn't seem to care about how she looks. . . ."

"Did I tell you that I brought presents for Alex and Alice?" Susan said loudly. "I left them by the door. Why don't I go downstairs and get them?"

Kathleen nodded over her sobbing children's shoulders. Susan hurried to the front hall only to hear a loud smack against the door as she arrived. She opened it to find the *Hancock Herald* on the front step. She bent down to pick it up and saw the banner headline as she did so.

JED HENSHAW, it read, ACCUSED OF BREAKING THE LAW BY NEIGHBOR AND FRIEND.

FOURTEEN

BUT WHAT ABOUT PEOPLE WHO DON'T READ THE article? What about them? They're going to imagine Jed has done heaven knows what! He could be a serial killer from that headline, for heaven's sake!"

"I think if he was a serial killer, the headline would have mentioned that," Kathleen said, handing Susan a large glass of Burgundy.

"But all he did was not pick up Clue's mess—once. The man admits to seeing it only once! Jed hardly ever walks the dog alone!" Susan cried, taking a big gulp from her glass.

"Susan, no one is going to take this seriously. Your neighbor who was telling the reporter about it said that he was only kidding. That much is clear from the article. Someone just thought that headline would sell more papers."

Susan looked down at the paper spread open on her lap. "Well, maybe . . ." she began.

"Look, maybe the paper can issue a retraction. But you yourself said that nothing could be done until Jed knows. And since his secretary said that he was going to be out of the office for the rest of the afternoon . . ."

"I wonder if I should go home. It's possible that Anthony Martel will call."

"Is your machine on?"

"Yes."

"Then drink your wine and let's talk. The kids will be watching Barney for the next half hour. What does Brett say about the murder?" Kathleen asked, kicking off her shoes and tucking her feet beneath her on the comfortable couch.

"Of course, under the circumstances, he can't say much of anything."

"The circumstances are unusual in this case, but I don't think he'll proceed with the investigation any differently than usual. In fact, if you think about it, it's all the more reason for him to make sure that everything goes by the book—and that a lot of people know that's the way things are being done."

"True," Susan mused. The wine was relaxing her enough that she could focus on something other than the horrible headline. "I talked with everyone on the Landmark Commission—except for Erika Eden—and, you know, those are pretty strange people."

"In what way?"

"In the first place they all think of Penelope Thomas as Wonder Woman—except for Lyman Nearing and he gave his vote on the commission away to his wife."

"How did he do that?"

Susan explained the situation. "I think, in fact, that Penelope probably asked Rosemary to be on the commission assuming that's what would happen."

"Sure. Two votes for the price of one," Kathleen agreed. "From what you're saying, Penelope could be pretty sure Rosemary would vote the way Penelope thought she should."

"Definitely. And I suppose that's what I'm going to find when I talk with Erika, too."

"You mean that she's on the commission because she'll go along with Penelope."

"Yes."

"You know, that doesn't sound like Brett to me," Kathleen said, taking another sip of her wine.

"Brett? What does Brett have to do with Erika?"

"They're pretty serious from what I've heard." Kathleen looked curiously at her friend. "They're dating. You didn't know? I thought that's why you were talking about this murder being different for Brett."

"Because he's dating a suspect?" Susan cried. "I had absolutely no idea!" She drained her glass. "I thought this case was different because he was going to be employed by one or another of the suspects after the election."

"You're right. I hadn't realized that," Kathleen said, refilling Susan's glass. "I just assumed it was because Brett was dating the murdered man's ex-wife."

Susan was stunned speechless. Brett, handsome, still fairly young, and certainly virile, had dated a number of women in Hancock. Most were divorced; it simply wasn't a town where many single women could afford to live. But, to Susan at least, his relationships had looked pretty casual.

"Are you telling me that you really didn't know? Susan, they were at the Dysans' party together a few weeks ago."

"We didn't go. There was an exhibit at Chrissy's school and she had three small sculptures on display.... Brett dates lots of women. Why do you think this relationship is serious?"

Kathleen shrugged her thin shoulders. "He told me so."

"What exactly did he say?"

"He said he thought it was possible that Erika was the woman he had been looking for."

"You're kidding. He really said that?"

"Exactly that. We were together in the kitchen. Brett had introduced Erika to me earlier in the evening and I said something about how attractive she is—you know how it is, I felt I had to say something nice."

"And she isn't attractive?" Susan interrupted.

"She's beautiful! Someone told me that she had done some modeling when she was young and I sure can believe it."

"So you said something polite about Erika's appearance and Brett replied that she was the woman he had been looking for."

"Yes. I asked if I should start picking out a wedding present and he said that he sure hoped so. And then we joked around about appropriate gifts for a police chief and his new wife."

"Nice," Susan muttered. "What do you know about Erika? All I know is that she was married to Ivan Deakin, was once a model, and now owns a flower shop downtown."

Kathleen frowned. "We've only spoken a few times. Frankly, she intimidates me."

"You! You're kidding!" That didn't sound like Kathleen.

"Well, she's so smart."

"Uses big words? Has a Ph.D. after her name?"

"Both. She does have a doctorate. I don't know what she studied, though."

"You just know she didn't go to graduate school to find a smart husband," Susan said rather sarcastically.

"Probably not." Kathleen sounded doubtful. "I would have thought she could just depend on her looks, if a husband was all she wanted."

"So she's smart and beautiful." Susan bit her lip. "I wonder why I haven't seen her around town."

"You know, I'm not sure. She travels a fair amount. At least she was going out of town the day after the Dysan party, and Brett said something about missing her when I ran into him last weekend at the inn—and I saw them together in between times. We all stood in line at the movies downtown a week ago," Kathleen said, getting up.

"Where are you going?"

"I thought I heard a scream. I'll just go check on the kids." Kathleen left the room without saying another word.

Susan stared at her glass. She knew it was foolish, but to tell the truth, she was feeling a bit jealous of this Erika Eden. She sounded like the luckiest woman in the world. She had looks, brains, education—and Brett. Susan frowned. It wasn't like she had a crush on Brett, for heaven's sake. She was married. He was just a good friend. But if he was such a good friend, why hadn't he told her about Erika? She was relieved when Kathleen returned and she wasn't forced to examine her feelings further.

"They're fine," Kathleen said. "Just getting hungry. Why don't we talk in the kitchen? I know I should be fixing something green and nourishing, but I think it's the orange meal—boxed macaroni and cheese and carrot sticks—again tonight. Jerry's working late."

"Your kids are thriving," Susan assured her. "And I should get going. Maybe I'll check and see if Erika is back on my way home."

"Good idea. I think you'll like her. Frankly, it's hard to imagine anyone not liking Erika."

"She sounds amazing," Susan commented, wondering if Kathleen noticed the sarcasm in her voice. She stood up. "Why don't I see myself out and you can get busy feeding your kids?"

Kathleen glanced at her gratefully. "Thanks. Call after you see Erika. I'm anxious to hear what you think."

Susan spent the entire drive back to the carriage house giving herself a lecture that any mother would have been proud to deliver. Selecting the foolishness of jealousy as her theme, she embellished it with examples from her past and the pasts of friends. By the time her car was turning into the driveway, she was fairly sure that she could meet Erika without any foolish, inappropriate feelings messing up the moment. Until she pulled up to the carriage house and parked behind a tiny yellow Miata convertible.

It was an adorable car. A car she had imagined herself driving in her fantasy life. Not that her fantasies were so very unusual or exotic; in them, she was beautiful, single, childless, and ever so slightly stressed by a successful career. (She wasn't sure what she did, but she was sure it paid very well and caused her to spend a lot of time living in expensive international hotels.) She got out of her Cherokee, glancing down at her wool slacks and matching turtleneck as she did so. In her dreams, she didn't wear clothing like this. She wore handwoven sweeping skirts and glamorous silk tunics. Clothes that she never seemed to be able to find in stores. Clothes sort of like the ones the woman coming toward her was wearing.

Susan reminded herself of all the good points she had made during her lecture on the way over here, put a smile on her face, and walked over to meet her.

Erika Eden was adorable; tiny and thin. The first thing Susan noticed was her astounding light blue eyes. Then she took the time to take in the short, curly black hair, the ivory skin that flushed slightly across the cheeks as she extended her hand in a welcoming gesture. "You must be Susan Henshaw. You're exactly the way Brett described you."

Middle-aged? Frumpy? Susan pushed the words from her mind and greeted Erika. "Then he told you that I wanted to talk with you?"

"He said that he thought you would be speaking with everyone on the Landmark Commission. He didn't think you would be able to resist investigating Ivan Deakin's murder—because your husband is involved," she added quickly.

Susan wondered if there was a frown on her face. Had Brett been complaining about her sleuthing? She had always assumed he appreciated her help. "Yes, this murder is different from others that I've been involved in," she admitted, deciding to keep those questions to herself.

"Would you like to come in and have a drink?" Erika offered. "Brett is supposed to be over for dinner, but I'm expecting him to be late. He usually is these days," she added with a smile. "So we probably have a lot of time."

"Great," Susan said, feeling a little guilty about her family's dinner. "Could I use your phone, though? I need to let my son know I'm going to be late."

"Of course. Come on in." Erika walked up three stone steps and opened the door for Susan.

The cottage was as tiny and adorable as Erika herself. Large quarry tiles covered the floor and the front wall was made up of five French doors leading to a small deck. Inside, white walls were hung with bright abstract art, a dramatic contrast to the two couches covered in raw silk. A coffee table, a wall of books, and a couple of floor lamps were the only other furniture. A bar surrounded by bright red stools divided the room in half. A green Garland stove dominated the kitchen area. Next to the door, a circular stairway led up to what Susan assumed was the bedroom.

At the end of the bar, a tray bearing glasses and a bottle of pinot grigio waited. "Why don't you use the phone while I get some things from the refrigerator," Erika suggested.

Susan called her own number and left a message on her answering machine for whoever arrived first. She peeked over her shoulder at Erika, who was busy pulling bags of vegetables and Tupperware containers from the smallest refrigerator Susan had ever seen.

Erika smiled and waved to the couch. "Have a seat. Brett's worried about cholesterol, so we're into vegetables. I make these up in the evening in case I get home from work late."

"I don't want to eat your food," Susan said. Actually, she did. She was hoping it would keep her from getting giggly. She had already had more than enough wine, she realized as she accepted another full glass.

Erika put a tray of crudités and a bowl of dip on the coffee table, and perched on the other end of the couch where Susan sat. "So"—she took a sip from her glass—"do you usually start by asking the important questions or do you sort of soften up your subject by asking innocuous questions? Where they work and their background . . . things like that?"

"Well, I—"

"I graduated from the University of Wisconsin and did my graduate work at Harvard and UC Berkeley. I was in great danger of becoming a professional student until I discovered that I loved green things as much as I loved accumulating degrees." She grinned and lowered her eyes, giving Susan a good view of amazingly long lashes. "But you're probably more interested in my marriage to Ivan." She shrugged, a grin appearing on her face. "What can I say? I was only twenty-one, an idiot. It was a stupid thing to do. Of course, we were both so involved in school that we didn't see all that much of each other. That could be it. It's easy to be married to someone you don't see much. And it was lucky that we didn't have any children."

"You—"

"You're probably wondering why I don't seem terribly

upset by his death. I suppose that could make me a major suspect, couldn't it?"

"I—"

"Of course, we did have a somewhat amicable divorce—because we saw each other less than we did when we were married. We weren't even particular friends. More like old acquaintances who just happened to be living in the same town."

"Have you always lived in Hancock?" Susan finally managed to get a question asked.

"Heavens no. I moved here about three years ago. I was living in New York City and one day I just decided that I couldn't take it anymore. I talked with my boss and he agreed that I would work at home for two days a week, so I put my condo on the market and started looking for a new home. I was interested in Westport or Greenwich, but an old friend had just moved to Hancock and had bought the large Victorian by the street. She offered me this carriage house for a song and here I am."

"So—"

"I had to do a lot of remodeling, of course. But I love this place and would hate to have to give it up. So I didn't even think about leaving when I discovered that Ivan Deakin was living here, too."

"So you didn't know that he was living here when you moved in?" Susan took advantage of a moment when Erika put a large mushroom covered with dip in her mouth to ask another question.

"I hope you're not browbeating Erika, Susan. I thought you were a better judge of character than that." Brett Fortesque was standing in the doorway.

FIFTEEN

He wasn't smiling.

Susan opened her mouth to defend herself. She had not, after all, been doing anything that remotely resembled browbeating. But, once again, Erika beat her to the punch, jumping up and hurrying to Brett's side.

"Brett, how can you say that? Susan has been wonderful. I feel like we've been friends for years." She poured another glass of wine and handed it to him. "Come. Sit down and have some vegetables. I'll bet you've been existing on fried takeout ever since Ivan's murder."

Brett accepted the glass and dropped wearily on the couch across from Susan. "I guess you're right. I'm starved. The last meal I remember was an Egg McMuffin sometime around six A.M." He took a large piece of cauliflower and, drowning it in dip, stuffed it in his mouth.

Susan, who had been sipping her wine slowly, began to play with the almost full glass, managing to spill most of it in her lap. "Damn!" She leaped up.

"Let me get you a sponge," Erika offered, starting for the kitchen.

"Maybe . . ." Susan looked around. "Is the bathroom upstairs?"

"At the top of the stairs to your right," Brett answered quickly.

"If you don't mind . . ." Susan said to Erika.

"No, of course not. Go on up. The towels next to the sink are clean."

Susan trotted up the stairway, blotting her chest with a napkin as she went.

She found the bathroom easily and spent what she thought was enough time to dry off her blouse up there, peering out the doorway into the bedroom. The ceiling was slanted with one dormer and three large skylights providing the only light. She noticed French doors on the opposite side of the room from the bathroom; there had been no other exit visible from the driveway. The furniture was simple: a large brass bed, two white-painted chests, and a television on a bookshelf stood on the cheerful rag rug that covered the floor; it was comfortable, simple, and elegant.

Susan stared at the piles of white pillows and blankets covering the bed while she tried to listen to Brett and Erika's whispered conversation. Although she couldn't make out the words, she decided to wait until they had finished speaking to reappear. They needed some time alone. That was why she had spilled her wine—although she hadn't meant to spill so much.

She started down the steps when she heard someone start up.

"Did you find everything you need?" Erika asked.

"Yes. I just wanted to freshen up." She wished she had had the sense to flush the toilet. "Brett looks tired. I suppose I should leave the two of you alone so you can serve him some dinner. We could talk some other time. Maybe tomorrow."

"I may have to go into the city tomorrow," Erika said, frowning. "For my work."

Susan wondered if Erika really needed to make the trip to support one small suburban store.

"But I might be able to get home early in the afternoon."

"I . . ." Susan didn't know whether to see Erika then or not.

"After all, even though Brett might not want to admit it, I must be the major suspect in the case," Erika continued. "I was married to Ivan as well as being on the Landmark Commission."

"Erika!" Brett sounded tired and exasperated.

"Well, Brett, that's got to be what everyone is saying. And I'd rather speak with Susan about this than anyone else. Her opinion is respected in Hancock. If people believe that she's on my side, it will help my reputation—and that means a lot to me."

"Look, I only have half an hour or so—I really shouldn't be taking even that much time for dinner," Brett began.

Susan was surprised to hear the desperation in his voice. "Why don't I go and leave you two alone, then?" she offered. "You can call me about tomorrow," she suggested to Erika. "I'll be in all evening."

"Excellent idea," Brett said before Erika could reply. "Why don't you heat up dinner while I walk Susan to her car?" He led Susan to the door, barely allowing enough time for her to put on her coat.

"I'll call!" Erika's words floated out the doorway as Susan got in her car.

"She needs some time alone," Brett said, not really explaining. "She's fragile. A lot more fragile than she looks," he added, slamming Susan's car door, turning, and heading back to the carriage house.

Susan put the key in the ignition and glanced back through the French doors into the well-lit interior in time to see Brett enfold Erika in his arms. She wondered if Erika had been crying and needed comfort. She steered her car around the circular driveway and down to the road, thinking about the last few minutes.

Erika was charming, attractive, and well educated. She had original and excellent taste. It was obvious that Brett cared deeply about her. It was also obvious that he was worried about the situation she found herself in. Did that mean that he believed she might be guilty? Did Brett think he had fallen in love with a murderer?

She thought it over during the short drive home, finally deciding that the only thing she could do was help prove Erika's innocence—by finding the real murderer.

The outside lights had gone on automatically at dusk and Susan spied a huge bouquet sitting on the middle of her doorstep as she drove up. She parked out front and followed the walk to her home, wondering if someone had died or what Jed could possibly have done to feel quite this guilty. The bouquet was one of the largest she had ever seen, certainly the largest outside of a church or a funeral parlor. A white envelope was tied to the cellophane surrounding the flowers. Susan removed and opened it.

Then she chuckled. It was from the neighbor who had been quoted in the newspaper article, apologizing for speaking to the press, assuring her that he had only been joking about Jed and Clue's droppings.

She was still chuckling after she had unlocked the door to her house and struggled to get the immense bouquet inside.

Clue was sleeping on the needlepoint rug in the hallway. The dog opened one eye, saw that Susan's burden was inedible, and returned to her nap.

Susan carried the bouquet to the library and checked the answering machine. She was astonished by the number displayed on the black box. Who would have thought there was space for twenty-six messages on that little tape? She flung her jacket on Jed's desk chair, found a sheet of paper and a pen that worked, and pressed the replay button.

Ten minutes later she sat back and stared at the list she had made. It wasn't going to be as difficult as she had expected to return the calls. Penelope Thomas, both Nearings, and Foster Wade had all called twice. Lyman Nearing apologized for bothering her. Chad had called saying that he was going to be late and that he would pick up some pizza between school and soccer practice (she should not worry; he was leaving plenty of time for homework; he had even gotten an A on his French test last week). Jed had called because he, too, was going to be late. He also would pick up something to eat before the meeting Anthony Martel had arranged for tonight. Anthony Martel called twice. The first time he was looking for Jed. The second time he was looking for Theresa. Susan probably could have told him where she was: some fourteen calls were from Theresa.

In the first few calls, Theresa sounded relaxed, almost apologetic for bothering Susan, and not terribly concerned about when Susan called her back. With the fourth or fifth call, she began to sound a little desperate, asking Susan to call her as soon as possible and emphasizing the importance of what she had to say. After the sixth call, the messages were identical: "Susan. This is Theresa Martel again. I'm at 555-1234. Please call me immediately. I will wait here for your call. Please. This is very, very important." The phrases were punctuated by loud sighs that Susan assumed were the sounds of Theresa exhaling cigarette smoke. This campaign was certainly shortening Theresa's life, she thought, dialing the number.

No one answered.

Susan frowned and tried again.

Still no answer.

Susan hung up and stared at the notes she had taken while listening to the messages. Her machine announced the time each call came in (sort of; the owner's manual had been lost, so the machine was permanently on Daylight Savings Time) and she had noted this on her list. She glanced at her watch. The last call from Theresa had been made less than fifteen minutes ago. Susan frowned and dialed the number again. After all, maybe Theresa had needed to go to the bathroom.

This time her call was answered—the voice of a young male who apparently thought "Yeah, man," was an appropriate greeting to offer a stranger.

"Hello. I'm looking for Theresa Martel," Susan said slowly. "Perhaps I dialed the wrong number?"

"Yo! Anyone here named Terry Martin?" The words were shouted into the receiver, leaving Susan's ear ringing.

"No. Theresa Martel."

"Terry Martel!" was shouted into the phone again.

Susan gave up. "Where are you?" she asked the person on the other end of the line a question she assumed he could answer.

"Here, man. Here at the satellite."

Susan wondered if someone who thought she was male could possibly be accurate about his location. "The satellite to what?" she asked, raising her voice an octave.

"The satellite. The blue satellite. You know, out on the highway."

Susan realized that she did know. The Blue Satellite was a sleazy bar and bowling alley that was, indeed, on the highway, where it had been since it was built in the early sixties. It could politely be called a dive. She couldn't even begin to imagine Theresa Martel being there. "Could you tell me the number of the phone you're on?" she asked the man on the other end of the line.

"Do I sound like some sort of faggy waggy secretary?"

"Please. It's important," Susan asked, resisting the urge to hang up on this rude person.

"Five-five-five–one-two-three-four. And this is a public phone and I think you've used up all your time, lady."

A loud click told Susan she had been hung up on. Well, at least he had finally gotten her sex correct. She wondered what she should do next.

The doorbell's discreet chime answered her question: she should go rescue whoever was at the door from one of Clue's overly enthusiastic greetings. She hurried to the front of the house, grabbed the dog's collar, and opened the door.

"Oh. I'd forgotten about your dog." The aroma of cigarette smoke preceded Theresa Martel into the hallway.

"I'll just put her in the backyard," Susan said, trying to look casual as she dragged almost a hundred pounds of dog across the floor. "Go on into the living room. It's that way." She nodded in the correct direction and continued with her task. She didn't want to leave Theresa alone for long. The woman looked terrible.

She pushed the dog into her pen, pausing only long enough to scratch the poor animal behind her ears and promise a long run in the woods when all this was over. Then she hurried back to her guest.

Theresa was standing in the middle of the living room, flicking cigarette ashes into the fireplace. "You don't seem to have any ashtrays around," she stated apologetically.

"We have some somewhere that we put out for parties," Susan muttered, pulling out the drawers of the end tables near the couch. She found a stray saucer, which she handed to her guest. "Use this, if you want."

"Thanks." Theresa looked at Susan. "Did you get my phone messages?"

"Yes. In fact, I had just finished calling you back when you rang. Well, I dialed the number that you left, but you weren't there." She looked at Theresa. The woman didn't look like she had been drinking, but she hadn't been bowling in that suit she was wearing either and why else go to the Blue Satellite?

"I couldn't stand waiting there any longer. I only stopped in to get some cigarettes, but then I decided to call you, and after I had left the number, I thought I should hang around until you called back. But other people wanted to use the phone, so I thought I would just drive over here in case you were home and not answering the phone. You know, if you were sleeping or something."

"I was out," Susan said, not bothering to explain. "Why did you want to talk to me so badly? Does it have to do with that newspaper headline?"

"What news . . ." A look of understanding appeared on Theresa's face. "Oh, you mean the thing about Jed and the dog poop?" She began what Susan thought was going to turn into a chuckle, but chuckling and inhaling are difficult to accomplish simultaneously and she began to choke.

Susan dashed over and slapped her on the back. "Are you all right?" she asked anxiously. "Can I get you something to drink? Some water?"

"No. I . . . I just need someone to talk with." Theresa looked up and Susan couldn't tell if the tears in her eyes were from choking or strong emotion. "You see, I was in love with Ivan Deakin."

SIXTEEN

SUSAN WAS SITTING ON THE CORNER OF JED'S DESK trying to get his attention while he peered into the screen of his laptop. "She was really upset, Jed. After making this ridiculous confession—after all, they hadn't had an affair or anything—and smoking up a storm, she even asked if she could go see Clue in the dog run—and she hates dogs! And I think what she's afraid of the most is that the wrong person will find out about this crush," she was saying, wondering if her husband was listening to her.

"Uh-huh." He typed a few words.

"It's that she thinks Tom Davidson may suspect," Susan continued. "She's afraid he'll report it on television. But I don't think he will, do you?"

"Uh-huh."

"Because he seems to have some principles and I think if you approach him correctly, he'll just have to understand that this has nothing to do with the murder and—"

"If I approach who correctly?"

"Tom Davidson." Susan looked at her husband. "You said you could write and listen to me at the same time."

"I thought I could."

"Jed! You can't even think and talk at the same time!"

"I'm sorry." Jed yawned, leaned back in his chair, and closed his eyes.

Susan immediately felt guilty. "You're exhausted!" she cried. "Listen, there is no reason to make yourself ill over your work. There's nothing that can't wait."

"It's not my work. I'm so far behind at work that I don't even worry about getting caught up—it's impossible." He opened one eye and offered his wife a wry half smile.

"So what are you doing sitting in front of your computer at midnight?"

"Rewriting my speech for tomorrow night. But it actually is Friday already, isn't it? The debate is tonight, isn't it?"

"Less than twenty-four hours away. But why are you worrying about this? I thought the debate was between the three mayoral candidates, not the people running for town council."

"I'm filler," Jed said.

"What?"

"Or maybe a pinch hitter. I don't know. It's too late to think. The problem is that with Ivan Deakin dead, there was a feeling that the debate might be a little . . . well, a little . . ."

"Dull is the word you're looking for."

"Yes. And, in fact, it's a very good idea for all the candidates for town council to get exposure. People should have the opportunity to find out who they're voting for."

Susan thought there had been ample opportunity for that. Interviews had been running in the local paper for weeks and weeks. Every candidate had spoken to every civic group in town—in some cases two or three times. She didn't know about everyone else, but she was pretty sick of the candidates—except for Jed, of course. She smiled at her husband. "So why do you have to write out something? It's a debate, isn't it? Isn't there a moderator to ask questions?"

"The point," Jed informed her seriously, "is to make the points that I think are important."

And to avoid answering the questions at all costs, Susan thought. It was an election year; she had been listening to people not answer questions for months and months. "You probably should go to bed. You just used the word 'point' twice in one sentence."

"I need—"

"I could read your speech and maybe make some suggestions and you could work on it on the train ride into the city."

Jed stood up. "I'm going to drive in tomorrow. I'll set the alarm a few minutes early and go over it before I leave. You're sure you don't mind doing this for me?"

"Of course not." Actually, she was curious to see what he had written.

"This is just a first draft," Jed reminded her after explaining where she would find the file his speech was listed under. "It needs work. I know that—"

"Go to bed. You're exhausted. It's probably better than you think it is."

"Yeah, maybe," Jed said. "But you'll wake me up if it needs any major work? I won't have all that much time in the morning."

"I will. Now go." Susan dropped into his chair before he could sit down again and flicked the computer back on. Trying to find the appropriate spot to peer through her bifocals, she squinted at the screen and started to read.

Five minutes later she got up and began to pace the room. Jed's speech was dreadful. Unlike his simple statement on television a few days ago, it was rambling, pompous, and pedantic. In only a few months he seemed to have picked up the oratorical style of both mayoral candidates. Susan frowned. The only solution was to rewrite it from the beginning. She would take his points and rewrite around them. She knew there was a way to split the screen so that she could—

Shit! The screen went blank. Or blue rather.

Susan pressed another key. Then another. Then she tried out various combinations. The blue square remained . . . one vast blue field that might remind a poet of spring . . . life renewed . . . infinity. It reminded Susan of how tired she was. People who were depressed were often said to be blue, and staring at the empty screen, she could understand why. Fortunately, Jed was probably too weak from fatigue to kill her. Besides, being a murderer wasn't exactly a qualification for political office. So if she could just prove that Bradley Chadwick had murdered Ivan Deakin, there would be nothing to worry about. It would be a landslide for the Martel ticket, no matter what happened during the debate.

Unless, of course, Anthony Martel had discovered that his wife was in love with Ivan Deakin and killed him. It didn't make a lot of sense. She turned off the monitor and thought over what Theresa had told her this evening.

The story had struck Susan as being almost innocuous. Embarrassing, but innocuous. Theresa had met Ivan Deakin a few years before, when they served together on a special committee the mayor had set up to study whether an old lumberyard should be allowed to become a small shopping mall. As far as Susan could tell from Theresa's garbled narration, the woman had become infatuated while reviewing diagrams of traffic patterns and reports on possible increases in tax revenue. Susan found it hard to believe, but she was wise enough to know that sexual attraction was completely illogical—and old enough to be thankful of the fact.

The committee had been disbanded after presenting its conclusions to the town council. (Which, after voting to allow the shopping mall to be built, received so many petitions from outraged citizens, that it ended up placing a series of restrictions on the mall's developers that led to a cancellation of the project. Now the old lumberyard was the delight of nocturnal teenagers, keeping the Hancock Police Department busy with calls from neighbors about strange lights from inside the wooden building, and Susan had to go to a neighboring town to buy yarn at a charming shop that had opened in the new mall there.) But according to Theresa, it hadn't been all that difficult to find excuses to see Ivan Deakin even after the committee broke up.

The Martels belonged to the local Unitarian church, but Theresa hadn't been going much until she discovered that Ivan led a discussion group there. She then found that she had a passionate interest in what Susan seemed to remember was something like "Sexual Ethics in Modern Society." She picked up a sheet of blank paper and made a note. It would be interesting to see if she could find someone else who had attended those discussions, Ivan's sexual ethics being rather well known by those she had interviewed recently.

Anyway, by the time that group disbanded, Theresa had gotten Ivan to join her as an adjunct professor at the local community college. Susan didn't think she had been told what his field of expertise was; Theresa had been more interested in waxing eloquent about his speeches at faculty meetings.

The puzzling thing, as Susan saw it, was that apparently their relationship hadn't been sexual. Although, she reminded herself, it was possible that Theresa, embarrassed, had lied and the two of them had been meeting regularly at a sleazy motel in the afternoon for months. (Although not in Hancock. Zoning had taken care of that. Unless people were willing to risk meeting their friends and neighbors in the lobby of the very chic Hancock Inn, they had to go out of town to rent hotel rooms.) But why would a man who was a notorious philanderer pass up Theresa? According to the latter, he had never even made a tiny pass in her direction.

In fact, she thought the man was a saint. This did not sound like the Ivan Deakin that Susan was coming to know. She turned off Jed's computer and started upstairs thinking. She would ask Erika about this when they met tomorrow.

She was exhausted and decided to shower in the morning. Remembering Rosemary Nearing, she put her dirty clothing in the hamper before slipping into a heavy flannel nightgown and climbing into bed. It was cold, and shivering, she snuggled next to her husband.

He responded by snoring loudly. Lulled by the familiar sound, Susan drifted off to sleep.

And woke up almost five hours later to one of the strangest sounds she had ever heard. Realizing groggily that she was alone in the dark, she turned on the light next to her bed and, squinting in the sudden brightness, ran out the door. The sound, she realized as she got to the hallway, was coming from the first floor.

"What's going on?" Chad appeared in the doorway across the hall, his hair standing on end.

"I don't . . ." Susan began, then became motherly. "Aren't those the same sweatpants you wear to soccer practice? Shouldn't you be sleeping in clean clothes?"

"Mom! What is that noise?"

"I—"

"Susan, what did you do to my computer?" Jed appeared at the bottom of the stairway, his face scarlet.

"I think I lost your speech, Jed. I'm so sorry. It was late and I was tired."

"You didn't just lose the speech. You lost everything.

Even the operating systems! I can't believe it." He turned and wandered out of sight, probably back to his study.

"You really did it this time, Mom," Chad commented. "I have a big day today, so I think I'd better get back to bed. Tell Dad if he divorces you, I'll understand. I'll miss your cheese soufflés, but I'll understand."

Susan scowled at the door as it closed behind her son. Then she frowned. She should, she knew, go downstairs and see if she could help her husband out. On the other hand, in the mood he was in, he would probably say things that he would later regret, so it could be argued that she was doing him a favor by returning to bed and hiding under the blankets. She turned and went back into her bedroom. Clue was sprawled across the bed, managing to occupy both sides. It was a sign, Susan decided, and started toward the bathroom.

No matter what the crisis, the day began with the same routine, and she had showered, gotten dressed, walked the dog (who had decided to get up when she realized Susan was wearing shoes), and was leaning over *The New York Times* as her coffeemaker began to produce a seductively fragrant brew when there was a knock at the front door. Susan trotted off to answer it, hoping that Jed had called someone who could help him retrieve whatever it was that she had lost in cyberspace.

But their early-morning caller turned out to be Tom Davidson. Not surprisingly, he began his greeting with an apology. "I'm so sorry to bother you so early, Mrs. Henshaw—"

"Don't worry. We've been up for quite a while," Susan said, opening the door wider for him to enter. "I don't suppose you know anything about computers."

"Computer programming was my minor in college," he answered, apparently unsurprised by the question. "In fact, it was my major until I took my first journalism course in the second semester of my junior year. That's why I graduated a semester after the rest of my class—I had to get in some extra courses."

"My husband is having a terrible problem with his laptop and he has to fix it before he leaves for work," Susan explained. "He's in his study."

"Lead me to him. I can ask him questions at the same time. What sort of laptop does he have?"

Susan frowned. She knew that "gray" wasn't the answer he was looking for, but it was the only one she could come up with. "Why don't you let him show you and I'll go get some coffee. Do you take it black?"

"No, white with lots of sugar," the healthy young man answered, following her directions to Jed's study.

Susan dashed to the kitchen. If Tom could quickly fix the computer, if she managed to get enough caffeine into her husband in the next twenty minutes, and if the Merritt Parkway wasn't crowded, he might just make it to work on time. She filled two mugs with coffee, put the sugar bowl and a small pitcher of milk on a tray, and ran to the study with it.

The two men were huddled over the computer, reminding her of doctors examining an ill patient. She put the tray down on a nearby coffee table and fled back to the kitchen. She would have loved to ask if they were making progress; and assuming Chad hadn't eaten them, there was a box of doughnuts she wanted to offer the men. Susan had an unjustified belief in the benefits of sugar and caffeine when problem solving.

The doughnuts turned out to be untouched and Susan hurried back to the study with a plateful. She could hear the men talking before she entered the room. Jed was sitting at his desk; Tom was leaning back in a nearby chair. The computer was closed.

"Everything all right?" she asked with as positive a voice as she could manage this early in the morning.

"Well, let's see," Jed answered slowly, taking a chocolate-covered doughnut off the plate. "My computer is empty. There are no files. No running systems. It's blank."

Susan started to apologize profusely.

"But that's okay. The programs can be reinstalled and I can get almost all my files from the machine at work. I've lost all the files having to do with the election, but that doesn't matter now."

"Because someone else has those files, too, and you can copy them?" Susan asked, thinking that she was finally catching on.

"Because I'm going to withdraw from the race," Jed answered, looking at her with a serious expression on his face.

"But, Jed . . ."

"I have to, Susan. Someone has been looking into our financial records and a serious conflict of interest has been discovered."

"I don't understand!" Susan cried.

"Then you'll be able to hear about it all on your local cable channel news tonight. Or maybe your friend Mr. Davidson will share a prebroadcast version of his story with you." With that, he got up and stalked from the room.

SEVENTEEN

"WHAT HAVE YOU DONE TO MY HUSBAND?" SUSAN screeched, slamming her hands on the desk and causing coffee and doughnuts to fly in all directions.

"Blaming the messenger is a common response. But we don't make the news, we just report the news," Tom Davidson reminded her calmly.

"Don't give me that shit! My husband is one of the most unselfish people in the world. He got involved in this campaign because he wanted to contribute to Hancock. He had—and has—no intention of benefiting from office—financially or otherwise. He—why are you writing this down?"

"I thought a personal statement from the wife—"

Any and all beliefs in a free press vanished from Susan's mind as she whipped the notebook from his hands, flinging his pen across the room in the process.

"Hey! That's a real Mont Blanc! It was a graduation present!" He scrambled over the couch to find his treasure.

"What is this story about my husband?" she muttered, flipping through the pages.

"What are you doing? I would go to jail to protect my sources. You're not supposed to know who I speak with." He grabbed his notebook out of her hands.

Susan saw a name she recognized on the page before her. "If you're depending upon Cassandra Chadwick for the truth, you're making a huge mistake. The woman is as phony as her face!"

"Huh?" Tom looked as though he thought she was going mad. "Listen, Mrs. Henshaw, why don't I get you a copy of the story we're going to run tonight and—"

"Where?"

"What?"

"Where is that copy?"

"I have the story in my computer." He looked at her with horror, possibly thinking about what she had done to Jed's laptop. "Down at the station. And the only person who knows the password to get in is me."

"So let's go." Susan headed for the door. "Do you want to drive or shall I? Or maybe I should follow you. I don't know exactly where the station is."

"I'll drive. But don't you want to tell your husband where you're going?"

"I'll call him at work when I've solved this problem," she insisted. "Just let me get my purse and my coat." A few seconds later she was suitably attired and opening the door for the young man. "We'll go down to the television station, but you can explain more fully to me on the way."

"I—"

"First, I want to know what Cassandra Chadwick has to do with this. Was she your source—is this your car?" she interrupted herself to ask.

It was still dark, but the bright orange Volkswagen Beetle was illuminated by the Henshaws' porch lights.

"Sure is. My parents gave it to me for graduation."

"It's wonderful." Susan slipped into the passenger's seat. "You might not believe this, but four friends and I once traveled almost all the way across the country in a car just like this during my last spring break from college."

"On your way to Fort Lauderdale, right?"

"Actually, we were going to a peace rally in Washington D.C.," Susan said. "There were thousands of these little guys there," she added, running her hand across the dashboard.

"Yeah, we saw old network news stories about that in one of my American history classes. Those must have been interesting times to live in."

She noticed the strange glance he gave her as he shifted into reverse. "What's wrong?"

"I can't see you as a longhaired, dope-smoking hippie. . . . Not that I mean to insult you!" he added quickly, driving up over the edge of the curb on the way to the street.

"You haven't," she said, smiling at his comment. "A lot of very different types of people were against the Vietnam War . . . and as a matter of fact, I looked very nice in tie-dyed T-shirts and bell-bottoms . . . and if you say anything at all about me and drugs on the air, I'll sue the pants off you!"

"Yes, ma'am," he said meekly. "I know things were different back then."

"Do me a favor," Susan requested. "Assume nothing and please don't keep talking as though I was born sometime in the Dark Ages. I can assure you I've never been on speaking terms with a dinosaur."

"Fine."

"Maybe you could tell me exactly what Jed is being accused of," Susan suggested now that they were getting along better.

"Jed—and you, in fact—stand to benefit financially if the Landmark Commission is not given the power that it will receive if Bradley Chadwick is elected."

"But our house was built after nineteen—"

"It has nothing to do with the house you live in," he interrupted.

"Then how will we benefit?" Susan was sincerely puzzled.

"Does the Malloy Fund mean anything to you?"

She thought for a moment before answering. "I've never heard of it."

"You actually own over nine percent of it. You and your husband, that is. You bought slightly over eight percent, but the dividends are reinvested biannually."

"Does this have something to do with that apartment complex over in Westport we invested in years and years ago?" Susan began slowly.

"Exactly."

"So where does this fund come in?"

"They bought the apartment complex. And then they sold that particular apartment complex and invested in a company that was building some single-family homes in this area. Then—"

"Could you just tell me exactly what the connection is now—right now?" Susan asked, completely confused.

"What the whole story comes down to over a dozen years later is that after a lot of buying and selling and a rather unusual trade of property a few months ago, you are one of the owners of a fund that owns property that will someday be an expensive single-family home in a desirable part of town where there are many other expensive single-family homes for sale—if the Landmark Commission has its way. Or, if Tony Martel wins and limits the power of the commission, the property is going to become two duplexes that, considering the shortage of rental property in Hancock, are guaranteed to be money-makers."

"Are you sure that Jed knew about this? I remember we talked about buying into the apartment complex—it was being developed by a neighbor about the time that we were beginning to think about retirement—that's the reason we chose to reinvest the dividends, I think. And as long as it was paying well, Jed never mentioned it to me. Maybe he didn't even know."

"Maybe he didn't, but that doesn't really matter, does it? What matters is that he will benefit financially if Tony Martel wins and will lose financially if Bradley Chadwick does. And the voters deserve to know that. Think of Whitewater. Think of Teapot Dome. Think of—"

"Wasn't there a reporter killed during an election someplace out west?" Susan interrupted. "Maybe you should think about that!"

Tom Davidson smiled knowingly. "But you wouldn't ever kill me. . . ."

"And Jed wouldn't ever run for office hoping to benefit financially. And you know what I wonder about? I wonder how Cassandra knew about the Malloy Fund, don't you?"

"My sources are private. You may have seen Cassandra's name in my notebook, but that doesn't mean that she was a source. She might even own shares in the Malloy Fund herself."

"Is she mentioned in the story?"

"No, but—"

"Then she's your source. And I'd sure like to know who told her about it. We're here, aren't we?"

"We are." The tiny car slipped into the parking spot reserved for the station's reporter.

Susan got out and followed the young man into the building. She had once accompanied Chrissy's fourth-grade class to Rockefeller Center on a tour of NBC. Tom's entire station would have fit in one of the larger closets at that network's facilities. There was a small office with three desks and an even smaller studio with two cameras, three chairs, a coffee table, and some equipment Susan couldn't identify.

Tom sat down before one of the computers and turned it on. "Why don't you sit right there," he suggested, nodding toward another desk. "But don't touch anything!"

"I don't usually mess around with other people's possessions," Susan insisted, rather indignantly.

"I'm sorry," Tom apologized sincerely, and Susan remembered that he was a nice young man who was just slightly overenthusiastic about his first real job. "Here's the story. I'll print it out for you." He pressed a few keys and a printer at Susan's elbow started to churn out paper. She grabbed the sheets before they hit the floor and started to read immediately.

"Why is this only printed on one side of the sheet?"

"That's the way we do things in my business," Tom answered, emphasizing the personal pronouns.

"Are you going to read this on the air?" Susan asked, realizing that she had never watched the daily news show that the cable company produced.

"Yes. The news is rescheduled this evening because we're covering the debate live at eight o'clock tonight. So we'll go with this an hour earlier at seven. I told your husband that he is welcome to come on the show and respond. But he said he wouldn't have time between work and the debate. . . . Say, you could do it for him," Tom suggested.

Susan thought quickly. Respond meant that she would have the last word, didn't it? She glanced back down at the script in her hand. In it Jed was condemned as a man who was running for office merely to pad his own pocket. It was an easy decision; she couldn't let that statement stand unchallenged. "I'll be here at seven," she answered.

"Make it six-thirty so we have time to get you made up." Tom Davidson was so enthusiastic that Susan began to doubt the wisdom of her decision.

"Okay," she said slowly. "I guess I'd better think about what I'm going to say."

"Bring your script along and we'll put it in the teleprompter," he suggested, standing up.

Susan followed suit. She was frowning. "You'll give me a ride back home?"

"Sure. We'd better get going. I have a lot of work to do today."

Susan had to dash to stay close behind him as he headed back to his car. She got in and barely managed to slam the door on the passenger's side before he had started the car and was backing out of the space. "How long can my response be?" she asked, taking an old grocery list from her purse and beginning to take notes.

"As long as you want—within reason. The story runs about four minutes, so your response can be any length up to four minutes."

"How do I know how long it will take?"

"Read what you write and time it. Simple."

It was, of course. She frowned and tried to think of a punchy first line. She had promised to visit Erika today, but how long could it take to write a four-minute statement?

An hour later she was beginning to think the answer to that question was forever. Of course, she had had a lot of distractions. Chad had just been leaving for school as she entered the house and she had managed to pry less than a dozen words out of him about his plans for the evening (he might be home for dinner or he might not) before he ran to the bright red BMW waiting in the street. (If she had noticed the car earlier, she wouldn't have bothered to concern herself with his plan to return home. Who is the blond girl driving that car and how old is she? were the questions she would have asked.)

Then, before turning on her answering machine, she

had gotten four calls from friends and neighbors about the election and/or the murder. Susan had answered the questions as tersely as possible, realizing that she was doing exactly what she had condemned her husband for trying to do last night. She made a few calls on her own, leaving messages on both Kathleen's and Erika's answering machines before turning her own on and sitting down at the kitchen table to think of that elusive punchy first line.

But, of course, she should be able to wipe down the kitchen counters while she thought, she decided, getting up and doing just that. And then there was her oven, which could use cleaning. . . .

She might have had the cleanest kitchen in town and the shortest speech ("Hello, I'm Susan Henshaw" was as far as she'd gotten—but she had crossed that out, deciding it was duller than dull) if she hadn't heard Brett's message on her answering machine. He was brief and to the point. He needed to talk with her. Immediately. It was important.

She called the police station and was put right through. "Brett, it's Susan."

"Susan. Thank goodness. Could you meet me at Erika's house?"

"Sure. When?"

"Right away."

"But I called and she wasn't—"

"She wasn't there. I know. She's vanished."

"But how do you know?"

"She dropped a note in my mailbox sometime during the night. Listen, it's a long story. I can tell it to you while we search her place."

Susan had no idea how to respond to that, so she hung up, checked Clue's water dish, grabbed her coat and purse, and headed for her car.

EIGHTEEN

IF WRITING A PUNCHY FIRST LINE HAD TURNED OUT
to be one of Susan's least favorite activities, she knew
that searching through another woman's private possessions was going to be the opposite.

It was true there was a murderer around, and concerns
about Erika's safety had filled her mind as she drove over
to the carriage house, but Brett's first words had cleared
that matter up.

"I suppose you may as well read this—it's the note she
dropped off at my house during the night," he explained.

Susan accepted the sheet of paper that he offered,
taking a moment to appreciate its thickness and unusual
appearance.

"It's hers," Brett said.

"What?" She wondered if he was talking about the elegant handwriting.

"That's some of the notepaper she carries in her stores.
You seemed to be staring at it," he explained further.

Susan decided she would read first and try to deter-
mine whether Erika Eden owned a stationery store or a
plant shop later. But the note was brief, to the point, and
really told her nothing: *I'm sorry. But I can't take this
anymore. I'm going on a short vacation. I'll call you
when I return. Much love, Erika.*

Susan handed the note back to Brett. "Erika carries this paper at Stems and Twigs?" she asked.

"Maybe. I guess. I know she has an extensive line of handmade paper at the store on Madison," he answered, rereading the note as he spoke.

"Madison Avenue? Erika has a flower store on Madison Avenue?"

"Yes. And one down in SoHo. There's also one opening somewhere in Westchester County next month. Larchmont, I think. That's why she's been so busy recently."

"Now, wait a second," Susan said as Brett took a key from his pocket and fit it into the door of the carriage house. "I thought Erika owned Stems and Twigs here in town. I didn't know there were other stores."

"She started with Stems and Twigs here, but wanted to carry other products—things related to plants, of course, but different. Like that paper. So, anyway, she opened a larger store out in East Hampton. The next logical move, as she explains it, was to the city. She opened a small store on Madison Avenue a few years ago, then moved downtown. The store down in SoHo is the largest. It also carries household goods made from natural fibers as well as organic oils, soaps, candles. You know the type of thing."

Susan did. And if Erika was a good businesswoman and had gotten in at the beginning of the natural-products boom, she might be a very wealthy woman.

"She does a lot of her own importing," Brett continued. "She was supposed to be going on a buying trip to China next week. But I was trying to talk her into hanging around here until we knew who murdered her ex-husband."

"Couldn't you have insisted that she stay around?" Susan asked, following him into the room. "After all, you could consider her a suspect. Not that I think you would. Or that she did," she added quickly, seeing the stricken look on Brett's face. "I mean, I don't think she murdered Ivan Deakin. Why would she?"

Rather than answer, Brett took off his heavy jacket and hung it on one of four hooks that were mounted on the wall beside the circular stairway.

The other hooks were full, Susan noticed. She pulled off her jacket and draped it over the banister.

"Erika always says that this place was designed for one person only," Brett said, a sad smile on his handsome face.

Susan decided not to pursue that fertile subject. "Why did you want me to come here?" she asked. It impressed her as much today as it had yesterday. But she didn't say anything more, noticing that Brett was standing in the middle of the room, staring at the wall of books. She leaned back against the banister and waited for him to answer her question.

Brett turned around. "I needed a witness—and I wanted one who was likely to be sympathetic."

To whom? was what she wanted to ask. "What are we supposed to be looking for?" was what she did ask.

"I'm hoping to find something that will tell me where she's gone." He looked into Susan's eyes. "And I'm hoping that I won't find anything that will incriminate her in Ivan Deakin's murder."

"Then this is an official search."

Brett nodded. "I have a search warrant. This is irregular, but legal."

The answering machine on the counter was flashing the number "2" and Brett pressed the play button. The first message was from someone named Barbara, complaining about a supplier who had promised delivery a week ago. Maybe a call from Erika herself might jog the order loose. Brett frowned and reset the machine.

"So where do you want to start?" Susan asked.

Brett turned and looked around. "How about the kitchen?"

Susan had been dying to get a closer look at that green Garland stove. She hurried behind the bar that separated the cooking area from the rest of the room. The stove dominated the space, leaving room only for a tiny refrigerator-freezer, a single sink, and a cupboard. The back of the bar was made up of open shelves, covered with glasses, china, crockery, and a surprisingly extensive collection of pans.

"There's no place to store food," Susan muttered, bending down and looking in the oven. It was full of baking equipment.

"Erika spent two years in Denmark. She learned to cook there—and she says that she became accustomed to shopping every day. She's a wonderful baker," Brett said wistfully.

Susan had been examining the *batterie de cuisine* and didn't find his statement surprising. She looked at all the food in the refrigerator and cupboard and at the small collection of cleaning supplies under the sink, but there weren't any bottles marked "poison" or receipts for airplane tickets issued that day. "I don't think there's anything here that might tell us more than that she is a fine cook," she commented, moving around the counter.

"Well, then let's look in here," Brett said, glancing around the rest of the room. "The bookshelf is the logical place to start."

The floor-to-ceiling bookshelves were built into the entire far wall of the room. Small objets d'art and dozens of tiny boxes separated the books. "Why don't I sit on the floor and go through the bottom shelves and you grab a stool and start at the top," she said.

"Sounds good to me," Brett agreed.

It took over an hour, but when they were done, they were fairly sure they hadn't missed anything. Early in the search, Susan had discovered an extensive collection of travel guides, language books, and maps. Hidden behind them were dozens of envelopes. She had excitedly looked in each and every one and found neat packets of foreign currency, sorted and accompanied by fairly current sheets noting the rate of exchange. Such organization turned out to be typical of Erika, who had sorted her books according to subject. Susan hoped if she ever had a long illness she would be allowed to recuperate here. The collection of English women's fiction alone would keep her happy for months. And the books about plants were extraordinary. There were also books in French and Italian.

After discovering that one of the couches was a sofa bed, Susan followed Brett up the circular stairway to the second floor and to a bedroom that was as orderly as the living room. Susan was surprised. When she left on a trip, her bedroom usually looked like the aftermath of a maelstrom.

Instead of getting to work and searching, Brett walked over to the window and was staring out.

"Why don't I start in the bathroom?" she suggested, thinking he needed some privacy.

"Fine," he muttered, preoccupied and distracted, it seemed.

Susan turned and entered the bathroom. Late one night at a party, she had got involved in a rather silly discussion about how most people could be divided into two groups, those who peeked in medicine cabinets in other people's homes and those who didn't. Susan fell into the latter category, but after listening to the confessions of her friends and neighbors, she had gone home and looked at what she had stashed in the metal box above the sink with a new eye. What did all this say about her? she had wondered, thinking the jar of cream that promised firm thighs if rubbed in nightly probably belonged in her dresser drawer. Now she pulled back the mirror over Erika's sink, wondering what she would find there.

And was not at all surprised when what she found was orderly, elegant, and organic—except for a can of Gillette shaving cream, a used razor, and a bright blue toothbrush. It wasn't hard to figure out that these items were Brett's contribution. Susan reached up to the top shelf and examined the labels on the little amber prescription bottles. Apparently the extensive supply of vitamins that accompanied them kept Erika healthy. Except for a prescription cold medication, the other bottles contained common antibiotics and a painkiller prescribed by her dentist a year ago.

There was a wonderful collection of makeup, sponges, wooden combs, and natural-bristle brushes. Little ceramic pots and tiny crystal jars were filled with creams and perfumes. Susan opened a corked glass vial and peered in, wondering if the white powder was an illegal drug, and decided probably not, unless cocaine smelled like violets. She closed the cabinet and examined the glass shelves built into the white tiled walls. Large bottles of herbal salts showed Erika to be a woman who enjoyed her baths, as did the thick beige unbleached cotton towels that hung on towel bars and filled the minuscule linen closet. Susan dutifully unfolded each and every one, succeeding only in spilling bundles of lavender on the floor. When she returned to the bedroom, Brett was still staring out the window.

"Nothing significant in there," she announced.

"Well, let's get to work in here."

The bedroom turned out to be where Erika kept her personal papers. Like the rest of the house, it was neat, organized—and dense. Closets were built into each wall. Drawers pulled out from under the bed. Books stood behind books on the deep shelves. They spent hours there, going through clothing, linens, and each and every notebook, pamphlet, and receipt in her desk and in the elegant wicker baskets on her shelves. It was a fascinating way to get to know a person.

And searching with Brett was a fascinating way to get a closer look at his relationship with Erika. For instance, he had been astounded to find a letter from Erika's accountant informing her of another offer to buy her stores and her name. The offer was, in the accountant's opinion, a little low: only eleven million dollars.

"Who would have thought there was so much money to be made from plants?" Susan commented, feeling that she had to say something.

"Amazing, isn't it?" Brett agreed slowly. "Erika told me that she began her business on a shoestring—I think she took out a bank loan for a little more than ten thousand dollars."

"Wow." Susan had always thought about beginning a small business . . . maybe something to do with food. Ten thousand dollars . . .

"Of course, she's worked night and day for the past ten years. She deserves every bit of her success," Brett continued.

But he sounded uncomfortable and Susan wondered how he felt about discovering that the woman he loved was so much wealthier than he. Then she realized that perhaps he was thinking that Erika could well afford to stay away for a long time. She shuffled through the rest of the papers as quickly as possible.

"What are you looking for?" Brett asked.

"I just wondered if she was thinking of selling her business."

"And using the money to move to Brazil?"

"I really don't think she killed Ivan," Susan protested quickly.

"And if you did, you would still say that to me. I know, you're a good friend," Brett insisted.

Susan took a deep breath. "Maybe we should talk about it. Do you think there's a chance that she killed him?" she asked quietly.

Brett sat down on the edge of the bed and shook his head. "I don't know. I know that she didn't like him much. And I know that she's a very passionate woman. But a murderer? I can't see her murdering anyone. But, of course, I love her."

"I know," Susan said, sitting down next to him. "Why did she dislike Ivan? They haven't been married for years. They don't have any children. They just happen to live in the same town." Susan wanted to hear the story. "I understood that they were married when they were young."

"That's true. In college, in fact."

"And married for how long?"

"For five years. But that figure is really deceiving. They lived together only a little more than two years."

"What did she tell you about the marriage?" Susan hoped that he would keep talking.

"That it was a mistake from the beginning. That they were both too young. They moved from their dorms into married student housing and fought for two years until she moved out."

"Why did it take so long to get divorced if there weren't any children?" Susan asked.

"Ivan refused to get a no-fault divorce—which had just

become possible in the state they were living in. She also didn't have any grounds for divorce—remember, years ago these things were more difficult."

"So what did she do?"

"She said she just waited. She assumed that there would come a time when Ivan wanted his freedom."

"And he did."

"Yes. Apparently he started seeing a woman who refused to date a married man. So he agreed to get a no-fault divorce. They filed the papers and then had to wait a year for it to go through."

"Which accounts for the final three years of their marriage."

"Yes."

"Did they see a lot of each other during those three years?"

"I don't think so," Brett answered slowly. "I know Ivan changed colleges—but I think they were still in the same state. In fact, I'm sure of it. She once said that she had to wait until the divorce went through to move out of state to do her graduate work."

Susan wondered what Erika's field had been, but there were more important questions to ask.

"But Ivan is known as a philanderer—or whatever you call a man who is involved with many women. Wasn't he behaving like that when they were married?"

"You know, Erika did mention that once. She says she must have been one of the most naive people in the world because she had no idea he was like that back then. Evidently she met an old classmate a couple of years ago and the other woman confessed to having an affair with Ivan while he and Erika were still together."

"How did they end up living in the same town?"

"Well, Erika got into plants and things like that while she was in California. She had planned to teach—"

"What's her field?" Susan asked quickly.

"Women's studies." He grimaced. "Not too practical and apparently she realized that about the time she finished up her doctorate. Anyway, she had gotten a job at some sort of organic farm while she was in school, and by the time she had her degree, she had fallen in love with flowers and knew that she wanted to own a store like Stems and Twigs. She thought the East Coast was a good location and stumbled into Hancock when she was visiting a friend."

"The friend who owns this carriage house?"

"Exactly. The carriage house was empty and so Erika moved in, borrowed money, and started the first store."

"And Ivan Deakin was here all this time?"

"That's an interesting question," Brett said, frowning. "You see, Ivan Deakin has a very interesting personal history."

NINETEEN

SUSAN LEANED BACK AGAINST THE FOOTBOARD OF the bed and thought for a moment. "I know I've read his bio in the papers, but I don't remember anything odd about it."

"Those bios don't tell much. Degrees and jobs mainly. And Ivan's is shorter than any of the other candidates— he not only doesn't have a family, but he didn't do a lot of volunteer work in town. Just a commission or two."

Susan nodded. That had been a tough part for Jed to fill out, too. They had finally translated the time that he ran the rides at the elementary-school carnival and the afternoon he planted bulbs in one of the parks (Kathleen had talked each and every one of her friends into volunteering for at least one afternoon or morning) into "extensive work in the local schools and parks." Fortunately, he had coached both his daughter's and his son's soccer teams when they were young, so the list was not entirely bogus. The amount of volunteer work some of the candidates had done amazed the Henshaws. Susan, for one, had great doubts that Bradley Chadwick could possibly have served on as many committees and boards as he claimed: the man had to work, eat, and sleep sometime, didn't he?

"I don't remember very much about Ivan's bio. He

graduated from some small college in Massachusetts, didn't he?" Susan asked, returning to the subject.

"Yes, barely . . . Remember, I've had men researching his background for the past two days, so I know more about him than most people," Brett explained, noticing her surprised expression. "His bio doesn't explain that he went to four different schools of higher education for five and a half years to obtain a degree from a college that no one can remember—it closed about six years ago, in fact. He did, however, get a graduate degree about ten years later from Cornell."

"After barely managing to get through his under-graduate work?"

"Interesting, but not unheard of," Brett said. "When you start looking into people's background, you realize that there are a lot of second chances in this life."

"What did he get the degree in?"

"Business the first time and then hotel and restaurant management."

"Well, he's certainly used his education, hasn't he?" Susan commented. In the early eighties, Ivan had been a famous enough restaurateur to be mentioned in *The New York Times*. In the current decade, he had branched out into the suburbs, buying, running, and selling the intimate French inns and bistros that were so popular—at least that's what Susan had heard. But as she listened to Brett's story she realized that the reality was very different than the image.

The story Brett told was of a man who traded friendship and a lot of free meals for publicity—and who ended up with flash-in-the-pan popularity that he was unable to turn into lasting success. Ivan Deakin was well known, but what was less well known was that he was a failure. In a little more than a dozen years he had moved from owning a popular restaurant in the heart of Greenwich

Village to owning an unpopular bistro near Greenwich, Connecticut.

"Didn't he make a lot of enemies along the way?" Susan asked.

"If you're thinking of people who might have had a reason to want him dead, believe me, we thought of that, too. And unless our information is incorrect, there's no one. It's his own money that he lost—or his uncle's money."

"His uncle?"

"Yes, it was an inheritance. He bought his first restaurant—the successful one—with an inheritance from his mother's brother. In fact, that inheritance may be the reason he agreed to a divorce. His uncle died right before he called Erika and suggested filing. He probably didn't want to be forced by a court to share the money with her."

"It must have been a lot of money."

"A couple of million. He was pretty much able to buy the restaurant outright."

"And how much of it is left?"

"Well, he drove an eleven-year-old Mercedes that is paid for, but there doesn't seem to be anything else."

"He didn't have any other money?"

"None. On the other hand, he didn't owe a lot either— probably because his credit rating was so bad that no one in their right mind would loan him money."

"What about Erika?" Susan asked.

"I've been wondering about that myself. She never told me that she had loaned or given him money—but I never asked either. What made you think of that?"

"Well, she was worth so much money and he had so little—it just made sense. Except that you think she hated him—" Susan snapped her mouth shut. The expression on Brett's face told her that she had said too much. "How did they happen to end up living in the same town?" she asked quickly.

"It could have been an accident," Brett said. "I mean, he might not have known that she was living here when he moved in. His restaurants in the city failed one after the other and he moved up to Westchester and bought a little inn up there, and, typically, that one didn't do very well and he sold it for less than he had bought it for, and then he opened a restaurant in Westport." Brett shrugged. "He was working in the suburbs and living in the city. Many people eventually move out under those circumstances. Besides, he probably needed the money that he got from selling his co-op. He got less for that than he had paid, too. But this had more to do with the market in the nineties than any lack of business sense."

"Did he own a home here?" Susan asked.

"He rented a very nice Tudor near the municipal center. That is, it looks nice from the outside. Inside it's a mess. Beige furniture rented from a company in Stamford, a huge entertainment system, and not much else. He was not, apparently, a man whose home was his castle."

"What a depressing story," Susan muttered, looking around the carriage house and thinking how differently Ivan's life had turned out from his wife's.

"Apparently he wouldn't have agreed with you. According to everyone who knew Ivan Deakin, he always believed that he was going to make it big with the next restaurant. He was even teaching a community-college course on how to run a successful restaurant. Seriously! You'd think that he'd just stand up in front of the room on the first day of class and say, 'Do as I say not as I do.' "

Susan wondered if she should explain how Ivan had come to be considered an expert in a field in which he had apparently failed. She suspected that Theresa Martel would prefer Brett not to know, but he was being so open with her and he had asked her to come here. She made up her mind and began her explanation.

"Yes, we know about that," Brett interrupted her. "Just another woman who found Ivan Deakin irresistible and would do anything for him. It seems to be a common theme in his life. His restaurants would have failed much more quickly if women hadn't helped out by sending him business or finding friends who gave him free publicity. One woman rented the restaurant in White Plains for her daughter's wedding, but on the day of the event, Ivan's suppliers refused him more credit and there would have been no food if a deli nearby hadn't agreed to send over three dozen foot-long hoagies. They didn't exactly go with the vintage champagne and out-of-season lilacs that had been flown in from Central America for the reception. And amazingly enough, when the mother of the bride was interviewed by one of my men, she had nothing bad to say about Ivan—of course, she was saving her venom for her son-in-law, soon to become her ex-son-in-law. He had arranged the reception."

"What about her husband?" Susan asked, thinking that this was another area to investigate.

"Ex-husband. There's no evidence that Ivan got involved with married women."

"But Theresa—"

"She may have had a crush on him, but she didn't say anything about an affair, did she?"

"No, in fact, the story was quite tame. More like a schoolgirl crush than anything else."

"That's the impression the officer I sent to the college got from whomever he spoke to there," Brett admitted.

"I wonder if any other candidates' wives could have been involved with him."

"We checked that out, too," Brett admitted. "And found nothing."

"I suppose an unsuccessful businessman is not the type of person to appeal to Cassandra Chadwick," Susan mused.

"Do you have any reason to suspect her?" Brett asked quickly.

"She's such a bitch," Susan muttered. "You wouldn't believe what she did to Jed."

"What?"

"She told that young reporter—Tom What's-his-name—"

"Davidson. What did she tell him?"

"That Jed invested in this thing called the Malloy Fund and that this fund would make lots of money if Anthony Martel wins—oh, shit. What time is it?" She jumped up off the bed. "I have to write a response to the story that's going to be on television tonight."

"Really? Network or local New York news?"

"Actually the cable channel. The Hancock news on Channel 46."

"Susan, no one watches that channel."

"Someone must. And every vote counts!" It had better. Otherwise she had wasted the last month making calls, writing notes, and being exceptionally nice to the most boring people in Hancock. "I really have to go," she insisted.

"Susan."

She stopped, unable to ignore the sadness in her friend's voice. "What, Brett?"

"She didn't kill him. I love her. Erika didn't kill Ivan Deakin."

"Then I guess we'd better get busy and find the real murderer," she said, putting a hand on his shoulder. "But first . . ."

"Go defend your husband," Brett said, almost smiling. "And if you think of anything . . ." He looked around the bedroom as though expecting to see something they had missed that would answer all their questions.

"If I think of anything, I'll give you a call right away," she promised. Like him, she glanced around the room one last time before leaving. Something was missing here; she just didn't know what. She frowned.

"Worrying about what to say on TV?" Brett asked, getting up.

"It's not easy," Susan began.

"Just remember Nixon and the Checkers speech. Don't worry about answering the question—and let everyone know how humble your family is."

"Not a bad idea," Susan agreed, heading down the stairway. "Especially since I don't actually understand how some apartments in Westport became the Malloy Fund in Hancock."

"Maybe you could mention Clue," Brett called down the stairs.

"And my cloth coat," Susan muttered, appreciating how nice he was to even think about her problems when he was so worried about Erika.

The phone rang as she reached the first floor and she paused to listen as the answering machine picked up.

"Erika, this is Theresa Martel. We need to talk about Ivan Deakin's murder. Something strange has happened and I think you might be able to help me with it. I just don't understand . . ."

Susan stood still as the message continued with the Martel phone number. Before she hung up, Theresa said, "It's important, very, very important."

"Did you hear that?" she called up to Brett.

"Sure did. I'll give her a call. Not that I think she'll confess to anything."

"But why is she so upset?" Susan muttered, leaving the house and heading out to her car. A glance at her watch

told her she had just enough time to walk Clue, give
Kathleen a call, leave a note for her son on the kitchen
table about his choices for dinner, eat something herself,
and write that damn speech before she was due down at
the station.

But she hadn't reckoned with the time it would take to
answer all the messages on her answering machine that
the callers had deemed important. After almost an hour
of sitting by the phone, she was wishing she could ask
people if their message was important to her or her
family or to them before returning their calls. The most
innocuous of the calls were jokes about Jed and dog
walking. The most irritating concerned the Landmark
Commission and the election. Susan, remembering that a
vote was a vote, dutifully listened to those callers, trying
to write her response to Tom's story in between "uh-
huhs." Around five o'clock, she realized that while there
might be a makeup artist at the station, she was going to
have to do her own hair. She spent an hour in the bathroom, washing, setting, and blow-drying, and was almost
completely satisfied with her appearance when she came
back downstairs.

Clue was waiting by the front door. "Okay, sweetie,
we'll take a quick walk before I leave." Mindful of Jed's
political problems, she tossed a large garment bag of
blouses she was taking along to the station over a chair,
grabbed a handful of plastic bags, stuffed them in her
pockets, and led the dog out the door.

She would have looked better when she arrived back
home if it hadn't begun to rain during her trip around the
block. She pulled her damp hair into an unflattering bun
and drove to the station, remembering Brett's assurance
that no one watched the cable channel.

TWENTY

Unfortunately, lots of people were going to see her photograph on the front page of tomorrow's *Hancock Herald,* Susan thought as another flashbulb went off in her face.

"Mrs. Henshaw, we understand that Tony Martel is thinking of forcing your husband off his ticket."

"Does the Malloy Fund have anything to do with the murder of Ivan Deakin?"

She could only hear pieces of the questions that were tossed at her as she walked into the building. Who were these people?

She asked the question of Tom Davidson immediately after stepping into the building.

"Don't you recognize them? That's the press," he explained, a grin on his face.

"And what are they doing here asking me questions? Don't they have better things to do? Don't they know we're about to elect a president in just a few days?" Susan asked, pulling her barrette from her hair. A glance at her reflection in the glass door to the station had convinced her that it would look better loose.

"Conflicts of interest are always news in an election year. Besides, those are third-string reporters. If anything else happens tonight, their stories will end up in the dump."

"Their photographs, too, I hope. Where are we going?"

she asked, surprised as he jumped up from the desk he had been leaning against and started from the room.

"Makeup."

"Good! Maybe she can do something—what is this?" Susan asked as he opened what appeared to be a storage closet and flicked on a lightbulb hanging from the ceiling.

"Makeup," he repeated, reaching out and picking up a battered tin box.

"You do the makeup?" Susan asked, realizing what was happening.

"Sure. What did you think?"

"I had sort of envisioned a woman in a pink coverall sitting before a mirrored wall."

"Look, I run my own camera. I edit my own tape. The station car is a Rent-A-Wreck reject. And you thought there would be a luxurious makeup room. . . ." He began to chuckle. "What did you think this was? The *Today* show?" He picked up a tube of pinkish greasepaint. "Do you want to do your own or do you want me to give it a try?"

"I can put on my own makeup," Susan assured him quickly.

"Well, add a lot of blush. We don't want you to look washed-out . . . or worried."

"I have nothing at all to be worried about," Susan assured him. "I called Jed at work and he explained everything. He had no idea that the Malloy Fund even owned property in Hancock. He doesn't pay much attention to that type of thing. He just knew that they were making money, so he figured—what's wrong?" Susan asked, noticing that Tom had dropped the makeup and was furiously taking notes. "What did I say? What's so interesting?"

"Look, you're a very nice lady. And I understand that you're pretty smart when it comes to solving murders, but you know nothing about running for political office. What do you think the voters would think about what you just told me?"

"Well, I—"

"Who would elect a man to public office who doesn't even understand his own financial affairs? He's either too rich to bother, too ignorant to understand, too lazy to—"

"Jed's not any of those things!" Susan protested, making one cheek twice as red as the other.

"I didn't say he was. I said it could be interpreted like that."

"By the other political candidates at the debate tonight," Susan said, realizing what he was saying.

"Exactly."

Susan frowned. "Shit. What am I going to say tonight?"

"I don't know, but you have about six minutes to figure it out. Think of that speech Nixon made when Eisenhower wanted to dump him from the ticket. I don't remember much of it, but it worked for him. We saw a tape of it in one of my—"

"American history classes," Susan ended for him.

"Yup," Tom said cheerfully. "I have to get to the studio. See you there."

"Where's the ladies' room?" Susan asked quickly.

"Down the hall and to the left. You only have five minutes."

Susan fled. She found the bathroom and would have been back in the studio with plenty of time to spare—if she had been able to find the studio. As it was, she arrived breathlessly as Tom Davidson was introducing himself.

"And here's our guest now," was the smooth transition he made as she walked into the room.

Susan blinked at the bright lights and sat down in the

black leather chair that he indicated. She smiled, reminded herself to sit up straight, and tried to look relaxed.

She was terrified. Too terrified to listen to what Tom was saying, so she was stunned when he turned to her and said something like "and we've given Mrs. Jed Henshaw the opportunity to respond to this story. Susan?"

She took a deep breath and started to talk about Clue. Then she talked about her children growing up in Hancock. She mentioned her husband's experiences coaching soccer. She chatted about the PTA. She probably would have mentioned the fact that she had worn a cloth coat to the studio if Tom Davidson hadn't placed a restraining hand on her arm.

"I'm afraid that's all we have time for during this special edition of the Hancock news. We will be covering the debate tonight from the beginning to the end. Now here's this from the quilting lady, Mrs. Patch."

Susan remained frozen in place until he stood up. "Isn't someone going to tell us we're off the air?"

"I'm telling you," Tom said, walking across the room and flipping a switch. Normal lighting returned. They were alone.

"There's no one here," Susan commented idiotically.

"I told you I ran my own camera, didn't I?"

"Oh, well . . . How did I do?"

He frowned. "Okay, I guess. What was all the stuff about your dog?"

"Well, everyone kept mentioning the Checkers speech. . . ."

"That's right. Checkers was the name of Nixon's dog, wasn't it?"

Susan tried not to wonder what this younger generation was coming to. "I guess I'd better get on over to the debate. Jed will be expecting me. Are those reporters still outside?"

"Probably not. They were around to interview Cassandra Chadwick and you just sort of happened on the scene."

"Why was Cassandra here? Did her husband invest in something like the Malloy Fund?" It was too much to expect. . . .

The next words out of Tom's mouth convinced her that she was right. "She was here to appear on the knitting woman's show. It was more interesting than I thought it would be. Did you know that Cassandra Chadwick spins and dyes her own yarns?"

"Does she raise the sheep, too?" Susan asked rather sarcastically.

"She said something about an island they own off the coast of Maine where there's a herd of sheep to keep down the natural grasses. But they won't have it for long. It's being deeded to the Nature Conservancy."

"Of course," Susan said, putting on the cloth coat that she had neither woven nor spun.

"That's why she called out the press. She wanted to announce the land donation. Your problem with the Malloy Fund just happened to come up."

"Of course," Susan repeated, reminding herself that there was nothing to be gained by antagonizing the press. And wondering why she hadn't thought of appearing on a crafts show of some sort. She could do crafts, couldn't she? Well, not really—maybe a cooking show, she thought, leaving the station and getting into her car.

By the time she arrived at the junior-high-school auditorium for the debate, she was imagining herself competently demonstrating her special recipe for beef bourguignonne to Julia Childs (who might, of course, recognize it as being from the original *New York Times Cookbook*). After the debate tonight, she would find Tom Davidson and see if there was a cooking program on the schedule down at his station. She followed the crowd walking down the hallway toward the auditorium. The walls were decorated by the art classes and Halloween had been the theme. Junior high kids being what they were, many of the posters rivaled the goriest of the horror movies now on the market and she overheard one knowing onlooker explaining that the art teacher had edited out the bloodiest ones in deference to parental sensibilities. Susan stared at a half-naked monster with blood oozing from some rather exotic piercing and mentally thanked the teacher.

"Susan!"

She turned around to see who was calling to her.

"Hi! Susan! Over here!"

Kathleen was standing on one side of the hallway, waving. "Over here," she repeated. "Come on." She pointed to the door marked LADIES.

Susan hurried over to her friend. "I really should go get a seat near the front."

"In here," Kathleen insisted, pushing her friend ahead of her through the swinging door.

"Smells like cigarettes," Susan muttered, looking around.

"You never sneaked cigarettes in the bathroom in junior high school? Never mind that now," Kathleen continued. "Thank goodness we're alone. Where did you put on that makeup? In the dark?"

Susan slapped her hands across her face. "I forgot! It was for TV." She peered into the mirror. "Oh, I look like a clown."

"Maybe you should put your hair up," Kathleen suggested.

"I tried that. It looked even worse." Susan was busy scrubbing the garish pink blotches from her cheeks. She spent a few minutes with the contents of her purse before turning back to her friend. "What do you think?"

"Much better," Kathleen said. "How's Jed holding up?"

"What do you mean?"

"Well, that story about the Malloy Fund . . ."

"I was hoping no one would see the show," Susan muttered, trying one last time to do something with her hair. "Everyone keeps saying that they don't watch public-access cable."

"But everyone watches Channel three and Bradley Chadwick made a pretty powerful statement about the whole situation to that cute little redheaded reporter. I don't remember her name."

"And it ran on the local news tonight?"

"Top story. It was used as a local tie-in with something presidential—I actually don't remember what, I was so stunned to hear Jed's name like that."

"Oh damn." Susan leaned against the sink. "Jed must be dying. Have you seen him?"

"Not yet. Jerry drove over here right away. I called your house and no one was there and we thought Jed could use a little moral support. So Jerry left immediately and I found a sitter and came on down myself. I was actually in the hallway looking for you."

"Thanks. I'm glad you did. Did you happen to hear anyone talking about the Malloy Fund?"

"No. Most of the chat seemed to be about Bradley's generous donation to the Nature Conservancy."

Susan frowned. "Probably just a tax dodge," she muttered.

"It may be, but he sure got a lot of good publicity out of it."

"Did you happen to see me tonight on Channel forty-six?"

"Just the beginning of the show. I had to give the sitter instructions and come on over here."

Susan knew an evasion when she heard one. "Kath, be

honest. If you don't tell me that I was terrible, no one will," she insisted. "Except, of course, Chad—who will never see me unless I appear on MTV."

"I really didn't see much of you, but I have to confess that I didn't understand why you started out talking about Clue. It seemed a little strange."

"Everyone told me to think about the Checkers speech—so I thought of Clue. I suppose it was pretty stupid." She raised her eyebrows, knowing she didn't want to hear the answer to that question.

"A little unusual," Kathleen conceded. "You did look remarkably relaxed, though. I know I used to be a wreck when I was on television back when I was a cop."

Susan appreciated Kathleen's kindness. "Well, maybe no one else saw the show." She dropped her makeup bag back in her purse and snapped it shut. "We'd better get going. I hope we can find good seats. I want Jed to know that I'm here."

"Don't worry. Jerry promised to save seats for us. He said he'd be near the front on the left side of the auditorium."

"Good thinking." Susan took a deep breath. "Let's go be supportive."

"You're a good wife," Kathleen said.

"If there's an award for great wife, I think every woman whose husband is running for public office deserves to win it."

"Even Cassandra Chadwick?" Kathleen teased, holding the door open for her friend.

"Well, let's not get carried away." Susan pulled back her shoulders, lifted her head up high, put what she had come to think of as her election-season smile on her face, and joined the crowd heading into the auditorium.

TWENTY-ONE

THE MAYORAL DEBATE ITSELF COULD HARDLY TURN out to be more acrimonious than the days of discussion over the choice of moderator had been. The first choice, a popular minister of the large Episcopalian church downtown, had excused himself on the grounds that the church and its manse had both been built before 1939 and he didn't want to be accused of conflict of interest. The second choice, a famous anchorman who lived in Hancock, expressed his appreciation at being considered, but claimed prior commitments. One of the more gossipy travel agents in town claimed the anchorman had made reservations for Bermuda the day after this statement, but no one blamed him for not wanting to get involved. There were other nominations for the job, but they were all miraculously busy or conflicted. All three candidates finally agreed on the dynamic new head librarian, a woman who had become well liked and respected in the three years since her arrival.

Unfortunately, she was nowhere to be seen when Susan and Kathleen joined Jerry in the front row of the auditorium. "What's going on?" Susan leaned around Kathleen to ask Jerry Gordon.

Two podiums dominated the center of the stage. A wing chair stood between the two. Seven folding chairs lined up on either side of the stage. The folding chairs were empty.

The wing chair was occupied by Agatha Rickert, a woman who had been the town clerk for the past thirty years. She was smiling like a cat stuffed with cream.

"No one seems to know." Jerry leaned closer and whispered into his wife's ear. "The couple behind us decided that Agatha finally went nuts and killed off all the candidates."

Kathleen chuckled and passed the message on to Susan.

Susan just continued to look worried. "But why is she even here?"

"I don't know. Where's—" Kathleen began. The entrance of the candidates interrupted her question.

Susan smiled up at her husband, but either he didn't see her or he thought a response might be interpreted as frivolous. He followed Tony Martel across the stage and found his seat. When the candidates were seated and had made their first major decision of the evening—legs crossed? ankles crossed? feet flat on the floor?—Agatha Rickert stood and trotted up to the podium.

"Good evening, ladies and gentlemen," she twittered in a voice most people in town knew—and many had come to dread. "There's been a tiny change in the program this evening. Not that there actually is a program. At least not a printed one," she added, giggling, "but you know what I mean." She smiled at the audience, turned to her left and to her right, and bestowed smiles on each candidate individually. "I'm afraid that the flu going around has claimed another victim and I'm going to be your moderator this evening." She smiled. "I hope you don't mind."

Susan noticed that Kathleen and her husband had exchanged looks. She suspected that many of the other people in the audience were doing the same. Agatha Rickert was a lovely lady. She was born to pour tea from a silver service as the sun set over manicured green lawns every afternoon. She would have been in her element ordering meals in the morning, arranging flowers in the afternoon, and tatting edges around endless handkerchiefs in the evening by the fire. No one was sure exactly how she had ended up doing what amounted to directing traffic down at town hall. It was a job for which she was singularly unsuited.

Agatha was unfailingly cheerful, even when guiding people to the wrong office. She was always helpful, although frequently she only helped make problems bigger than they were to begin with. She was sweet and fluttery—and dealing with her had raised the blood pressure of more than one "accustomed to getting my own way with a single phone call" executive in town. Susan loved the woman. She leaned forward in her chair. This debate was going to be more interesting than she had imagined.

After a slightly difficult time finding the beginning of the sheet of paper she had been asked to read, Agatha suggested that the mayoral candidates make their opening statements.

Bradley Chadwick stood and approached the microphone.

"And don't go over your time limit," Agatha reminded him coyly, wagging a warning finger in his direction before resuming her seat.

Susan was happy to see Jed smiling. He had once told her being with Agatha reminded him that kindness was more important than efficiency. Then he left the rest of the family's dealings with town hall up to his wife.

Bradley had barely begun his speech when Agatha stood up again and interrupted. "I should tell everyone that a bell will go off if either of the candidates goes over the time allowed them. Not that I think they would do it intentionally, of course. But I don't want anyone to get a surprise."

Bradley Chadwick smiled flatly. "Thank you, Miss Rickert. We don't want any voters frightened by a bell either."

She smiled pertly at him, then at the audience, and resumed her seat, dropping her notes on the floor as she did so. By the time Bradley had retrieved them for her and was back at the podium, most of the members of the audience were chuckling. Bradley was obviously working very hard not to scowl.

Susan was thinking of baking a loaf of her special raisin egg bread and taking it down to Agatha first thing tomorrow morning. The woman was making Bradley look like the pompous fool he was. She could not have been more thrilled.

But her pleasure diminished considerably as Bradley began his opening statement. When he worked off a written speech, the man was good. Very good, she realized. It was difficult not to sigh with relief when he sat down without mentioning either the Malloy Fund, dog walking, or her husband.

Agatha's introduction of Anthony Martel was neither quick nor to the point. She worked hard to refer to him as Tony, but, giggling like a schoolgirl, gave up and reverted to Anthony midway through her speech. In the interests of fairness, she repeated her admonition about time limits and bells. This time she didn't drop anything on her way back to her seat.

Unlike his opponent, Anthony Martel was rather long-winded and boring. Susan, who had been listening to him speak for months now, found herself thinking about Jed. He was sitting still, watching Anthony with what Susan kiddingly called his "almost Nancy Reagan" look on his face—not adoring, but interested. She wondered what he was thinking, if he was nervous, if he had heard about her version of the Checkers speech. . . .

The opening statements ended and the questions began. Susan wondered how they had been chosen—but just for a moment. Then she began to wonder who hated her husband.

The first question Agatha read was not, as Susan was expecting, about the Landmark Commission, but about the Malloy Fund—and Jed's investment in it. The question was asked of Anthony Martel and challenged him to justify keeping Jed on the ticket under these circumstances. Susan took a deep breath and leaned forward to hear the answer.

Kathleen unobtrusively put a restraining hand on Susan's arm and Susan remembered that she was the object of a certain amount of attention. She bit her bottom lip and wished she'd had the sense to sit in the back of the room where her anguish would be comparatively private. Anthony Martel was denying any intention of taking Jed off his ticket and trying to explain that Jed had acted out of ignorance rather than greed.

Susan, listening to this, realized the truth of what Tom Davidson had been telling her: Jed did sound like an incompetent manager of his own financial affairs, certainly a man incapable of taking on any extra civic responsibilities.

Jed seemed aware of the situation, too. He stood up and began to move closer to Anthony Martel.

But Bradley Chadwick was quicker. He was on his feet and appealing to Agatha Rickert before Jed could get a word out of his mouth. "I believe, Miss Rickert, that the plan is for the mayoral candidates to speak and then, if one of us wanted to cede some of our time to one of our running mates, to do so at the end of the debate. Am I right?"

Well, it was obvious to anyone who ever had needed a quick answer from Agatha Rickert that this was not going to go smoothly. Agatha fluttered, and twittered, and mussed around generally, shuffling through the papers on her lap, glancing off stage right and then stage left as though expecting an answer to be flashing in the wings. Finally she smiled weakly at the audience, took her place in front of the microphone, and breathed, "I honestly don't know." With another smile, she returned to her seat.

Meanwhile Anthony Martel and Bradley Chadwick stood at their respective podiums and glared at each other. Anthony looked furious, clenching the edge of the podium, his knuckles white. Chadwick, in contrast, seemed completely relaxed, his lips twisted into a very slight smile, his hands crossed over each other, only his eyes betraying his anger.

Susan took a deep breath. These men were ready to fight to the death. Stupidly, she had assumed that the other candidates' feelings were more like her husband's: they wanted to win, but it certainly wasn't essential to their mental well-being. She glanced at her husband and changed her mind. Jed was looking pretty angry himself.

There were a few moments of silence and Susan was beginning to wonder how this situation was going to be resolved when Agatha Rickert came through, as she always did.

Agatha moved into the few feet between the two men and wagged her finger first at one and then the other. "Oh, you naughty boys. Fighting when you're supposed to be debating. What are we going to do with you?"

It brought the house down. Suffering from delight and relief, Susan laughed so hard, tears came to her eyes. She scrounged in her purse for a handkerchief, noticing that Jed seemed to be equally delighted by Agatha's performance.

"Now, I don't know about you all," the older woman continued, speaking directly to the audience, "but I think that when a man is accused of something, he should be allowed a few minutes to defend himself. Maybe our mayoral candidates will allow Mr. Henshaw to speak for himself about this Maloney . . . Malone . . . well, whatever the name of the dang fund thing is!"

"I certainly agree," Anthony Martel said quickly, backing away from the podium and motioning for Jed to take his place.

There wasn't much that Bradley Chadwick could do but graciously agree.

Susan covered her mouth with her handkerchief, took a deep breath, and offered a tiny prayer for her husband.

Either her prayer was heard, or he didn't need it. Jed did just fine. He took a moment to explain how and when he had invested in the Malloy Fund. He was slightly self-deprecating about his inattention to his holdings, but, after all, he reminded them, he wasn't a particularly wealthy man. He worked at an advertising agency, and it was his job, his family, and his community that dominated his time and his attention. He came across as successful, caring, and civic-minded—also succinct. Remembering the speech she had blown away on his computer last night, Susan was amazed. Jed had always told her that he used speech writing as a jumping-off point, but she had never really believed him. Forgetting the misery of the past few days, she wondered for a moment if not starting him on a political career years and years ago hadn't been a mistake. The next question, however, kept that pink bubble from floating in the air.

"What precisely does Jed Henshaw's wife have to do

with the ongoing investigation of the murder of Ivan Deakin?"

Anthony Martel got up from his seat and resumed his place at the podium.

"Don't they have any questions for Bradley Chadwick?" Susan whispered angrily to Kathleen.

"It will be his turn soon," Kathleen said soothingly.

Jerry looked around her and smiled at Susan. "Don't worry," he whispered. "Bradley will get his."

Anthony Martel was busy explaining that he wasn't privy to any more information about the investigation than everyone else and that, as far as he knew, Mrs. Henshaw was doing nothing in this investigation that she hadn't done before.

"Of course, that's not saying much. After all, no one actually knows what she has done before," someone whispered.

"You're right. Even Lyman once said that she just makes herself sound like a one-woman police department. She probably just gets the publicity because she's a female. And Chief Fortesque, because he's such a gentleman, doesn't bother to tell the truth," came a whispered response.

Susan sat up straighter, wondering to whom the voices behind her belonged.

"Don't move!" Kathleen whispered urgently. "I'll wait a few minutes and turn around and find out."

What a friend, Susan thought. Not only could Kathleen read her mind, but she did exactly what Susan would have asked of her without Susan asking.

"I—" Susan began before realizing that Jed had been called back up to the podium to speak for himself—or for his family, as the case may be.

This time Jed didn't do quite so well. Susan wasn't surprised. He was angry. It had apparently been one thing to attack his business sense, but it was another to attack his wife. He was practically sputtering and, in fact, what could he really say?

Susan found herself wanting to get up and defend herself, but the next words from the woman behind her grabbed her attention.

"You know," the voice said, "I think that Brett Fortesque calls Susan Henshaw in on a case at times when he wants to muddy the waters."

"Sure. Especially times when the murderer is his new girlfriend."

"Or maybe Jed Henshaw himself."

At this point Susan gave up any pretense of civility, swung around in her seat, and glared at Penelope Thomas and Rosemary Nearing.

TWENTY-TWO

As it turned out, Kathleen came through again.

"Don't say anything," she whispered to Susan. "Half the eyes in this place are on you. You'll only give them something else to talk about—and Jed won't benefit."

Susan swung around in her seat until she was again facing the front of the room. She was so furious that she was quaking. The next few questions were about the Landmark Commission. But Susan couldn't relax. She passed the rest of the debate in a blur of rage, which had only increased by the time the candidates were shaking hands and chuckling together like members of the same men's club.

Susan stood up stiffly, having no idea where to look. Jed had seemed to be studiously avoiding her eyes during the last part of the debate. The whispering behind her back had continued, but had become unclear. Within moments, she was surrounded by friends and well-wishers, and their assurances cheered her up a bit. Peering around the shoulders of friends, she realized that Jed was also surrounded by people and she hoped he, too, was finding support. She noticed Penelope Thomas still standing beside Rosemary Nearing, but neither Lyman nor Foster Wade seemed present. But the biggest surprise was Chad leaning against the back wall of the room.

"Kath, Chad's here!" Susan said, grabbing her friend's arm.

"Good for him!" Kathleen said. "I gather you didn't know he was going to come?"

"No. And this will thrill Jed," Susan told her. "He's been hoping both the kids would get a little more involved in his campaign, but Chrissy is away and Chad's busy with his own life—and Jed was convinced they should volunteer instead of being forced to do anything."

"Why don't you grab Chad before he gets away?" Kathleen suggested to her husband.

"Sure will." Jerry took off and Susan turned back to her friends. Kathleen was accosted by Alex's first-grade teacher and moved off to one side of the room to chat.

Susan, returning to the role of good candidate's wife, chatted, smiled, and allowed herself to be assured that the Martel ticket had been the winner in the debate. Once again, she glanced around the room as unobtrusively as possible. She noticed that Jerry had found her son and the two of them were chuckling together. Brett was also near the back of the room. He was listening to a woman who was holding his attention by physically putting a hand on his arm. As Susan watched they turned slightly and she saw that his demanding companion was Theresa Martel.

"Oh, there's Theresa Martel . . . I have something to tell her," Susan said to the people she was chatting with. "Would you excuse me?" Actually, she wanted to ask Theresa about the call she had made to Erika Eden.

"Sure, we'll let the candidates' wives commiserate with each other." Dan Hallard chortled. "They probably want to talk about what they're going to wear at the victory party on Tuesday night."

Susan loved the man. He was a good neighbor, friendly, unfailingly helpful in a crisis—so why was he always saying the type of thing that drove her nuts? She smiled at him and headed toward Theresa and Brett.

The crowd in the auditorium was thinning out, most of the spectators hanging around chatting with friends and neighbors. The debate over, almost everyone appeared to be having a good time. Everyone but Brett, that is. He was looking uncharacteristically tense. Susan wondered if that meant he had heard from Erika or if it meant that he hadn't—or, possibly, if it was only an indication that Theresa was driving him crazy.

Certainly, she realized immediately as she approached the couple, Brett was happier to see her than he usually was.

"Susan, I was going to look for you," he called out when she was still halfway across the room. "I need just a few minutes of your time."

Giggles and whispers greeted his remark, which had obviously recalled, for some, the question about Susan and the police chief's relationship that had been asked during the debate.

"I must speak with Susan alone for a minute," Brett continued to Theresa.

"But you understand what I'm telling you, don't you?"

Susan heard the anxiety in Theresa's voice, but was unprepared for the sight of the misery that was readily apparent on the woman's face. Theresa looked like she hadn't slept for days. Poorly applied makeup didn't disguise the dark circles under her eyes, her thick hair was lank and stringy, and she seemed to be eating the lipstick from her lips as though starving.

"Of course." Brett smiled kindly at Theresa. "Don't worry. I'll look into it." He paused. "But right now I really must speak with Mrs. Henshaw."

"Theresa, I thought the debate went pretty well, didn't you?" Susan asked, trying to be friendly.

"I—I suppose so." Theresa looked anxiously at Brett, ignored Susan, and then walked off, heading not to her husband, who remained on stage with the other candidates, but toward the doors at the back of the auditorium.

"You wanted to talk to me?" Susan asked, moving closer to Brett so that their conversation wouldn't be overheard.

"What do you know about that woman?" Brett asked, looking at Theresa Martel. "She seems to be falling apart."

"I know. She's drinking—and she started smoking after quitting years ago," Susan explained.

"She told me some sort of strange story about not being able to get rid of something her husband said—or wrote and didn't say. She doesn't make much sense." Brett frowned. "Do you think she might be dangerous? I sure hope it's just a case of the d.t.'s."

"I hope so, too," Susan said. "Have you checked out the carriage house again? Erika hasn't returned, has she?"

"Not that I know of. But I was hoping you might go over there and check things out. I'd send a man, except—"

He stopped. Susan understood that he wanted to keep his other officers away from his personal life—and Erika's—as long as possible. "I'd be happy to check it out. I won't be able to get out of here right away, though—I really have to see Jed," she added, knowing he would understand.

"Sure. Here's the key. And please call me. At home, if I'm not down at the station . . ."

"Of course. Did Theresa say anything else?" she asked quickly.

"She has some sort of strange idea about the murder. I think she's just trying to convince me that her husband couldn't possibly have done it," Brett said, explaining nothing.

"But—"

"I'll tell you about it later," Brett promised. "There's someone on the other side of the room that I have to see."

"Fine," Susan said, knowing there was no point in protesting. She could push him to tell her later when they spoke more privately. And it was time for her to see Jed.

Chad was standing on the stage with his father, broad smiles on both their faces. Susan hurried up. "So why didn't you tell us that you were coming?" she asked her son.

"You must be kidding. You didn't actually think I would miss this, did you?" her son answered.

"Chad promised Chrissy that he would report to her— just in case I said something embarrassing," Jed said, smiling at his son.

"I thought—" Susan began.

"He was pretty great, wasn't he, Mom?" Chad interrupted. "I mean, I was really surprised."

"Thank you," Jed said sincerely.

"Of course, that question about Mom and the murders was out of left field, wasn't it? I wasn't at all surprised that you got so mad over it. I hate it when people talk about that."

"I—" Susan tried again.

"How about getting some pizza?" Jed suggested to his family.

"Great!"

"I . . . I have something I have to do," Susan managed an entire sentence.

"That's fine. Dad and I will just stop at the pizza place on the way home, won't we?" Chad insisted, adding, "I'm starving."

"So am I," Jed agreed. "I haven't had anything to eat since lunch."

"Oh, then, Jed, I'll come home and make you something more nutritious," Susan offered.

"No. Pizza sounds great. And Chad and I haven't had much time together," he reminded Susan.

She took the hint. As he grew older Chad and his father had become closer. Susan felt this was the way it should be, but she still missed the closeness she'd had with her son when he was younger. "I thought it all went pretty well, didn't you?" she asked her husband.

"I don't know." Susan realized that he sounded tired—and irritated.

"Hey, you were great, Dad," his son repeated.

"Thanks," Jed said again. "But, you know, there is something about this election that . . . that I just don't get."

Susan would have loved to hear more about this, but Anthony Martel was heading their way. "Jed, I want to thank you. You did a wonderful job—and you took the brunt of the lousy questions."

Susan started to ask how the questions had been chosen, but was afraid that it would be morning before they got out of there if Anthony began explaining. "I saw Theresa a few moments ago," was all she said.

"Really?" He looked surprised. "When I left home tonight she said she wasn't going to attend. She wasn't feeling very well," he explained further. "She thought she might be getting a cold or something."

"There's a lot going around," Jed said heartily.

"There certainly is," Susan agreed.

Chad looked like he thought his parents were complete dorks—or whatever the current insulting term was. "It's Friday, the pizza place is going to be jammed," he reminded his father.

"Would you like to come with us?" Jed asked his wife, more from politeness than any real desire for her company, she suspected.

"No—but if you get home before I do, be sure to take Clue around the block—and bring the pooper-scooper. We don't want you to lose the election because you didn't pick up after the dog again," Susan kidded her husband.

"You're not going to be late, are you?" Jed asked.

"I have to see someone—nothing serious. If I'm going to be late, I'll call," she answered. It shouldn't take long for her to check out Erika's home—if she got going.

The parking lot was almost deserted when she went out to her car and she was on her way to Erika's without further interruption.

The owners of the large house to which the carriage house belonged were obviously giving a party, and Susan pulled her Cherokee in behind a long line of cars parked on the street and walked up the driveway to her destination.

The lights from the main house were bright enough for Susan to see the keyhole in the door and she gained entrance to the carriage house without any trouble. Long drapes that she hadn't noticed before hung on the wall of French doors; Susan pulled them closed and turned on the light by the couch. The room, which had been charming with daylight streaming through the many windowpanes, was equally appealing in lamplight. Susan walked around slowly, realizing that Brett had offered her an almost impossible task. She had only been here twice before. How could she possibly know if anything was different now?

She wandered about, picking up magazines and putting them down, removing books from the shelves and glancing at them. Since Brett had searched the top shelves, Susan had not noticed the many Italian gardening books that were collected there. She resisted opening some herb guides and cookbooks, reminding herself that she wasn't there to read.

She confined herself to a quick glance around the kitchen, decided it was unlikely that Erika had stopped in to fix herself a small snack, and headed upstairs on the circular stairway. Mindful of the people in the house next door, she again pulled the curtains across the windows before turning on the lights.

She was sure a woman as organized as Erika would have a reading lamp placed by her bed, so Susan was sitting on the bed with her hand still on the light switch when she realized that the sticky feeling beneath her was rosy-red blood.

TWENTY-THREE

Later Susan couldn't actually remember dialing the phone beside the bed, and she had no idea how she managed to pull Brett's home phone number from the recesses of her mind. She did, however, remember thinking that Brett was crazy when he ordered her to touch nothing. No one had to tell her that, she thought, running back down the circular stairway. She would wait for Brett as far away from that mess as she could possibly get without leaving the carriage house.

Her heart was still threatening to explode when a young policeman that Susan didn't recognize appeared at the door. "But Brett—" she began.

"Chief Fortesque is on his way. He called the station house and I just happened to be cruising nearby. Where's the blood?"

Susan raised her soiled hand. "Upstairs on the bed—"

"Do we need an ambulance?" he asked quickly, taking her hand in both of his. "Hey, you're not wounded!"

"No, no one is. The blood is upstairs on the bed—but there isn't anyone up there. That I saw," she added quickly, realizing that she hadn't gone into the bathroom or really searched that floor at all. "Do you want me to go up with you?"

"No. You stay here and wait for the chief."

Susan was fairly sure she could do that—barely. She

sat down on the bottom step and put her head in her hands. She looked up as Brett burst in the door. "Brett, there's another officer here. He's—"

"Your face. What happened to you? I thought you said—"

"I'm fine," Susan assured him. "There's just so much blood on the bed that I smeared some on me—what's wrong?"

Brett was looking at her, frowning.

"Oh, my God," Susan said, panicking. "AIDS! I never thought . . ."

"You don't have anything to worry about. I don't think you can catch anything from this," Brett said, touching her forehead with a clean handkerchief and sniffing it. "This isn't blood."

"Karo syrup, food coloring, and maybe something else," the police officer announced from upstairs. "I collected a sample for the lab."

"Good." Brett nodded. "You look a little pale. Do you want to sit down?"

Susan glanced up at the other officer.

"I was talking about you," Brett said, chuckling.

"I'm . . . I guess I'm fine if it's not blood." She started up the steps, mumbling, "I want to see it again."

Both policemen followed her back up the narrow stairway. Susan took a deep breath, but knowing that the stuff on the bed wasn't blood made it easier to walk into the room. All the lights had been turned on and the scene before her now seemed more like an amateur stage set than a murder scene. She walked over to the bed and began to put her hand into the damp mess.

"This really doesn't look much like blood, does it?" she asked, beginning to feel foolish.

"It fooled all of us when we first saw it," Brett reminded her.

"Why do you think she would do this?" Susan asked him.

Brett looked at her. "You mean Erika? Erika didn't do this."

"I'll go call for the crime kit." The other officer started back down the stairs.

"Smart kid," Brett muttered as the young man disappeared. "I'd stay as far away from this one as possible if I was in his position, too."

"You were saying that Erika didn't do this," Susan reminded him.

"Erika is a classy lady. Does this look like something a classy lady would do?"

Only if she were smart enough to know that you would say that, Susan thought. "Why would anyone do this?"

"Damn good question," Brett said. "It's more like an adolescent prank than part of a criminal investigation."

"I gather this wasn't here before? You did come upstairs, didn't you?"

"Of course, and it wasn't here. I wouldn't have sent you if it had looked like this." He glanced up at her. "You didn't notice anything else, did you?"

"I didn't really look," Susan said. "I could now, of course. . . ."

"Just don't touch anything," Brett warned her. "We have no choice but to regard this as a crime scene—even if it turns out to have nothing to do with the murder."

"Are you going to try to find out if anyone was seen around here tonight?" Susan asked.

"Sure."

"Maybe someone at the party saw something," she said, wandering around the small room.

"We'll check that out."

"I'm not trying to tell you how to do your job." Susan

nudged open an unlatched closet door. "She didn't take many clothes with her, did she?"

"What do you mean?" Brett asked, standing up.

"There's only one empty hanger here. . . . Look."

Brett did just that.

"Of course, maybe she didn't plan on staying away for very long," Susan suggested.

"Or maybe," Brett said, "she didn't plan on going away at all. Maybe she was kidnapped. Damn it!" He slammed his hand down on the tiny bedside table, smashing it to the floor. "I've been an idiot. She could have been kidnapped. I've been trying to protect her and I could be protecting someone who wishes to harm her. . . . What am I saying? There's a murderer loose out there. She might have been murdered." He dashed from the room, leaving Susan alone once more.

Frowning, Susan opened the closet door more fully. The closet was as well organized as the rest of the house, each article of clothing hanging on a padded hanger, herbal sachets tied up in corners, fabric-covered boxes arranged by size on the shelf. Shoes and boots were lined up on the floor; it looked like one pair, at the most, was missing. Puzzled, she returned the door to its previous position and tiptoed to the stairway. Silence from below encouraged her to believe that she had more time alone. Despite Brett's admonition to disturb nothing, she quickly went through the dresser drawers. Like the closet, they suggested that either Erika was a marvelous example of traveling light or she hadn't planned to stay away for long.

If, Susan reminded herself, she had planned this absence at all. Could Erika have been kidnapped, as Brett suggested, she wondered. Or possibly murdered? But by whom? Why would anyone kill Ivan Deakin and then kill the woman who had divorced him years and years ago?

She wandered into the bathroom, thinking over these questions. As before, the room revealed little of the personality of the person who lived here. Susan thought about her own home. She had built the bathroom of her dreams a little over a year ago. And there were frequently towels on the floor, stockings drying in the shower, makeup and soaps lying around—and that was just *her* mess. Jed's apparent belief in the decorative value of his worn socks never ceased to surprise her. Susan opened the medicine cabinet, wondering if anyone could possibly be this neat all the time or if it was Erika's housekeeper who cleaned up after her.

Interesting question, she realized, sliding the door closed. And it should be fairly easy to answer. Certainly the woman living in the large house would know the schedule of Erika's cleaning woman. Susan glanced out the tiny bathroom window. The party was still going strong. She noticed Brett standing on the side porch of the house, talking earnestly with another man.

It was time to go home. The Henshaw males would be done with their pizza feast and Jed, at least, would be at home, possibly worrying about her. She had accomplished little by coming here. She went downstairs and let herself out of the carriage house. "I have to go," she called to Brett as she passed him by.

"I'll talk to you tomorrow," he replied, waving rather absentmindedly.

Susan found her car keys, got in her car, and drove home quickly. The front porch lights were on, as were the lights in her bedroom. She let herself into the house, noticing with amusement that Clue was completely uninterested in her entrance. "You're a wonderful advertisement for a burglar alarm system," she commented, bending down to pat the dog's head.

Clue opened one eye and resumed snoring. Susan

started toward the kitchen, remembering a bag of leftover Halloween candy. She could use a Snickers bar or two. . . .

Or a dozen, she thought, turning around and heading up the steps. After midnight, she had no self-discipline when it came to sugar. If she started, she wouldn't stop. The only alternative was not to start.

The television was on, but Jed was asleep, snoring loudly. Susan headed into the bathroom and, a little later, was slipping into bed when she realized that Jed had been watching a videotape. Curious and trying to stop thinking about those candy bars, she punched a few buttons on the remote. What appeared on the screen was her interview with Tom Davidson earlier in the evening.

She sat up and watched carefully. Starting out talking about the dog did, in fact, seem a little strange. Perhaps she should have mentioned Nixon and the Checkers speech—not that she wanted to be compared with Richard Nixon. Although there were days when she could feel a growing empathy for Pat—and Betty; and Rosalind; and Barbara; and Hillary; and whoever was to become their first lady in January.

She watched with a growing feeling of relief that the cable station had few viewers. It wasn't that she was terrible, but she didn't exactly help Jed's chances at winning. The show ended and a homebody-type woman came on the air, promising viewers an opportunity to see a fascinating show about knitting featuring the "ever-chic Cassandra Chadwick." Susan was glad the tape had ended.

No one would ever refer to her as "ever-chic" she realized, turning off the light and snuggling down next to her husband. It had been a long and difficult day, and she expected to be asleep in minutes.

Half an hour later she was sitting at her kitchen table, a

pile of candy wrappers before her. She had been wrong. It wasn't Snickers that she needed, it was Butterfingers. Or, she thought, reaching into the large wooden bowl of candy, *both*.

A loud commotion in the hallway announced her son's arrival.

"Hey, you're still up," Chad said, walking into the room and opening the door of the SubZero.

Susan wondered, for the millionth time, if her son was capable of entering the kitchen without checking out the refrigerator. Or drinking something out of a container— as he was doing now. "Chad, please don't. . . ." she began her traditional protest.

"Hey, candy!" he said, seeming to notice what she was doing for the first time. He reached out and grabbed two Baby Ruths. "Do you know what I've always wondered?"

"No. What?"

"Did you and Dad steal Halloween candy from me? You know, when I was a kid and all."

"I wouldn't say steal," Susan began. "Sometimes we borrowed a bar or two. When you were young. You used to spend hours and hours trick-or-treating, even coming home and emptying your plastic pumpkin before going out again—and you had more candy than anyone could possibly want."

"Hey, I don't mind," Chad said cheerfully, grabbing another handful of candy and sitting down at the table. "I was just curious. Say, do you think Dad is going to win?"

"He sure deserves to," Susan said. "Did he say anything about it to you at the pizza place?"

"Yeah, but just the normal father-type stuff. You know, the best man will win and he's glad that he's given it his best shot and if he doesn't win he'll still feel like he's benefited from the experience. That type of stuff—

it's supposed to inspire me to run for president or something."

"You know that we don't want to influence you to do things you don't want to," Susan lied. In fact, they wanted him to do absolutely nothing without checking it out with his parents first. They were probably lucky that Chad had always been too independent for such silliness.

"Sure, Mom." He was grinning. "Well, it's late. According to the coach, I should have been in bed two hours ago. Big game tomorrow, you know."

"Who are you playing?"

"McKnight Prep. I hear they're pretty good, too. The captain of their soccer team is the kid whose father is running against Anthony Martel."

"Really?" Susan asked, suddenly interested. "You mean Bradley Chadwick?"

"Yeah. They call the kid Junior like in some old black-and-white movie. But he's supposed to be a monster on the field. Cheats, too, I hear."

"Really?" Susan wondered if it ran in the family. Then she had another thought. "Did you mention that to your father tonight?"

"You mean about Junior being the captain of the other team?"

"Yes."

"No. Why? Do you think he would be interested?"

"Yes. In fact, I think tomorrow should be a family day—and we should both come and watch you play."

"You're not going to scream loudly like you did when I was a kid, are you?" her son asked suspiciously.

"Of course not. I'm going to be completely dignified and . . . and 'ever-chic.' "

Chad looked as though he thought she had gone crazy.

TWENTY-FOUR

It was a beautiful day for a soccer game. Huge hardwood trees, their leaves scarlet, maize, and burnt sienna, lined the soccer field. The sky was brilliant blue, the air crisp, windy, and brisk. In the tradition of the Connecticut suburbs, parents wore wool crew socks under their Docksides, and navy pea coats were draped with tartan scarves. Susan had abandoned her usual blue jeans and was wearing camel-hair wool slacks with a favorite red Guernsey sweater that she had bought in Bermuda a few years before. She might not be ever-chic, but this was the first time she could remember wearing full makeup to one of the high-school playing fields.

Over a huge breakfast of pancakes, sausage, and baked apples, Jed had greeted her idea of campaigning by the playing field with limited enthusiasm. "At least I'll get to spend some time outside," had been his comment. But Susan noticed that he seemed to be having a wonderful time cheering on Chad and his teammates.

Hancock High was winning, much to her delight. Chad had made two goals—and it was only halftime. Bradley Chadwick, Junior, had not yet scored—and had fallen down and gotten a bloody nose.

Susan was walking up and down the lines, chatting with friends and neighbors, expressing optimism about the election on Tuesday, and listening to various people discuss Ivan Deakin's murder.

It was interesting, she thought, waving at her son's math teacher, how the murder had transformed the town. Only a week ago every single citizen over the age of twenty-one had seemed to be obsessed with the Landmark Commission; now all anyone seemed to want to talk about was who had killed Ivan. If she hadn't known better, she might have thought that Ivan Deakin had been killed to deflect attention from the election and its primary issue.

She was thinking about that when Lyman Nearing approached her.

"Mrs. Henshaw. Susan. How nice to see you here. I've been admiring your son's athletic abilities all fall," he said.

"How nice of you to say that." She beamed. "Do you come to a lot of the games?"

"All of them," he replied. "I love soccer. My son played it when he was at Hancock High and also was junior varsity up at Cornell for two years. Nearing Rings now offers a scholarship for a deserving player. And two of my managers are very involved in the fund-raising efforts of the high school team."

"That's right. You said that you encouraged your employees to get involved in community activities, didn't you?"

"You have an excellent memory. Not that I'm surprised. Still can't get over the fact that you don't take notes during your investigations. Amazing."

Susan smiled modestly.

"And how is your investigation going? Found the murderer yet?"

"No."

"But I bet you're getting closer, aren't you?"

Susan frowned. "I don't think so," she admitted. "In

fact, I don't seem to be going anywhere. Ivan lived a very odd life, systematically going through his inheritance by starting unsuccessful restaurants, but he didn't seem to invest other people's money or make a lot of enemies along the way." She paused and then continued speaking as the teams resumed the field. "In fact, the only person who seemed to hate Ivan Deakin was his ex-wife, and she's disappeared."

"So she's your primary suspect?"

"Not actually," Susan admitted. "There are . . . reasons that we don't believe she killed him."

He nodded, not appearing to expect her to say more. "What about the speech?" he asked.

"What . . . Ivan's speech!" Susan exclaimed, remembering that she had gone to the police station for it, but came up empty-handed. "You know, I really should start writing things down. I had forgotten all about the copy of the speech. Thank you for mentioning it."

"Anytime. Maybe I'll put on my thinking cap and I can be of more help."

"Great. You know, there was something else that I was wondering about," Susan said, "but I don't remember."

"Give me a call anytime," Lyman said. "I'd be happy to help. Just don't call tomorrow night. I'll be at the commission meeting."

"The Landmark Commission?"

"Yup. It's the last scheduled meeting before the election. I wasn't even notified, but I noticed it on the original schedule that was sent out months ago. After your visit to the factory, I decided I had been avoiding my responsibilities by turning my vote over to my wife, so I'm becoming more personally involved. Besides, it might be interesting to see exactly what they want to push through before the election."

"You're right. It should be very interesting. I don't suppose the public is invited?"

"Commission meetings are, by law, open to anyone who wants to attend. Although I don't think there are usually many spectators. Most people are willing to postpone their protests until an issue comes before the town council." He looked at her curiously. "Are you planning to attend?"

"It might be interesting." Susan was scheduled to spend the evening on the phone, schmoozing with potential voters, but maybe she could get that done in the afternoon.

"Maybe you would accompany me?" he surprised her by suggesting. "Then, if anyone objects to your presence, I would be right there with the appropriate city ordinance to quash their protests."

Susan smiled broadly. "That would be wonderful."

"So I'll pick you up at your home at seven-fifteen."

"I'll be ready." She started to move away and then had another thought. "Do you think it would be a good idea to notify the media about the meeting? I was thinking of Tom Davidson. He's been covering the election for the cable channel in town."

Lyman nodded slowly. "It's an excellent idea. But why don't I do it? After all, no one in my family is running for office. We don't want people to think you're arranging these things—like Cassandra Chadwick."

"Good thought. Thanks. I'll see you tomorrow night."

The teams were dashing up and down the field with renewed energy as Susan and Lyman went their separate ways. Susan, remembering her son's admonition, moved behind a group of onlookers to cheer him on anonymously. Lyman Nearing stood so close to the line that an official asked him to move back.

As the game continued Susan decided it was time to join her husband when she overheard Brett's name. The speaker also mentioned Erika Eden. Susan froze, pretending to be intent on the game and hoping to hear more.

"I've been calling and calling, but all I get is her answering machine," one woman was saying.

"But I had no idea that she was once married to Ivan Deakin—and I've known her for years," the other woman replied. "It's so strange."

"Maybe, but they were married for so short a time . . . and so long ago."

"But why isn't she answering the phone?"

"I'm more interested in knowing why she never mentioned that she and that sexy Brett Fortesque were dating."

"Hmmm . . . My husband accused me of stealing bicycles from our own garage just so I would get a visit from him."

"Wish I'd thought of that. The sexiest males in our house are my daughter's boyfriends—and I don't want to know what that means."

Laughing together, the women moved away. Susan wondered if it would be bad policy to visit the away team's side of the field. Bradley and Cassandra, due to their patrician height, were clearly visible across the field and she thought it might be interesting to take a peek at the enemy on its home ground. Well, why not?

She thought about McKnight Prep as she wandered around the end of the field. Connecticut was as full of excellent public-school systems as it was of prestigious private schools. Parents in Hancock who wanted their children to get a private-school education had more than a few choices. But McKnight Prep was known to Susan only as a group of gray fieldstone buildings surrounded by large green playing fields in a neighboring town.

The McKnight Prep parents were an even preppier group than those on the other side of the field. Plaid prevailed. As did loafers that looked like traditional Bass

Weejuns—were such things still made? Susan wondered. She wandered around, keeping one eye on the game and looking for the Chadwicks with the other. Of course, she ended up running smack into a man wearing an itchy-looking Harris-tweed jacket.

It turned out to be Bradley Chadwick. Ever the good candidate, he grabbed her shoulders, stabilized her, and then shook her hand and asked for her vote.

"This is Susan Henshaw, dear." Cassandra Chadwick appeared at her husband's side. "You know, her husband, Jed, is the candidate who invested in the Malloy Fund."

Bradley smiled. "Well, I guess your husband did my side a little favor when he did that, didn't he?"

"You know, Jed would never, ever—"

"I think it's charming that you continue to defend him," Cassandra interrupted, slipping her hand through her husband's arm. "We both do, don't we, dear? Loyalty is such an important family value."

"Essential." He agreed, smiling to the surrounding crowd, but not looking directly at Susan. "In fact, loyalty is in many ways the basis for any relationship—a fact that is well known to the people who are here today, cheering on their children." Suddenly his general beam dissolved into a scowl. "Dear, what are the girls up to?" he asked his wife.

"Well, Blake is helping out at the boosters' club booth, and the last time I looked, Brooke and Brittany were sitting in the bleachers cheering on their brother." A brief frown crossed her unlined face. "Why do you ask, dear?"

"They seem to be standing together at the end of the bleachers talking with some horrible upper-school boys. I thought you said you were going to stop gadding around and pay more attention to the children."

"I'll go check on them," Cassandra offered. "You know how children are," she said to Susan.

"Of course," Susan agreed, trying to hide her delight at the other woman's obvious distress. It was tempting to investigate this particular mystery. But she knew she wouldn't: children were to be protected not used.

"Your son is quite a soccer player," Bradley commented.

Susan wondered if he had been reading her mind. "Your son seems to be good, too," she offered an exchange of compliments.

"Yes, Junior has had opportunities to go to many of the Ivies, but instead he has decided to follow me to my own alma mater. He'll be captain of the soccer team there as I was in my time, I predict."

"How wonderful," Susan said. She thought about the pile of college applications on her son's desk. He probably hadn't touched them in weeks. "Princeton?" she asked, noticing the orange-and-black scarf Bradley wore around his neck.

"Peterborough."

"I don't think I've heard . . ." Susan began.

"It's small and selective. I've always thought a small liberal-arts college offered the best chance for a well-rounded education, don't you?"

Susan was beginning to realize that Bradley asked questions in a manner that implied that you were somehow lacking if you didn't agree with the opinion he had just expressed. "Where did you go to medical school?" she asked.

"I went abroad. I was very interested in exploring other cultures when I was young and adventurous. I think that's the way to be when you're still unformed."

Susan found herself wondering about Bradley's ability to make a less than illustrious education sound like an enviable choice. "Were you involved in politics in college?" she asked, wondering if he would answer that he was president of the student council or make something less than that sound important.

"I have always been seriously committed to community service. It is as important to me as the air that I breathe. And I have instilled that belief in my children. My God, what is your son doing to my son Bradley! Junior!" With that, the public-spirited mayoral candidate dashed onto the playing field.

Susan jumped up and down, trying to see what was happening over the crowd of spectators.

"Public schools simply don't teach morals or civility," a man next to her said.

"Of course, you're right," someone agreed. "How could they? They take absolutely everyone."

Susan realized that she was standing on the wrong side of the field.

There was a time-out on the field and she took advantage of it to dash across to her husband, who was standing by Hancock High's bench.

"Is Chad okay?" she asked anxiously, glancing at the young men from both teams standing or squatting in the middle of the field. It was impossible to pick out her own son from the pack.

Jed nodded. "He sure is. It's someone on the other team who fell. I don't think it's serious. Only the coaches and a few parents are out there and no one has called for doctors.

"Where are you going?" he asked as Susan turned and started to walk away.

"I think that's Brett over by the police car," she said. "I need to talk to him." Now that she was sure her son was unhurt, she could get on with her investigation—and find out what had happened to Ivan Deakin's speech.

TWENTY-FIVE

Ivan Deakin's speech had spent the week sitting on the edge of Brett's desk. And that's the spot Susan returned it to when she had finished reading it.

"So?"

Susan looked at Brett, who had been watching her as she read. "I certainly don't see anything there to murder someone over."

"That's what everyone around here who's read it thought."

"Unless, of course, someone decided to kill him for breaking his promise," Susan mused. "After all, he did announce that he would offer a solution to the Landmark Commission mess that would please everyone—and I don't see anything there that would please anyone."

Brett read through the speech again. "Nope. The concept of voluntary preservation is rather quaint in its belief in human goodness, but that's about as interesting as this speech gets."

"Of course, he might have gotten a number of votes just because people are tired of the squabbling between the other two candidates. I mean, coming in at the last minute like he did gave him a sort of glamour . . . or maybe it also gave the election a boost," she added slowly.

"What do you mean?"

"Well, attendance had really dropped at most of the

election events and speeches the candidates were giving"—she tried not to think about the possibility that
attendance had only dropped at the Martel events—it
wasn't possible, she decided—"and when Deakin called
this meeting, not only did a record number of people
show up, but they appeared at the debate last night."

"You don't think the debate would have been popular
without Ivan's candidacy?"

"I don't think the debate would have been as popular if
Ivan hadn't died and I think he wouldn't have died if he
hadn't announced his candidacy."

"Are you sure? Think about it," Brett said. "People are
involved in this election."

"Yes, but I've been getting the impression for weeks
that most people have pretty much made up their mind
about who they're going to vote for. So why would
anyone go to the debate—except to support a friend?
There are certainly a lot more interesting things to do on
Friday night. I mean, these debates happen every two
years and I've never even considered attending one."

"The election and the murder sure have taken the
attention away from other things—like the national election," Brett said, tucking the speech away in a folder.

"What else?"

"What?"

"You said the election and the murder had taken
people's attention away from other things ... what
things?"

Brett looked at her with a frown on his face. "Now that
you mention it, I can't think of anything else that is going
on in town."

"Maybe that just proves your point. Maybe if the election hadn't been causing such a furor, we would know
about other things."

"Possibly. But I know that nothing unusual has been

happening down at the station. It's just been the usual round of traffic violations, burglaries, petty crimes downtown, and some rather sad domestic disturbances in the past few weeks. And I don't know how you might find a record of anything else without going through records of every meeting and committee in town."

"But I do," Susan said. "In fact, I know someone who has gone through it all for me: Tom Davidson." She stood up. "I think I'll go find that young man."

"You'll let me know right away if he tells you anything that might have some bearing on all this?"

"Sure will." She paused with her hand on the doorknob. "Any news about Erika?"

Brett sighed and shook his head. "And I sure wish there were. I can dismiss the fake blood on her bed as a prank, but I've been thinking over what you said yesterday—that she didn't take any clothing with her—and I can't think of a single explanation that doesn't worry me. Where would a woman go with no clothing?"

Susan stood still as an answer occurred to her. "Maybe a health spa?"

Brett didn't move for a minute and then a large smile broke out on his face. "You know what? Erika mentioned a few weeks ago that she was negotiating with someplace in upstate New York—they wanted to carry a line of all-natural products that she's importing from Sweden—or Denmark—or someplace Scandinavian. Now, where did she say it was?"

"Maybe Holland?"

"I mean the health spa."

"Give Kathleen a call," Susan suggested. "She's been collecting pamphlets and rate cards from spas around here ever since Alice was born."

His hand was on the phone before she had closed the door behind her.

Susan was in her car and halfway to the cable station before she realized that it might have been smart to call first. But as she arrived at the station she noticed a car in the reporter's spot and Tom Davidson was getting into it.

Susan honked loudly and pulled her car in behind his. "I need to talk to you!" she called out.

"I have to cover the end of the junior high girls' soccer game. It's important. The niece of the station's owner is on the team."

"I could drive you to the playing field," Susan suggested. "Then we would have time to talk. It's important."

"Is it about the murder or the election?"

"Both."

"And you'll share the story with me first?"

"If Brett says I can."

Tom pulled a huge black canvas bag from his trunk, threw it in the backseat of her Jeep, and climbed in. "You know where the games are played?"

"I've spent more fall afternoons there than I'd care to count," she answered, backing into the street. She had often thought that the extraordinary amount of time suburban parents spent watching their children perform probably had something to do with the decline of the gross national product.

"So what can I help you with?" he asked.

Susan explained her mission.

"Everything that's been happening since the election began to take up everyone's attention, heh?" he mused.

"Exactly. Brett says there haven't been any notable things happening at the police station—at least nothing they're aware of down there," she amended.

"Nothing I can think of either. Let's think about the rest of Hancock. You're not interested in things like school events . . . or church events."

"Not unless you can somehow relate them to the election or the Landmark Commission or the murder."

"There seem to be some women in the PTA at the elementary school who would like to murder each other," he muttered.

So what else is new? she thought. "What about the historical society—or maybe there's something going on in the parks department that the Landmark Commission decision would affect."

"Nothing I know about. The historical society has been pretty quiet in recent months—maybe waiting to see what the Landmark Commission is going to do."

"And, of course, there is the summer lull," Susan said, pulling up to her second soccer game of the day.

"Yeah, I know what you mean," Tom said, pulling his equipment from the car. "No one is around here for most of the month of August. By Labor Day, the station had even run out of human-interest stories about children, cats, and dogs. And then, the second week of September, every organization in town has a meeting or two and we run our butts off trying to find airtime for them all."

"Do you want me to help you carry anything?" She was astounded by the amount of equipment he was hanging on various parts of his body.

"Nope. I'm fine. Follow me. I think we should tape from the other side of the field—not into the sun. Too much glare."

"What about the garden clubs?" she asked, trotting to keep up with him. Oh, to be young.

"They've spent most of the fall having bulb-planting parties, getting ready for their holiday fund-raisers . . . and there was some sort of participation in the Fall Festival, I think. I don't know how any of the things we're concerned with might be affected by those things."

"What about—"

"On the other hand, the Zoning Board has been going through a lot of brouhaha recently."

"I didn't think the Landmark Commission and the Zoning Board had much to do with each other." She remembered her husband saying something about this in fact.

"Well, not now. But if Bradley Chadwick wins and the Landmark Commission is given the power they want, the Zoning Board's powers will be severely limited."

"Which might infuriate someone on the Zoning Board," Susan said, wondering if she had checked out the members of the wrong group.

"Sounds possible to me." Tom hiked the camera up on his shoulder. "Unless, of course, you were one of the people who are on both the Zoning Board and the Landmark Commission."

"Some people are on both?"

He frowned. "Penelope Thomas, of course, and . . ."

"And who?" Susan prompted when he stopped, hitched the camera up on his shoulder, and began taping. "Who?" she repeated.

"That man," he answered. "I don't remember his name. He owns a large company . . . part of the military-industrial complex."

"Lyman Nearing? Lyman Nearing is on both the Landmark Commission and the Zoning Board?"

"That's his name. Who would name a poor innocent baby Lyman? I think—hey, where are you going?"

"I have to go talk with Lyman Nearing."

"Not until we're done taping this thing. You brought me here, remember?"

"But—"

"And maybe you could learn more if you go back to the station with me and watch the tapes of the meetings of the Commission and—"

"You have their meetings on tape?"

"Sure do. There are notes taken by secretaries, of course, but they're not complete—and you can tell more from the tapes. Facial expressions and all that."

"And if I wait here with you until you've finished this story, you can get the tapes for me?"

"Sure."

"And I'll be able to take them home and watch them?"

"It's against station policy to allow our materials to be given out."

"But—"

"But I don't see what's wrong with allowing you to view them down at the station. We recently allowed a high school student to do that—he was doing some sort of term paper on local government or something. Poor guy fell asleep over them. He was real enthusiastic about going to college and majoring in political science when he came in—but not when he left. That's probably how colleges end up with so many art-history majors."

"How long do you think this will take?" Susan asked, not terribly interested in his opinions about higher education at this particular moment. "It looks to me like the game is just beginning."

He glanced at his watch. "It is. It should have started six minutes ago—if it started on time, that is."

"But we'll be here over an hour more!"

"So sit down and enjoy the game," he suggested, moving down the field as the action changed direction.

Now, attending a game in which your child is playing is one thing; attending a game and watching other people's children play is another. Susan had no intention of doing the latter. She didn't know anyone who would—except Lyman Nearing, she realized. Lyman Nearing, a man whose name did keep popping up, didn't it?

The sun was getting lower in the sky and Susan was

beginning to wish she'd worn a jacket over her favorite sweater. Trying to warm up, she paced back and forth along the field, thinking about Lyman Nearing. She liked the man. He was charming, enthusiastic, and appeared to have a firm moral center, valuing his adopted son and showing a real commitment to his community. He even enjoyed standing around chatting with neighbors. He would, she realized, have been a natural to run for mayor. He'd be good at the job—and he'd even love the campaigning. It was, Susan had realized in the past few months, a rare person who was a natural campaigner. The ability to be friendly with strangers, most of whom wanted something, was less common than the perfect noses Bradley Chadwick made a living creating.

She mused, also not for the first time, that it was an even rarer person who coupled the qualities of a natural campaigner with the dedication, intelligence, morality, and empathy that made a great leader. A person unlike Bradley Chadwick, she thought, noticing the man himself walking toward her.

"Mrs. Henshaw." He beamed, apparently thrilled that he had remembered her name. "First we meet at the high-school soccer game and now here. Do you have a daughter who plays on one of these teams?"

"I have a daughter, but she's in college," Susan said.

Bradley Chadwick, she noticed, did not say that she looked much too young to have a daughter in college. Perhaps plastic surgeons weren't accustomed to telling lies of that nature about age. "How nice," he muttered, looking out across the field.

"Are you watching your daughter?" Susan asked politely, turning to see if she recognized one of the blond Chadwick daughters. But Bradley, she realized, wasn't watching the players. He was watching his wife.

And Cassandra Chadwick was watching Tom Davidson.

TWENTY-SIX

"SHE WAS STARING AT YOU."

"I gather you don't think it was my animal magnetism," Tom said, dropping two tapes on the floor of her car and bending down to pick them up.

"It's not that. It just seemed a little strange. . . . She looked so . . . like she was concentrating so hard." She wondered if he thought she couldn't drive and talk at the same time.

"She's a real piece of work—a very tense woman."

"Everyone involved in the election is tense these days. After all, the election is only three days away. Look at Theresa Martel—she's probably going nuts at this point."

"She hasn't been around much recently, has she?"

Susan frowned. "Did you see her at the debate last night?"

Tom shook his head. "Nope."

"That's odd."

"There was a huge crowd there. I might have missed her. Not all the family members sat in the front like you did."

"True." Susan steered her car into the parking lot and put on the brake. "Is there a phone around here that I can use? I should let my family know I'm going to be late."

"You're not attending any last-minute cottage parties?" Tom asked, getting out of the car.

"There aren't any—thank goodness. And the last mailings have gone out. I'm supposed to be spending the weekend on the phone calling up supporters to make sure they vote. I think it's a pointless task myself, but it's one of the duties of a candidate's wife." She followed him into the station and to his office, stopping to use the phone on his desk to leave a message for Jed, before entering a tiny room furnished with two folding chairs, five television monitors, and two tape machines. A gigantic metal cabinet covered one wall and Tom opened this. Susan peered over his shoulder at its contents. What looked like hundreds of tapes were stacked on shelves. Some had peeling labels hanging from them. "These are the tapes of the town meetings?" she asked, hoping the answer was no.

Fat chance. "Sure are." He started to take tapes out and toss them across the room onto a ledge above twin tape machines.

"How do you know what is what?"

"Simple. Town council meetings on the top shelf. Then it goes down in alphabetical order. So these are the Landmark Commission." He grabbed a couple more tapes and added them to the pile. "And the Zoning Board is here on the floor."

Susan looked at the rising towers. "Are you sure I can't take these home?" It was going to take forever— even if she fast-forwarded through most of the meetings.

"Station policy," Tom repeated. "There are two tape machines. Maybe you could call your husband to help out?"

Susan thought for a few minutes. She didn't think Jed would want his every word recorded by the enthusiastic reporter. "He's busy . . . but maybe Kathleen could help out." It was an inspired idea. "Do you mind if I use the phone again?"

Tom motioned to one hanging on the wall. "Feel free."

Kathleen answered and listened as Susan made her request for help. "What's Jed doing this evening?" she asked when Susan had ended.

"Well, he needs a break," Susan began, glancing at Tom.

"Good. Then maybe he can go to the new Arnold Schwarzenegger movie with Jerry and I'll come help you. Jerry's mom arrived for the weekend, so I don't have to worry about getting a sitter."

"That bad, is it?" Susan knew that no matter how wonderful the mother-in-law, it could be a stressful relationship.

"We'll talk when I get there," Kathleen promised. "Which should be soon. Jerry can take everyone out to dinner someplace. See you soon."

"She's on her way over," Susan said.

"Fine. Do you want me to teach you to use this thing?"

Susan stared at the large tape player. "That's fast forward?" she pointed to a button with an arrow printed on it.

"Sure. Do you want to start with the Landmark Commission or the Zoning Board?"

"Well . . ."

"Or you could alternate between them in chronological order. You know, first the Zoning Board meeting the first week of the month and then the Landmark Commission meetings in the same month."

"The Landmark Commission meets more than the Zoning Board?"

"The Landmark Commission meets and meets and meets. And, believe me, they accomplish as little as possible in the longest time possible. That Penelope Thomas sure loves to listen to herself talk—in fact, they all do. . . . Well, you'll see for yourself in a few minutes. First the Zoning Board?"

"But how do you know where we should start?"

"I thought it made sense to start the week the Land-mark Commission was created." He popped a tape into the machine. "You'll see. It didn't go unnoticed by anyone on the Zoning Board."

Susan leaned forward as one of the small meeting rooms down at the town hall came into focus. People were walking in the door, greeting each other, and finding seats around the table set up before a couple of dozen folding chairs. The camera panned to the left and focused on a board announcing the date and the name of the group meeting. Then it wandered into the audience, recording for posterity (or whenever this tape was erased) two women she knew critically discussing another friend's new hairstyle. Susan relaxed. This might turn out to be fun.

When Kathleen arrived, less than half an hour later, she had changed her mind.

"Hi! I brought sandwiches from the deli," Kathleen announced, walking into the room with a large paper bag in her hand.

"Great!" Tom Davidson said enthusiastically. Then he looked at the two women with an embarrassed expression on his face. "I mean . . ." he began.

"I brought some for you, too," Kathleen hurried to assure him. "Roast beef on rye, corned beef on rye, ham and cheese on whole wheat with mayo. Take your pick."

The food was passed out and Susan began to eat without pressing pause on the machine she sat before. Kathleen leaned over her shoulder and peered at the screen. "I recognize Penelope Thomas, so this must be the Landmark Commission," she said.

"Nope. The Zoning Board. Penelope is on both. You

can tell the difference if you watch for Lyman Nearing. He's on both, too—but he only attends the Zoning Board meetings."

"That Penelope Thomas is a busy woman," Kathleen commented, sitting down by Susan. "Does she run the Zoning Board with as firm a hand as she does the Landmark Commission?"

"Not at all. This is only the second Zoning Board meeting I've watched, but so far she merely seems to be a thorn in the side of the rest of the board. Her view that nothing, absolutely nothing, should change in Hancock is consistent."

"I wonder why," Kathleen said.

"Some people just don't like change," Tom Davidson suggested. "They find it threatening."

"Sure," Susan agreed slowly. "But what exactly does Penelope gain if she actually manages to stop all change in Hancock?"

Tom Davidson stopped eating and looked at Susan. "That's a very good question, but I still don't understand why are you so sure this has something to do with Ivan Deakin's murder."

"I don't know yet. But there must be a connection somewhere. There just isn't anything in his private life that would cause anyone to kill him," Susan said, pushing the image of Erika Eden to the back of her brain. Brett had good instincts. If he said Erika wasn't guilty, she wasn't guilty. Probably.

"Perhaps he had extensive land holdings that would be affected by the election?" Tom suggested.

"Apparently the man was almost destitute. He was renting his home here actually," Susan answered. "And his current restaurant isn't in town."

"Oh, that's where Jerry is taking his mother and the

kids tonight," Kathleen said. "I thought someone should check it out and suggested it to him."

"Great idea," Susan said. "Is it still open?"

"They were taking reservations when Jerry called— but they may be desperate for business. Jerry said that they claimed it was fine to bring two small children."

"Maybe it's a family restaurant," Tom suggested.

"Maison Catherine? I doubt it," Kathleen said.

Tom appeared mystified. "Why not?"

"Family restaurants never have French words in their names," Susan explained. "If it's a chez something, maison de something, or the something bistro, they probably don't have high chairs waiting."

"Except in France," Kathleen added.

"Funny that things should be slow at Ivan's restaurant," Tom commented. "Usually any notoriety brings in the customers rather than keeps them away. Except for something like a salmonella scare, of course."

"Good point," Susan said.

"I guess you don't know much about Maison Catherine, do you?" Kathleen said. "It's gotten one of the worst reviews the *Hancock Herald* ever gave. I was going through old papers looking for someplace to hold the spring fashion show for Alex's school and I was astounded by the review. It all but said go to McDonald's before you go here."

"Must be pretty bad," Tom commented.

Susan wondered if Kathleen had learned absolutely nothing from the years of their friendship. The first rule of remaining sane in Hancock was "Avoid organizing charity fashion shows." She pressed the fast-forward button and sped through a plaintive plea for an exemption to the zoning laws by a man who wanted to add a four-car garage to his substandard property. The rest of the meeting was taken up by a developer asking to subdivide some land for sale on the river. Susan was flashing through the request when Tom reached out and stopped and rewound the machine to the beginning of the man's speech.

"Why did you—?" Susan began.

"Look at that."

Both women leaned into the screen—and then exchanged looks.

"Look at what?" Kathleen asked.

"Look at Penelope Thomas!" He pointed at the screen with his pen. "Watch her while the developer is talking."

The threesome watched closely. Susan was frowning, Kathleen puzzled, and Tom triumphant. "That's what we were looking for!" he said as the speaker resumed his seat.

"What?"

The women asked the question together.

"That man is talking about subdividing land down on the river."

"That's right. By the old gristmill," Susan said, leaning forward. "I heard something about that last summer."

"And Penelope Thomas looks happy about that—which is weird," Kathleen said. "That's a particularly historic part of town. Almost anyone would want to preserve it."

"And it's near her house," Susan added.

"But the board hasn't voted on it yet. She's sitting there happy as a clam listening to a man who is asking to do something she would find absolutely unacceptable if it were allowed to happen."

"And there's no way she can be sure his request will be denied, is there?" Kathleen asked.

"It *will* be denied," Tom insisted. "I've been through all these tapes already. It was denied at the next meeting of the board."

"And Penelope knew that would happen?" Kathleen asked.

"I don't see how. . . . Why don't we skip to that tape and maybe we can find out," Tom suggested.

"Good idea," Susan said. "If we can find it." She stopped, seeing that Tom was still able to put his hand right on the item that was needed.

"Here you are." He cheerfully ejected one tape and popped in another. "Let's see. . . ."

He reached out and pressed the stop button just as the same man they had seen at the earlier meeting stood up to speak. Tom turned up the volume and they all listened to the man's impassioned plea for free enterprise in Hancock. It was a good speech. Susan found herself wondering if he was a citizen—and could be convinced to run for office sometime in the future.

The point the man was making was that his project would be good for Hancock. An architect had apparently found a way to build three single-family homes on the empty three miles north of the old gristmill without impinging on the building. In fact, the plans would also include control of the flood plain that would keep the mill from being flooded each spring. Thus, the man argued, not only would the project expand the tax base for Hancock, but it would actually preserve the historic structure.

"His request is going to be denied?" Kathleen asked Tom.

"Watch," he insisted, pointing at the screen.

There was some general discussion of the request. Two members of the board had done their homework and precedents were brought up and explained. Another woman, apparently an expert in the laws regarding wetlands and the environment, expressed a lot of positive feelings about the project. No one watching could doubt that the man was going to be given permission to begin his project. Until Penelope Thomas took the floor.

She didn't waste any time arguing with the board members. She didn't even bother to address the man who had made the request. She simply explained that this particular property fell under the jurisdiction of the Landmark Commission and that, as chairperson of that commission, she was sure the request would be denied. The Zoning Board could do what they wished, of course, but an approval of this project would only be a waste of time—for the man making the request. She smiled at him and sat down.

The camera was at the rear of the room and only the back of the man's head was visible. But there was an unobstructed view of the members of the board. Some looked unhappy. Some looked furious. But all of them voted to turn down the man's request for a variance.

TWENTY-SEVEN

"WELL, WHAT DO YOU KNOW? THAT WOMAN HAS the most amazing power," Susan said, leaning back in her chair—and smacking her head against a pile of tapes, knocking them to the floor.

"I'll get them," Tom insisted. "That was some performance, wasn't it?" he added, stooping down.

"I told you so," Kathleen reminded her. "It's just like you said. The woman has the most amazing powers. How else would she ever have talked the Hancock Environmental Commission into having a booth at the Fall Festival?"

Susan looked at Kathleen, a puzzled expression on her face. "How did that happen exactly?"

Kathleen thought for a moment. "I'm not sure really. I heard that Penelope badgered the planning committee until they just couldn't say no." She pursed her lips and thought for a moment. "Maybe I could make a few calls and find out a little more than that."

"Sounds like a pretty good idea," Tom said, sorting through the tapes that had fallen.

"Is there anything else here that you think I should see?" Susan asked. "Because I don't think there's any way I'm going to get through all this tonight."

Tom started to answer when Kathleen interrupted him. "Anyone want to get dessert at the Hancock Inn?"

"Dessert?" Susan looked at the piles of tapes and back to her friend. "Are you still hungry?"

"That's where the answer to our question about the Fall Festival is. The steering committee is celebrating a birthday party there tonight," she explained. "I thought maybe we could go over and have dessert and coffee—or a glass of brandy—and ask a few questions."

"I was going to say that you've already gotten the gist of what is happening on these two committees by the tapes you've seen," Tom added.

"Then maybe we should get going," Susan said. "You'll come with us, won't you?" she added to the young man.

"I have some things to do here," he said slowly.

"You might miss a good story," Susan urged, thinking that he would like to accompany them if only she could assuage any guilt he might be feeling about leaving the station.

"Well, I'll probably be here late tonight," he said. "I do have more work to do."

"Then you can probably use the caffeine. And the inn makes great chocolate cheesecake," Susan added, knowing it was a favorite with people young enough and thin enough not to be worrying about either cholesterol or calories.

"We should get going," Kathleen urged them.

"I'm ready." Tom stood up.

"Shouldn't we clean up?" Susan asked, realizing, as soon as the words were out of her mouth, that she sounded just like a mother.

"Don't worry. I'll do it when I get back."

He sounded just like a son.

Susan led the other two from the building to the parking lot. They got in her car and, less than fifteen minutes later, were driving up to the inn.

"The lot's full," Kathleen said, looking around.

"It's Saturday night. They might not be able to take us," Tom said.

"There's always a seat for Susan here," Kathleen assured him, getting out of the car.

"I once helped solve a murder that took place in the wine cellar of the inn," Susan explained, seeing the mystified expression on his face.

But he didn't doubt the truth of her assertion when, busy though the inn obviously was, four people left their posts and other customers to greet and find a seat for Susan and her party.

They were seated in a small booth near the fireplace in the bar. Susan took a quick look around and made sure that Tom was seated with his back to the room. She and Kathleen exchanged glances over the tops of their large menus; they had both noticed the woman slumped across the bar.

Tom succumbed to Susan's description of the cheesecake. Kathleen and Susan stuck to decaf cappuccino. Kathleen had barely sipped hers before she took off to do some table hopping and find answers to their questions about the Fall Festival.

Susan looked at the young man tucking into dessert and decided to try for some answers, too. "I understand how you feel about not revealing your sources, but I was wondering if you had interviewed everyone on the Landmark Commission," she began.

"Most of them at least three times," he answered. "Except for Lyman Nearing. He's very forthright—and easy to talk to. I felt like I'd heard everything he had to say after we spoke twice."

"I know what you mean," Susan said. "It's easy to see why he's such a successful businessman. But what did

you think about the other commissioners? If you don't
mind my asking."

Apparently he didn't—and he didn't mind answering
either.

"Strange group is what I thought. Rosemary Nearing
and Foster Wade worship Penelope Thomas and will
approve any request that she makes. Lyman's not like
that—almost the opposite, in fact—but he's been so
uninvolved that he actually gave his vote away."

"Apparently he's taking it back," Susan interrupted,
and explained Nearing's intention of attending the
meeting tomorrow. "And what about Erika Eden?" she
then asked. "I didn't get the impression that she's an
automatic stamp-of-approval type of person."

"Not at all. She's an extraordinary lady. Did you know
that she built a tiny little store downtown into a major
player in the natural-products market? She travels all
over the world to do most of her own importing."

"And she's beautiful," Susan reminded him as if he
didn't know.

"I'll say. And it was very generous of her to volunteer
to serve on the Landmark Commission—being as busy as
she is and all. Of course you must know her real well—
being friends with Brett Fortesque like you are."

"We've met," Susan admitted, thinking rather about
two things. Had Brett intentionally kept the two of them
apart? After all, everyone else seemed to have known
about their relationship. And why, for heaven's sake, had
a young, single, beautiful, busy businesswoman wanted
to be on the Landmark Commission anyway? She sipped
her cappuccino and considered the questions. And
decided that, maybe, there was only one question. She
had been in Maine most of the summer and, since then,
the election had dominated her life. She hadn't seen

much of Brett, but she hadn't seen much of any of her friends, she realized.

"It is interesting that Erika Eden doesn't seem to be considered a major suspect in her ex-husband's death," Tom said. "You don't think it's a sign of police corruption here in town, do you?"

Apparently it was an interesting enough thought to cause him to ignore the last quarter of his cheesecake and Susan was glad Kathleen's return caused a distraction. She didn't want an exposé of Erika Eden on tomorrow night's news show.

"Well, that was interesting," Kathleen said, sitting back down at the table.

"Tell," Susan insisted.

"She—" Kathleen stopped and stared seriously at Tom. "This is completely off the record."

"Fine."

"This was told to me by a friend—and if it's published or reported in any way, I'll know exactly where it comes from," she said slowly.

"I know what off the record means."

"Tom's okay. I'm sure he won't report on this," Susan insisted. She was dying to know what had gotten Kathleen so excited.

"The reason the HEC manned a booth at the Fall Festival was that Penelope Thomas had made some sort of promise to the Chamber of Commerce that this last Fall Festival would be the best ever—meaning it would have the largest number of participants apparently. And when the HEC turned her down and explained that we don't participate in events in the fall, she threatened to have part of the park system declared a landmark."

"So the HEC would lose control over their gardens," Susan said, nodding.

"Exactly."

"Blackmail!" Tom stopped eating and pursed his lips.

Both women had no trouble discerning how the word thrilled him.

Susan just smiled at his enthusiasm.

"Not quite," Kathleen argued. "It was more an implied threat. Because no one said that the gardens would be destroyed—or anything else—just that the HEC would lose control."

"Hmm. So the important thing here is how much Penelope Thomas had to lose if the Landmark Commission wasn't given the power it requested," Susan added.

"And she was going to lose it if Anthony Martel won the election," Tom added.

"So she had a lot to lose if Ivan Deakin hadn't been killed," Susan added. It was an interesting thought.

Kathleen just nodded.

"God damn this town! No matter where I go, people are talking about my husband. You know what they say, 'In the rooms, the women come and go, talking of Anthony Martel-angelo.' " The loud voice rose above the general conversation in the room.

"Oh, shit. I thought she was dozing." Susan grabbed Kathleen's arm. "Help me get her out of here." She jumped out of her seat.

" 'I grow old. I grow old . . .' "

"Nice poetry," Susan said, putting her hand under one of Theresa's elbows.

"Why don't we check out the ladies' room?" Kathleen suggested, assuming a position on the other side of the intoxicated woman.

Theresa shook herself like one of the golden retrievers she didn't like and stood up a little straighter. "I may be drunk, but I can still walk," she insisted, taking a step forward and landing on her ankle.

"Why don't you take Mrs. Martel upstairs to the

office," the bartender suggested. "There's a couch up there and she's probably tired after all the campaigning. I know I would be," he added to the room at large.

"Thanks. We'll do that," Susan said.

This time they gave Theresa no choice but to go with them. With an obliging waitress bringing up the rear, they herded her up the stairs to one of the small rooms in which the business of the inn took place. There, on a chintz-covered couch, they deposited Theresa.

"Maybe I should bring up a pot of black coffee?" the waitress offered.

Kathleen nodded. "A large one."

"And maybe a tray with some pastries?" Susan asked. "Well, we're going to be here for a while, aren't we?" she added in response to Kathleen's change of expression.

The waitress hurried out of the room, whether to get on with her task or to avoid being part of any conflict, they would never know.

"Now what are we going to do?" Kathleen asked, looking down at the prostrate woman.

Theresa opened her eyes and looked straight up at Kathleen. "Bury it in a hole," she answered before closing them again.

"Don't tempt me," Kathleen muttered.

"Kath!" Susan elbowed her in the ribs.

"A hole. A hole. A hole. A hole," Theresa repeated in a singsong voice. "So why does it keep coming back?"

Susan looked at Kathleen. "What are we going to do with her?"

"We get her out of there. What else can we do?" Kathleen replied.

"You've done everything possible. I'll take over from here." Anthony Martel entered the room, a steaming coffeepot in his hands.

"This election has been quite a strain for all of us," Susan said.

"I suppose it's a good thing it looks like I'm going to lose. Who knows what the strain of being the mayor's wife might do to her." He knelt down by the couch. "And Cassandra Chadwick was here before—she'll probably make sure everyone knows about this."

"I'm sure Theresa'll be all right," Susan repeated inanely. "And it's possible that Cassandra won't say anything."

"If there's anything we can do . . ." Kathleen's hand was on the doorknob.

"No, nothing, thank you."

"Then we'll get going," Kathleen said. She and Susan started back down the stairs.

"You know what I'd like to do?" Susan said as they arrived at the ground floor.

"What?" Kathleen asked.

"I'd like to go and take a good look at the Women's Club."

"Returning to the scene of the crime?" Tom asked, coming up to them.

"It's where the murder took place and more than a few strange things happened that night."

"Like the person who followed you around the balcony," Kathleen added.

"And I'd like to check out the sequence of events. Who was where at what time," Susan explained further to Tom. She thought he looked impressed.

"Then let's get going," he suggested.

"Still off the record," Kathleen reminded him.

"Fine. But how are we going to get in? It's Saturday night. There isn't any political event scheduled there."

"Don't worry. We'll manage," Susan said with more assurance than she felt.

"I guess someone who can get a seat here on a busy night like this can go anywhere in town," he said enthusiastically, following the women out of the inn.

Kathleen and Susan weren't so sure.

TWENTY-EIGHT

Aren't we rather casually dressed to blend in with this group?" Kathleen commented, peering out the window of Susan's Jeep at the crowd strolling up the broad steps into the Hancock Women's Club.

The club was decked out for a party. Arches of silver and gold balloons framed the sidewalk to the front door. Banks of bronze and white chrysanthemums were visible inside. A banner proclaimed congratulations to Babs and Bobby. "Looks like a wedding reception," Susan said. "A very formal wedding reception."

"And we're not dressed for something like that," Kathleen repeated. "And we really can't just walk inside and ask to look around. Maybe we should come back tomorrow morning."

Susan thought for a moment. "I have a couple of silk blouses and some scarves in the back. I took them along with me to Tom's station when I was going to be on the air and I haven't had a chance to take them into the house. And, you know what?" she asked, remembering that she hadn't managed to get to the dry cleaner either. "Jed's good navy suit is there, too—and about a half-dozen ties." She glanced over at Tom. "He's not as thin as you are, but you're about his height—it might fit."

"You think we should put on this clothing and go in there acting like guests?" Tom looked dubious.

"Why not?" Kathleen asked.

"People are going to be wandering around, eating and drinking. We certainly won't be bothering anyone," Susan assured him.

As she suspected, the idea of food got to him. "Well, I suppose . . ."

"You'll be doing a lot stranger things than getting dressed in someone else's clothing and socializing at the reception of someone you don't know if you're going to be a reporter," Kathleen said.

"Well . . ."

"Good." Susan took his hesitation as acquiescence. "Everything is in the back. I'll just pull the car up into a dark spot and we can find a large bush and change behind it."

It was easier said than done. The Women's Club was in the middle of a residential section of town. Any and all dark corners had been illuminated (and eliminated) by expensive security companies. The trio was finally forced to change in the car.

Kathleen was wearing a silk skirt that, fortunately, matched the red silk blouse Susan had almost worn to be on TV. Susan, still in the camel slacks she had worn to the game this morning, put on the other shirt: a tailored white silk. She didn't look terribly festive—but Tom looked wonderful. Luckily, he had been wearing a beige dress shirt and Jed's suit looked fabulous on him. He would look just like all the other guests at the reception—as long as no one glanced down at his feet. Double-breasted Armanis aren't usually accessorized with old, slightly shabby hiking boots.

"Are we ready?" Kathleen asked.

Tom fell right into the role. "Ladies?" He offered his arms to them.

Kathleen took his arm immediately.

They made a charming couple, Susan thought. "Why don't you two go on without me?" she suggested. "You look great together and I'll just blend in with a larger group."

"You're sure?" Kathleen asked.

"Definitely. I may even try to get in the back way. Tell you what." She glanced at her watch. "I'll meet you up on the balcony in fifteen minutes."

"Why—" Tom began.

"I want to figure out how much can be seen from one side or the other. And how visible someone would be going up and down the stairway. Stuff like that."

"Then we'll be there in fifteen," Kathleen said, gently tugging Tom in the direction she wished him to go. "I don't want to wear my old car coat and I'm getting a little cold, Tom."

"Oh. Yeah. We'll be up there in fifteen minutes."

Susan watched them join the now thinning line going through the door. She looked down at her clothing and decided to try to sneak in through a side door. In the midst of all the glitter and gold lamé, she would stick out like a sore thumb going through the receiving line.

She headed around the right side of the building. The first windows she passed were apparently rest rooms and the glass was frosted. The next window peeked through two lines of furs and dress coats out to the large floor where dozens of tables were set with crystal, silver, and massive flower arrangements rising from dozens of shimmering brass votive-candle holders. Susan continued on along an unbroken wall until a door appeared before her. It was unlocked.

And led right into the middle of the kitchen. A very large and very busy kitchen. Susan had only limited experience with caterers, but it was obvious even to her that a crisis of some sort was going on here. She moved against the wall, not wanting to get in the way of the people rushing around, full trays held above their heads.

"Where the hell have you been? And what are you doing dressed like that? Did you think you were here to wait on tables?"

Susan blinked and stared at the plump woman standing before her. "Excuse me?"

"I hope you brought an apron, at least."

Susan looked over her shoulder, wondering if this person could be speaking to someone who had followed her into the room. She was alone. "Excuse me?" she repeated.

"You better get going. We don't have much time to waste."

Susan shrugged. She was inside. She was about to explain that she was a guest when she was interrupted by a rather hysterical waitress. The young woman's appearance answered one question: she was wearing camel slacks and a tailored white shirt. Just her luck, she was dressed like the help tonight, Susan thought.

"I can't believe it! There are more security people in here than at the White House!" the young woman cried.

"Those wedding presents are worth big money," the bossy woman who had greeted Susan explained.

"I—" Susan started.

"But I've never been fingerprinted for a job before," the young woman continued. "Who are these people?"

"I don't know. But they're wealthy enough to pay for a big spread like this and you better pick up a full tray and start to circulate. I don't know. . . ." She seemed to notice Susan again. "What are you doing? Why haven't you begun decorating those platters?"

Before she could start to explain, a burly man in a uniform walked in the door. "Who's she?" he asked, nodding in Susan's direction.

"The pastry chef we hired for the evening. Your employer wanted 'congratulations' written across little chocolate boxes full of chestnut mousse. She's the person we hired to do it."

Susan smiled. She had taken a course in cake decorating. She could do that and be upstairs in fifteen minutes—twenty at the most.

"Did she pass the security check?" he asked, looking at her like he couldn't believe such a thing was possible.

Susan started to answer, but he continued before she could utter a word.

" 'Cause if she didn't, I have orders to call the police."

"I better get to work on those desserts." Susan didn't want to end up explaining her presence to anyone. She'd just decorate those little chocolate boxes and get on with it.

"That wall."

Susan glanced over at the speckled counter that ran from one side of the room to the other. "Where—" she began to ask before realizing that she was looking at them. Every single speck was a small box created from six chocolate squares. "How many?" was what she changed her question to.

"Three hundred and forty-seven. You better get busy. You only have a couple of hours."

"You expect me to write 'congratulations' in tiny print three hundred and forty-seven times?" Susan asked, astounded. How could anyone do that?

"It's what you were hired to do, isn't it?" the guard asked her.

Susan just frowned and walked over to the counter. She'd spend a few minutes doing what was expected, and when everyone was busy—or when the real pastry chef arrived—she'd head up to the balcony. She frowned.

Her immediate problem was how to turn one class in

cake decorating at the local gourmet shop into practical experience. She'd never worked on anything so small. . . .

The next time Susan glanced at her watch, twenty minutes had passed, fifteen boxes were complete, and a couple of dozen were in the garbage can. The chocolate was thin and a single slip or bump caused the delicate boxes to crumble. She looked around the room—no one seemed to be paying any attention to her. She slipped out of the apron she had been loaned and took off.

The party was boisterous. In another hour the tiny writing on the boxes would be wasted. Very few members of this group would be up to reading anything small by then. Susan skimmed along the wall to the stairway and climbed.

Tom and Kathleen were sitting in the dark at the top of the stairs.

"We should have brought a flashlight," Susan stated flatly.

"Neither of us will argue with that," Kathleen said. "I cracked my elbow on a corner and Tom's tripped twice."

"I don't think we can risk turning on the lights up here. Someone might come up to investigate," Susan said, explaining about the guards who had been hired to protect the presents.

Tom was picking at the lapel of his suit and didn't join their conversation.

"Something wrong?"

"There's a lot of sticky stuff on this suit," he answered, sounding annoyed.

"I wasn't carrying it with me in case I found a good-looking young man who wanted to sneak into a wedding. The suit was on its way to the cleaners—because it needed cleaning."

"But what *is* this stuff?" he asked.

"Probably lunch or dinner. Jed is always either working or politicking during meals—so a lot of food ends up on his clothing these days." She looked around. "My eyes are actually beginning to adjust to this light. Do you think we could get going?"

Kathleen stood up. "Just tell us what you want us to do."

"Well, I came up the stairs and walked into the boardroom over there." She nodded to the closed door to the right. "And I was wondering where someone else would have to have been standing to have been watching me." She frowned. "If you understand what I mean."

"Sure. You walk to the door—very slowly—and then go into the room. What sort of lighting is in there?"

Susan thought for a moment before answering Kathleen. "There was lots of overhead lighting when I was there before. But I think I saw a table lamp on a credenza at the end of the room. I could try turning it on."

"Look, we don't want to be discovered wandering around up here because we'd be asked to leave and we wouldn't accomplish what we want to accomplish—but it wouldn't be that big a deal—no one is going to shoot us," Tom said. "And if you don't turn something on we're not going to be able to see you—or anything else."

Susan decided not to mention the presence of armed guards. Both Tom and Kathleen would be happier not knowing. "Okay. You two split up and I'll try to find a dim light and then we'll get started."

They each set off in opposite directions. Susan, ever aware of the danger of discovery, hurried over to the conference-room door and opened it slowly and quietly. The room, lit only by light coming through the windows overlooking the room below, was dark. The speakers were on and "Send in the Clowns" bounced from wall to wall. Susan tiptoed over to the place where she thought the light was located and reached out, hoping to touch the shade. What she touched felt like skin . . . a hand. . . .

Susan felt a scream gathering in her throat. But when it arrived, it seemed to come from outside of her.

"What the hell . . . ?"

Susan gasped. The scream was soprano but the voice was definitely male. She backed away, knocking over a chair or small table behind her.

"Daniel, what are you doing? Someone will hear!"

This time the voice was female. Susan moved back again and, catching her foot in the furniture behind her, crashed to the floor.

A light flashed on, giving Susan a clear view of the bride—Babs presumably—the top of her white dress farther off her shoulders than any designer had imagined, sprawled across the credenza. An elegant-looking young man lay across her.

"Turn that off!"

Her groom took orders well. The room was plunged into darkness.

"I'm sor—" Susan began.

"Shut up! Do you want someone to come up here?"

Susan smiled. Did this young woman think this was the first time a bride and groom started the honeymoon a little early? "I didn't mean to interrupt you. I just didn't know you were here. I'll—"

"Hush!"

Susan complied.

"If one of those damn guards comes up here to look around and sees us, and Daddy hears about it, he'll kill someone," the bride whispered.

"He'll kill me," her young man insisted. "And God knows what Bob will do."

Susan didn't say anything. If this man wasn't Bob, then the bride had a bigger problem that she wanted to know about. She started to speak, but the couple immediately shushed her.

"Okay, who's in here?" The door slammed open and the guard Susan had seen in the kitchen stood framed in the light.

Susan leaped to her feet. "It's me. The pastry chef!" she lied. She hurried to the door, hoping he wouldn't feel obliged to turn on the light and expose the couple behind her.

"Well, you, missy, are going to come with me. We're going to call the police."

Susan smiled up at him despite the rude way he had grabbed her arm. "I think that's an excellent idea," she announced, looking down at her hand. "I would like to speak with Brett about something myself."

TWENTY-NINE

"You are going to explain what you were doing up there, aren't you? I assume the story that you were moonlighting as a pastry chef was just a story?"

Susan assumed this was a rhetorical question and didn't answer. Besides, if she explained, she would be forced to mention Tom and Kathleen. She had seen them sneaking down the stairs as she was rushed from the building. "I was looking for clues—and look what I found. Blood. Fake blood like the stuff that was on Erika's bed. Only this was on Jed's jacket. And we know Jed didn't have anything to do with putting it in the carriage house!" She looked at Brett, hoping he would appreciate her point.

Brett looked tired—and miserable. His office, where the two of them were sitting, was a mess. "You haven't found Erika, have you?" she asked gently, changing the subject.

"If she's at a spa around here, she signed in under an assumed name. Not that there's any law against that." He frowned. "To tell you the truth, I'm going nuts. I can't believe she did it. But I know . . . I've seen people misjudge the women they love. . . . And, of course, this is destroying my credibility with my men. Some of them don't believe we can't find her. I hear the rumors—some of them actually believe I'm hiding her." He shook his head. "And I can't blame them. I'd be thinking the same thing if I were in their shoes. She can't be guilty. But—" He stopped.

"But why did she disappear?"

"Exactly."

"Just because she ran away after Ivan's death doesn't mean she's the person who killed him."

"So why did she run away? She got some sort of urge to exercise and diet that couldn't be denied?" Brett crossed his arms and put his head down on his desk.

Susan sat silently in the chair on the other side of the desk and waited for him to collect himself. When he looked up again, she thought there were tears in his eyes. "Is there any way we can get into Erika's store?" she asked.

"The one here in town?"

Susan nodded her yes.

"Actually I may have a key. She was having trouble with the alarm system a few months ago and I met the company's rep there when she had to be in the city. I think it's still here." He scrounged around in his pants pocket as he spoke. "Yup. You think there's something important there?"

"I don't know. She didn't do it. I agree with you there. And I think I may have a clue as to who did—but I need to think about it."

"Susan, I need to know—"

"Brett, trust me on this one. I don't have anything definite yet. Just a vague idea—and it doesn't have anything to do with Erika."

"Then why do you want to go to the store?"

"Because I want to know why Erika volunteered to serve on the Landmark Commission. She doesn't own the carriage house, so I was thinking that her store might have something to do with it."

Brett's handsome face crinkled up into a half grin. "You're right. Of course, I've been so worried about whether or not she murdered Ivan that I didn't stop to think about what had been going on."

"It sounds like Erika was a pretty busy woman. If she felt the need to serve her community, there are lots of things she could have done besides serving on the Landmark Commission. I don't know that the store is the answer, but—"

"But it's as good a place to start as we know of," Brett finished for her.

"Exactly."

"So let's get going." Brett leaped up and rushed over to open his office door for her.

"What are you going to tell that goon from the security company?" Susan asked, preceding him into the hallway.

"I don't think anything less than hours of torture will satisfy the man." Brett nodded to two of his officers seated in the lobby near the door of the police department. "So I'm going to ignore him. Someday you must tell me why you practically threw yourself into his arms at that wedding reception."

"Someday I will," she promised, knowing he had more important things on his mind right now. She followed him over to his unmarked police car and got in to the passenger's seat. "What do you know about the store?"

"Not a whole lot. I know the store has always been located there. It wasn't somewhere else before this. It's been around for quite a while. You've been there, haven't you?"

"Yes. Not recently, but I bought the big wheat wreath with gourds that I hang over the fireplace in Jed's study there and—I don't believe it. What is wrong with me this year?"

"What?"

"I've been so busy that I didn't even hang that wreath—it usually goes up the day before Halloween. I cannot believe it."

Brett apparently couldn't have cared less. They were almost at the store. "What precisely are you looking for?"

"I don't know—this is similar to what you were thinking about at the carriage house. Except this probably connects the store to the Landmark Commission in some way."

"Sounds like we should be doing a title search down at town hall, not looking around the store," Brett said, maneuvering his car into a loading zone.

"Could we go check that out?"

"It's closed."

"I just thought that since it looks like you can park anyplace you want . . ."

Brett got out of the car without saying a word. Susan followed quickly, but he had unlocked the front door of the shop and was punching buttons on the keypad inside the door when she joined him. "The office is through that door," he said, nodding toward the back of the store.

Susan headed in the direction he indicated, taking the time to notice the tiny arrangements of dried flowers on the way. They would look wonderful on the table at Thanksgiving. . . .

"Susan? You aren't listening to me, are you?"

"I was just thinking," Susan answered a little indignantly.

Brett stopped with his hand on the office door and turned to look at her. "I'm sorry. Really, really sorry. You've been a big help and there's no excuse for me snapping at you like that."

"You don't have to apologize. I know the strain you're

under. Once we find out who killed Ivan, everything will be okay."

"Everything will never be okay again." The speaker of these words—Erika Eden—walked out of her office, a sad expression on her face.

Without a word, Brett enfolded her in his arms, his lips lightly brushing her sleek cap of hair. Erika briefly closed her eyes, looking, Susan thought, like a cat who had just found a warm, sunny spot on a windowsill. Then she opened her eyelids wide and looked straight at Susan. "You said something about finding out who killed Ivan— are you really getting closer to that?"

"We may have some answers soon," Brett answered her.

"Nothing is definite," Susan insisted. Erika's misery was obvious and she didn't want to add to it with false hopes.

"Oh . . . I thought maybe you had come here to tell me it was all over . . . but, of course, you didn't even know I would be here, did you?" Erika looked up at Brett curiously. "Why are you here?"

"We wanted to look around. We were hoping for some answers," he explained.

"But now you can tell us what we want to know," Susan added.

Erika glanced up at Brett and took a deep breath. "Ask me anything," she insisted.

"Why did you join the Landmark Commission?"

Erika sighed. "I've been dreading answering this question—but you probably knew that," she said to Brett.

"I don't know anything about it," Susan said quickly. She thought Brett might not want to admit his ignorance of the situation. "But I do need to know the answer to the question."

"There's an easy answer," Erika said, moving out of

Brett's embrace and looking straight into Susan's eyes. "I joined the Landmark Commission because I wanted to protect my business. It's simple. In fact, almost everything I've done for the past decade has been done to protect my business or to help it grow." She looked up at Brett. "Except for getting involved with you. Of course, when I met you last summer, I thought everything was going to work out."

Susan resisted a strong urge to ask where they had met instead of a more relevant question. "How did you even hear about the Landmark Commission before it was formed?"

"Luck. I run all the stores from here—do all the paperwork. Hancock is a pretty high-rent district, but it's nothing compared to Madison Avenue or Southampton, so it's logical that the largest office is here. Besides, this is where I started. I just bumped out the back wall, moved up, and added lots of memory to my PC. Come see," she added, noticing the confused expression on Susan's face. She opened the door to her office, turned on the lights, and led them in.

"Wow. Who would have thought all this was back here?" Susan commented, looking around the two-story glassed-in atrium. "It's gorgeous."

"It is now," Erika said proudly. "When I expanded back here, it was also used as a storeroom. But I now have three warehouses."

"Not here in town," Brett added.

"No, they're all out in New Jersey."

"This is the only property you own in Hancock," Susan said.

"I don't own this. I rent. But I'm lucky enough to have had a long lease—one that is due to run out in September next year."

"And you'll move then? Or will you close the store?"

"I've known this was coming for almost two years and planned for it. There was never any real question of not having a store in Hancock. The whole healthy, wealthy Connecticut suburbia has gotten me a lot of publicity—and it's a hook. I'm not quite like all the other natural-products stores in New York—and I have a history. People come to me for help setting up new stores—and they come to me for the natural products that I import from all over the world. That's more and more a part of my company."

"You may not know this, but I went through your carriage house," Susan interrupted, not wanting to indict Brett in the activity. "And I saw a letter from someone offering a lot of money to buy your business."

"Eleven million dollars. A whole lot of money." Erika nodded seriously. "But it's not just money that I want. I'd like to be able to keep up the import part of the business and let someone else take over the stores." She smiled. "I've arranged and rearranged flowers and leaves until I'm sick of it. And you always have to have an edge—to make sure your look is just a little better than everyone else's." She shook her head. "There are a lot of people who do that type of thing better than I do. And I've been lucky enough to talk some of them into working for me. That part of the business can go on without me."

"Erika has been providing work for women in small villages in underdeveloped countries with her importing," Brett began proudly.

"And building a company and making a good living doing it," Erika added. "Brett sometimes makes me sound like the local missionary rather than an American entrepreneur."

"So what does all this have to do with the Landmark Commission?" Susan asked.

"Do you know the old gristmill?"

"Down by the river?"

Erika nodded. "I own it. And I have every intention of turning it into Stems and Twigs' flagship store. When it's opened, the publicity will be wonderful and it will set the tone for the rest of the stores. And, with luck, I will be able to sell the entire business, keeping the involvement that I want to have."

"But it's truly a historical landmark. There's no way the Landmark Commission will allow you to alter it," Susan said, remembering the videotape of the Zoning Board meeting she had watched.

"Not quite true," Erika answered. She looked embarrassed. "That's the shoddy part of the story. I knew the Landmark Commission was being created, because both of the Nearings are good customers. Nearing Rings has been using us to create their holiday decorations at the plant and for their parties since we were just a small business here in town. Lyman believes in using local businesses where he can. And his wife, Rosemary, has been a wonderful customer for a long time. In fact, we carry a very popular line of colonial herbs because of her support."

"And one of them told you about the Landmark Commission?"

Erika surprised her by chuckling. "Both of them told me, in fact. They don't, of course, talk to each other much, but they were both in the store in the same week and each of them mentioned it to me. Someone—I think it was Rosemary, but I'm not completely sure—mentioned that the commission would have jurisdiction over the historical buildings in town. I thought immediately of the mill. It was on my mind almost constantly since I had only closed on it the week before."

"So you volunteered to be on the commission?" Susan asked.

"I was a little more devious than that. I've had some dealings with Penelope Thomas—she's always running some function or another and that means she's always asking for donations for decorations or door prizes—you know the type of thing."

Susan nodded. She did indeed. She had made the begging rounds of the local merchants more than once. And she also knew how appreciative she was of the businesses that were generous.

"So I created a false overrun of wonderful natural bath products and called her and offered them to her current charity project."

"She must have been thrilled," Susan said. Penelope, she was sure, had certainly never had it so easy.

"She was appreciative. Thrilled is not a word I would use for Penelope."

"And then you volunteered to be on the commission?" Brett asked.

"I wish I could say that, but I can't. It's what I intended to happen, but no one ever accused Penelope of not doing her homework. She knew that I had just bought the mill and she didn't have any trouble figuring out what I was planning to do with it. She offered me a place on the Landmark Commission and, before I could answer her, explained that the members of the commission would have the ability to protect the properties that were special to them. I'm ashamed to admit it, but I said yes almost without thinking."

"You were protecting something that you had created over the years. Something more important to you than the ordinary business," Brett said, reaching out to put a hand on her shoulder.

"Is that what you would say to one of your officers who took a bribe to pay his mortgage?" Erika asked. "Brett, it was wrong. I knew it was wrong. And I did it. I mean, I tried to justify it. I said that I would give other business owners the same opportunities that I gave Stems and Twigs. But, of course, I didn't. There was no way I could do that. Penelope offered me a trade. I went along with what she wanted to do on the commission and she let me do what I had planned to do with the gristmill."

"That's why you left town?" Brett asked.

"It was so shabby. I didn't want you to know about it. And when Ivan was killed, I knew it would all come out in your investigations. So I took off for a spa that I'm going to be doing business with. I know how stupid it was. And I know what I'm going to do about it."

"What?"

"Go to the commission's meeting tomorrow night, announce my resignation, and tell the whole story."

"That should cause a sensation," Brett said, a frown on his face.

Susan also looked sad. She realized that Erika's decision was the right one, but the meeting, with so many raw nerves exposed, was going to be a sad event.

THIRTY

Fifteen minutes before the meeting of the Landmark Commission, she realized that she had been completely wrong. This meeting was going to be a joy. A long article on the front page of the Sunday edition of the *Hancock Herald* had guaranteed it.

Unaccustomed to much of an audience, the commission met in one of the smaller meeting rooms in the basement of the library. Susan and a few dozen other women had once attended a "Parenting Teenage Boys" symposium there and it had been crowded then. By the time the commission was called to order, a long line of people anxious to attend was snaking through the hallway.

Tom Davidson, excited, hair standing on end, was rushing through the crowd, toting television monitors and stringing wires in an attempt to broadcast the meeting to the crowd in the hallway. Other reporters, too young to be as bored as they looked, asked questions of various citizens, recording the answers in notebooks and on tiny tape machines. A couple of policemen stood at the bottom of the stairway, keeping an eye on the crowd, but Susan was pretty sure she wasn't the only person who was aware of Brett's absence.

Erika Eden had come to the meeting early, taken a seat at the table, removed a notebook from her purse, and sat reading to herself. As other commissioners entered the room and found seats, Erika looked up, smiled, and said nothing. When Penelope Thomas entered the room, Erika repeated the drill; except she didn't bother to smile.

Penelope, though, had scowled. And not just at Erika. She scowled at everyone in the room, scowled at the chair that was left for her, scowled at the pitcher of ice water in the middle of the table, and positively glared at the front page of the *Hancock Herald* that was sticking out of a spectator's handbag. Susan enjoyed every minute of it.

She had gotten very little sleep last night, worrying about this meeting and about whether Erika would be strong enough to do what she felt was necessary. But, of course, the *Hancock Herald* article meant that Erika wasn't alone. It turned out that, finally, Penelope Thomas tried to blackmail the wrong person. That person had called some friends who called some friends and the editor of the local paper had seen a wonderful two days before the election-story opportunity. The headline alone, PENNY THOMAS ACCUSED OF OFFERING FAVORS, had kept a smile on Susan's face since breakfast time.

Now she leaned back against the doorjamb where she was standing and watched as Penelope Thomas tried to call her meeting to order. First she rapped on the desk with her knuckles. Then she banged with an empty water glass. Finally she shrieked, "Shut up!"

The group—many, Susan realized, like her trying to hide their grins—followed her orders. As people out in the hall shushed each other and Tom dashed back to the table to adjust his camera, she glanced at Erika Eden. The young woman was still pale.

"I find myself forced to resign as chairman of the Landmark Commission," Penelope announced, fury in her voice.

Susan waited for the lies and the justifications that,

apparently, were not to come. There was only one more sentence.

"There is no Landmark Commission without me." The last words were coming out of Penelope's mouth as she pushed through the crowd and out of the room.

The audience was astounded, but Susan was more interested to note the reactions of the faces of the other commissioners, still sitting at the table.

Foster Wade, apparently at his sartorial peak in a wrinkled, ill-fitting navy wool blazer and dirty light gray polyester slacks, looked indignant. "What precisely did she mean by that?" he asked no one in particular.

Rosemary Nearing seemed to be near tears, her chubby cheeks flushed with excitement.

Lyman was clearly thrilled, and didn't care who knew it. "That Penny," he said cheerfully. "Takes herself too seriously. Always did."

But Erika was still pale, and miserable. Susan started to move toward her through the milling crowd. But Tom Davidson stuck a microphone under Erika's chin and asked a question.

"I have a statement to make." Erika's voice rang out through the electronic system. "Please, I would like you all to listen to me. I became a member of the Landmark Commission to protect my business interests—here in Hancock and elsewhere. I apologize to the community and . . . and I hope no one will judge the people around me harshly. No one knew what I had done. No one."

Susan knew Erika was trying to protect Brett, but she realized Tom had other aspects of the story on his mind. "What did Mrs. Thomas offer you to ensure that you would be loyal to her?"

"It wasn't quite like that," Erika insisted, but Tom, in the tradition of journalists everywhere, had already moved the microphone on down the table and was questioning Lyman Nearing. The print reporters were pushing and shoving to get into the room when Susan pulled Erika up from the table and nudged her toward the door.

"You're not going to be a help to anyone now," Susan said. "Why don't we get out of here?"

"I don't want anyone to think that I dodged questions about any of this," Erika insisted.

"Don't worry. After the revelations about Penelope Thomas, you really didn't have to say anything at all today. You don't notice anyone else running around talking about their involvement with the commission, do you?"

"No, but . . ." Erika looked around the humming room.

"So let's get out of here," Susan insisted. She didn't know about Erika, but she had more work to do. Knowing that Penelope Thomas was using the Landmark Commission as her own personal power base was only one small piece of the puzzle. Already, she heard one of the reporters in the hallway mentioning Ivan Deakin's name.

"Where are we going?" Erika asked, following Susan through the crowded halls. "I'm sorry. I already made my statement," she added to a reporter who stuck a microphone in her face. "I have nothing to add at this time."

"You sounded very professional," Susan said when they had reached the street. "Do you spend much time with reporters?"

"None. But I'm a big fan of CNN. In every big hotel in every big city in the world, people are saying just that thing.

"So where are we going?" she repeated.

Susan slowed down. "I have no idea. Now that the questions about the Landmark Commission are settled, I simply can't imagine where to look for Ivan's murderer."

"What was Ivan's solution to the Landmark Commission problem? What was he going to announce that night at the Women's Club?" Erika asked.

"Nothing."

"But his speech . . ."

"Oh, he had a speech, it just didn't say anything."

"What do you mean?"

"It was some sort of political pablum. He thought Hancock could depend upon the good sense of its citizens to make the correct decisions about their historical buildings. You know the type of thing—it's on CNN, too, isn't it?"

Erika smiled at the comment before continuing. "I know the type of thing. But it doesn't sound like Ivan. The man may have been wrong most of the time, but he was a risk taker, always coming up with a new scheme and always believing that the next scheme was going to work."

Susan thought about all the restaurants. "Well, you know him better than most people. . . ."

"And why would he run for office unless he had come up with something? It might help his failing business if he became mayor of Hancock, but that couldn't be the only reason he ran."

"But his speech. I read it in Brett's office. It was silly. It didn't say anything or offer any new solutions—" Susan stopped and looked at Erika. "It wasn't his speech. Of course, that explains everything. It wasn't his speech."

"You mean someone else wrote it?"

"I mean someone took advantage of the mayhem after Ivan's death to replace the speech that was on the podium with the innocuous one that the police picked up and that I read down at the station."

"You really think there was an opportunity for someone to do that? I thought the police were there right away and they usually seal the crime scene." She looked embarrassed. "I watch cop shows, too," she admitted.

"One of our country's most popular exports," Susan muttered. She was thinking back. Brett had walked in the door of the Women's Club, glanced at the body, and almost immediately began talking on a cellular phone. Possibly calling Erika? Susan thought it was likely. He knew Ivan Deakin and Erika had been married. He knew better than most that an ex-wife was bound to come under suspicion in a murder case. He would have tried to pin down Erika's whereabouts immediately. Susan sighed and looked at the other woman. "I think things were handled a little differently after Ivan died." Less professionally, she thought, but didn't say aloud.

"So what happened to the original speech?" Erika asked.

"Probably got tossed in a wastebasket—or maybe Long Island Sound. We'll never find it now. . . . Unless . . ."

" 'Unless'?"

"Unless what happened to the original script will answer a lot of the questions I've been asking all this last week. Unless the script moved from the Women's Club to the Martels' house to . . . to a hole in my backyard." Susan nodded. "That would explain it. That would explain why she came to visit me and why she was out in the yard visiting an animal that made her more than a little nervous. And it might explain why she's been drinking ever since the murder."

"Theresa Martel? You think Theresa Martel stole Ivan's speech?"

"I don't know why she did it or why she didn't just toss it in her garbage can right before the scheduled pickup, but I'll bet she did."

"What are you going to do now?"

"Drive to my house and dig a hole in my backyard,"

Susan said. "Then, if I find what I think I'm going to find, head over to the Martel house and check it out," Susan insisted. "Would you like to come with me?"

"I don't think—"

"I wish you would. I might need help." *If Theresa's guilty and I need someone to call the police,* was what she didn't say.

"Fine. Why don't I drive?" They had arrived at the tiny Miata.

"Okay."

"And why don't we get going before that man with the video camera catches up with us." Erika unlocked her door and slipped into the driver's seat as she spoke.

Susan was in complete agreement, and they headed down the road, leaving the press in their wake.

No one was home at Susan's house, except for the dog, who would never, ever understand why Susan chose to get a shovel and flashlight from the garage and dig a hole in the one place the entire household agreed belonged to the dog alone—so, to spare her sensitive nature, Susan left Clue in the house while she set about this task.

"Is that the speech?" Erika asked a few minutes later, beaming her flashlight down into the hole.

Susan frowned. "Well, it's what a speech looks like after a dog has dug it up, chewed on it, and reburied it at least once." Susan stared down at the mess in her hands. "Probably more than once."

"Impossible to read."

"Exactly." Susan nodded.

"So what do we do now?"

"Go over and see the Martels. Theresa must have buried this here and I think we can assume whoever buried it, read it—"

"And killed Ivan," Erika concluded.

"I think it's possible."

"So that her husband would win the election. Sort of a modern Lady Macbeth."

"I suppose so," Susan said. The only problem was that she didn't see Theresa Martel in that role. And what about Theresa's confession of love for Ivan—how did that fit into this story?

"Or do you think Anthony Martel is behind the murder?" Erika asked.

Susan remembered the books about poison in the Martels' master bath. "It's possible."

"What are you going to do? Just ask her if she buried the manuscript in your dog's cage?"

"It's a run."

"What?"

"It's a dog run," Susan repeated.

"What's the difference?"

"Probably a couple of hundred dollars," Susan said. "Park over there." She pointed to the street. "We don't want to get stuck in the driveway if someone arrives after we do."

"You don't think we're in any danger, do you?"

"No. But mainly because I cannot imagine either Theresa or her husband as the murderer. Anthony seems to be a rather dull, idealistic man who wanted to be mayor in order to do what he thought was good for the community."

"And what about Theresa?"

"Well, it's not what I would have said a few weeks ago, but the woman seems to be a garden-variety out-of-control drinker."

"So maybe she killed Ivan while she was out of control."

"It's possible."

"And then switched the speeches, hid the old one for a

couple of days, then buried it in your dog run. Does that seem like something a drunk would do?" Erika suggested.

"I can't imagine why anyone would do that," Susan said. "It seems to me that it's a better way for a murderer to draw attention to herself than to hide."

THIRTY-ONE

Aʜᴛʜᴏɴʏ Mᴀʀᴛᴇʟ ᴏᴘᴇɴᴇᴅ ᴛʜᴇ ᴅᴏᴏʀ ᴀᴛ Sᴜsᴀɴ's knock. "Susan, hello . . . Is Jed with you?" He peered out into the darkness.

"No, this is Erika Eden," Susan said, introducing her companion. "We came to talk to Theresa. Is she home?"

"Yes, but she may be napping."

"I'm here and I'm not napping." They looked up as Theresa wound her way down her cluttered stairway. "And I'm not hungover," she added.

"My wife hasn't been feeling very well," Anthony jumped in quickly.

"His wife has been drinking herself into a state of numbness by midafternoon each day. Most nights I've been flat-out drunk. And I have started each day with a hangover. Each day since Ivan was killed. Until today," she added. "Today I'm off to a new start. And my good husband is not going to have to make excuses for me. You," she added, looking at Erika, "you are Ivan Deakin's ex-wife, aren't you?"

"Yes."

"Anthony, I would like to speak to Susan and Erika alone."

"But, dear—"

"It's important," Theresa added firmly. "Why don't you go work on your acceptance speech?"

265

"I might, my dear, lose the election."

Theresa nodded. "You might, but no one ever listens to concession speeches, so there's no need to spend any time on that one. We will go to the kitchen. I think it's time I began cooking meals again."

Susan, thrilled to see that the sensible Theresa Martel was back, followed the other two women to the kitchen.

"Have a seat. We'll have some tea," Theresa stated. "You will have to move stuff off the chairs. I'm a rotten housekeeper—even when I'm not drinking."

Susan and Erika sat down and Theresa fussed around with water, kettles, mugs, and tea bags.

"Did you know my husband?" Erika asked politely.

"Yes. He made me love him, in fact," Theresa replied. She was busy at the stove, her back to the room.

Erika seemed startled, but Susan appreciated the fact that she quickly recovered herself and continued the conversation. "Did you have an affair?" she asked, as though it were an every-day occurrence. Which indeed, Susan thought, it had been much of the time.

"No. He never suggested it. And I wouldn't have anyway. I loved him, but I also love and respect both Anthony and my marriage to him."

"You're a wise woman," Erika commented a little grimly.

"I've been a fool," Theresa said angrily. "I was a fool to fall for Ivan, to be so upset by his death, to drink so much and do such foolish things this week." She slammed a full teapot onto the stove as an exclamation point.

Susan opened her mouth and then closed it again. How could she ask this unhappy woman if she had murdered Ivan Deakin? And what would she do if Theresa said yes?

Erika solved the problem for her. "Do you have any idea who killed Ivan?" she asked quietly.

"I thought for a while that Anthony must have done it." Theresa turned back to her guests. "Susan knows that. I even went over to her house and slobbered on and on about it. I was drunk," she said to Susan, "but not drunk enough to forget that—unfortunately. But I have thought and thought about it. And not only is Anthony just not a murderer, but he couldn't have killed Ivan. He was upstairs at the Women's Club when Ivan died. And if I hadn't been drinking so hard, I would have realized that earlier."

"True," Susan muttered. But was it? The murderer only had to put poison in the pitcher, he didn't have to stand around and make sure Ivan actually drank from it. And could Anthony have left the poison, gone upstairs to pretend to listen to the speech, waited for Ivan to die, dashed back downstairs, and switched the speeches right before the police collected them? To Susan, it sounded like a pretty athletic evening—as well as one that depended upon a lot of uncontrollable factors—the lights going out, Ivan drinking the water before he read the speech, being on hand to exchange speeches at the right moment. She shook her head. If that's what the murderer had planned on, he or she had been damn lucky things worked out the way they did. The opportunities to foul up were legion.

"But I was at your home more than once, wasn't I?" Theresa continued. "The other time I hid that damn speech in your dog's cage."

"It's a run," Susan corrected her absently.

"Wait a second!" Erika cried. "Are you talking about Ivan's speech?"

"Ivan's speech? No, I'm talking about the speech

my husband was going to make that slandered Bradley Chadwick."

Susan looked around the messy kitchen. There were empty ice-cube trays sitting on top of the microwave oven. Garbage overflowed its plastic pail and fell to the floor. Cookbooks were lying on the counter, still covered with a heavy coating of flour from a baking project. Maybe it was the environment, but she was becoming very, very confused. "Tell me about this speech that ended up in my dog run. Please."

"Well, I read all of Anthony's speeches—I've even helped him draft some of them—but this one . . ." She paused and looked at the other two women. "This one was different."

"You said it slandered Bradley Chadwick," Susan reminded her.

Theresa opened her eyes wide. "It did. I couldn't believe it. It accused him of all sorts of improprieties."

"Such as?" Erika prompted.

"Such as investing in all the towns around here in properties that would become substantially more valuable if he got elected, and being willing to give the Landmark Commission the power they want to have. There was a substantial list that included shopping centers, two apartment buildings, and I can't remember what else."

Susan nodded slowly, remembering the shopping center that had been built in a neighboring town when the plans for the lumberyard fell through. "Interesting," she said. "We were thinking that only investments in property here in Hancock were going to be affected by the election, but that's not true at all, is it? What isn't allowed to be built here will very possibly be built nearby."

"It's an interesting thought, isn't it?" Erika agreed. "Anything else?" she asked Theresa.

"The speech claimed that Dr. Chadwick and Mrs. Thomas—Penelope—had been in collusion and that it was really Bradley Chadwick who was running the Landmark Commission, not Penelope."

"Maybe it's all true. Why are you so sure this is slander?" Erika asked.

"Because when I asked Anthony about it, he said that as far as he knew, none of it was true." Theresa was looking into mugs, apparently hoping to find some that had been washed recently.

"I'm getting confused," Susan announced. "You're saying you read a speech that your husband wrote. That it said all these things about Bradley Chadwick, and that when you asked your husband about it, he said he had been writing lies?"

"I asked him about the stories, not the speech," Theresa answered, pouring water over the tea bags in mugs and passing them out.

"And he said they weren't true. But did he explain why he had written the speech?" Erika asked.

"Of course not," Susan said, putting down her mug. "Because Anthony didn't write the speech. Ivan Deakin did."

Theresa puckered her brow and thought about that one. "Ivan Deakin?" She looked confused. "I just assumed Anthony had written it, but maybe ... It was certainly more Ivan's style than Anthony's. It was almost inflammatory."

"No one would ever call your husband inflammatory," Susan agreed.

"But that doesn't explain why I found it in my purse. How would a speech that Ivan wrote end up in my purse? He was up on the podium. I never got close to him that night."

"You found the speech in your purse the night that Ivan was killed?" Susan asked.

"Yes. When I stopped at the bar on the way home—I was getting cigarettes, not a drink. I drank a lot, but I didn't drink and drive—I don't think." She frowned.

"And when you opened your purse, there was the speech waiting for you?"

Theresa nodded. "Yes, folded up neatly. I just assumed Anthony had put it there. He's always stuffing things in my purse—sunglasses, his cellular phone. You know."

Susan did. Jed seemed to think that her purse was common property, too.

"Well, I listened to the radio all the way home. I wanted to learn whatever there was to know about Ivan's murder. But when I got home, I read the speech and was shocked. The next day I asked Anthony about the accusations concerning Dr. Chadwick—and he said he had never heard anything so outrageous and that I should be very careful not to slander Chadwick. I—I was stunned."

"Of course, because you thought he had written that speech," Susan said slowly. "But it wasn't Anthony's speech. It was the one that Ivan was going to give the night he was killed. It was the speech that was going to blow up the Landmark Commission—and, in fact, probably give the election to Ivan Deakin."

"So how did it end up in Theresa's purse?" Erika asked. "And then buried in your dog run?"

"Yes, how?" Theresa asked.

"Someone must have put it in your purse—and you buried it in Clue's run, didn't you?" Susan reminded her.

"It's not that simple. You see, the damn thing just kept reappearing. First it was in my purse. And then, after Anthony said the stories were wrong, I threw it away—at least I thought I threw it away. But the next day I was driving down the road, opened my purse for a cigarette, and there it was again. I—well, I had been drinking a lot and I just figured I was having some short-term-memory problems. But I thought I tossed it on the floor of my backseat—I can actually remember twisting my shoulder when I did it. But then, when I was at your house that day, there it was again, in my purse."

"So you buried it?"

"No, I didn't do that. Your dog did. I just waved it at him . . . her?"

"Her," Susan said.

"Her . . . to keep her away from me, and she grabbed it. And you yourself had said that she was always eating tissues and pieces of paper towels. So when she took it from me, I just figured she would eat it. But then she turned and started digging a hole and you called me." Theresa shrugged. "The last time I saw the speech, your dog was hiding it in the dirt. I was so glad to get rid of it that I never thought of it again. Until today."

Susan took a deep breath. "Do you think it's possible that Anthony put Ivan's speech in your purse?"

Theresa took a sip of her tea, bag still in the mug, and thought. "I don't see how. I saw Anthony for just a few minutes after Ivan was killed—less than a few minutes, in fact. And I had my purse in my hand the entire time."

"Was it a shoulder bag?" Erika asked.

"Yes."

"And do you remember if you had it on your shoulder the entire time?"

"I don't know."

"I usually hang my purse over the back of my chair," Susan suggested.

"I don't—no, I do remember. Because the room was so crowded and Anthony and I got there really early. I thought there would be empty seats and so I dumped my purse and coat on the chair next to mine."

"Where did you sit?"

"Right near the front of the room. I was there early," Theresa repeated.

"But your coat and purse were moved before Ivan appeared—when the crowd came in."

"Yes. And I either put my purse on the back of my chair—or just stuck it on the floor under my seat." She looked around the room apologetically. "I'm not a very neat person, I'm afraid."

"Purses are always a problem. Did you see anyone around your purse? Or looking like they might be putting something into it?"

Theresa frowned. "Not that I remember. But it was so confusing—especially after the lights went out and the speech was canceled."

"What do you remember about that evening?" Susan asked.

"Well, we got there early—I told you that—and Anthony went right upstairs. He wanted to be there to greet the other people on his ticket. I went right in to find a seat downstairs." She looked down at the center of her kitchen table as though examining the pile of mail that seemed to be a permanent centerpiece. "I was, I admit, anxious to see Ivan."

"Did you talk to anyone? Do you remember who sat down nearby?" Susan asked.

"I spoke with dozens of people—maybe more. Since Anthony began his campaign, everyone in town thinks they own a piece of my time."

"I know what you mean," Susan agreed.

"And who was sitting near you?" Erika insisted on sticking to the point.

"Neighbors on either side."

"And who behind?" Susan asked, thinking of the purse strung over the chair back.

Theresa shrugged. "I don't know. And almost anyone could have walked by my chair after the speech was canceled and stuck the pages in my purse. That place was mayhem. I'm sorry I can't be more helpful."

"It's okay," Susan said. "I think there's only one person who could be orchestrating this thing."

"The murder?"

"The murder. The cover-up. The election. The Landmark Commission. Everything," Susan said.

THIRTY-TWO

IT's NOT MUCH OF A VICTORY PARTY WHEN THE opposition candidate bowed out of the election almost twenty-four hours ago," Kathleen said, handing Susan a fresh glass of champagne.

"It's hard to run for mayor when you and your wife have been arrested for murder," Susan answered, a wide smile on her face. "And I think you're wrong. This is one of the best parties I've ever given. If this election had gone down to the wire, I'd be exhausted. As it is, both Jed and I got a wonderful night's sleep last night and I spent all day today puttering around, getting the house in order, and preparing for our guests tonight." She took a long sip from the slender goblet. "I haven't been this relaxed in weeks."

"How did it feel to cast a vote for a Henshaw?" Kathleen asked.

"Fabulous. And, of course, it's wonderful to vote for someone you know is going to win. That's not usually true for me in national and state politics these days."

"What is happening outside of Hancock this evening? Any election results in yet?"

"I have no idea. There's a large group around the television in the living room, but I've voted and I can wait until tomorrow to find out whether or not I was in the majority. Tonight I'm doing nothing but relaxing and celebrating." She drained her glass and leaned back against the window behind her.

The Anthony Martel victory party had been going on for two hours now and Susan and Kathleen had just found a quiet place to sit, tucked away on a window seat in Jed's study.

"Theresa looks better, doesn't she?"

"Not drinking, I hope?" Susan asked.

"I think she's gone on the wagon. She was sipping Perrier the last time I passed by."

"If only she had done that a few weeks ago . . ." Susan shook her head ruefully. "It sure would have made things easier."

"For you, but not for Cassandra Chadwick."

"True. Cassandra benefited from Theresa's drunkenness. Although I think killing Ivan and switching his speech with the one that she and her husband had made up was a pretty gutsy thing to do. And it was brilliant to stash Ivan's speech in Theresa's purse like she did."

"Hmm. I'd love to know if she planned that or if she just noticed Theresa's purse and took advantage of a God-given opportunity," Kathleen mused.

"She sure must have recognized that Theresa's drinking made it possible to manipulate her. I mean, it was one thing to stick the speech in Theresa's purse, but to move it when Theresa finally thought she had gotten rid of the damn thing was almost genius."

"When did you realize Cassandra was behind all that?"

"Cassandra," Susan answered, exasperation in her voice, "was behind everything. She was on local TV shows, fed stories to Tom Davidson and to every reporter from here to Hartford to New York City. She was the person who spoke with our neighbor about Jed not picking up after the dog and then fed the story to the newspaper. It was easy for her to do because she was so busy getting all the good publicity she could for her husband. She put the fake blood on Erika's bed and then—stupidly—put some on one of Jed's coats in my car."

"Why was that stupid?"

"Because she was trying to scare me off. She knew the police would check it out and discover that it wasn't real blood, but she thought she could fool me—first into thinking it was blood and then into believing that Jed might have had something to do with Erika's disappearance. Of course, I would never believe Jed had anything to do with a murder. Besides, she risked being seen both at my car and at Erika's carriage house."

"Not at the carriage house. I think Brett worked very hard to keep everyone—including his own officers—away from the carriage house."

"And Erika," Susan agreed.

The two women were silent for a few moments. "You know," Susan began quietly, "Brett really screwed up this one."

Kathleen nodded. "He sure did."

"If he had properly sealed the crime scene as soon as he arrived at the Women's Club, the speech would have been found immediately and everyone would have realized that only Bradley Chadwick had a reason to want Ivan Deakin dead before he had a chance to deliver that speech."

"Has he said anything to you about that?" Kathleen asked.

"No. Actually, that's the reason I thought he might appear tonight."

"Any word from Erika?"

"Yes. She called this morning and said thank you for all that I'd done to help her. And then this afternoon that fabulous bouquet that's in the middle of the dining-room table was sent out from her store."

"Nice."

"You know, it is. The only person who's been calling is Tom Davidson. He's planning what he called 'extensive coverage' of the murder and now the arrest—and later a trial."

"We must know someone who works for a network," Kathleen said. "It's time we got that young man a job in the city. His enthusiasm is wasted here."

"Good idea. There will be more dirt for him to report on there."

"Well, maybe not more, but it probably won't be about people you know well," Kathleen said, draining her glass and smiling at her friend.

"True, and that will be a relief," Susan agreed as Jerry and Jed wandered into the room, full glasses in their hands.

"So, congratulations," Susan said, leaning across the pile of dirty glasses to kiss her husband. "You're going to be a wonderful councilman. And I'm sure Anthony Martel will be an excellent mayor—the man is always working. I even overheard him talking with our guests tonight, asking them to serve on committees."

"Oh, he's hardworking all right." Jed bent down to drop silverware in the dishwasher and she couldn't see his face. "You know, all the council men and women head committees or act as liaisons to different departments in Hancock."

"I know. You thought you were going to be asked to work on some new public-relations schemes, didn't you? You'd be so good at that. And with your background in advertising, you certainly have more experience than any of the other councilmen."

"But that's not the committee that I'm going to run. In fact, I'm not going to run any committee." He stood up and looked at Susan. "You will never believe what task Anthony has asked me to take on. Something more up your alley than mine, I'm afraid."

Susan thought furiously, not speaking for a few minutes. "Something to do with the schools?"

"No, something that has taken up your time more recently than the PTA."

Susan was completely perplexed. "Jed, tell me. What?"

"I'm going to be liaison from the Hancock Town Council to the Hancock Police Department. It seems that Anthony was very impressed with the relationship between our family and the chief of police."

"Oh . . ." Susan said, her heart sinking. This wasn't what Jed had wanted to do.

"And he made one request."

"What?"

"He asked that you not investigate any murders in Hancock for the two years he's in office."

Susan scowled. "What did you say to that?"

Jed grinned. "I told him that one of the things I love about my wife is that she never, ever listens when I tell her what to do."

Don't miss Valerie Wolzien's other mystery series, featuring contractor Josie Pigeon and her all-female construction crew, starting with SHORE TO DIE.

For a glimpse of SHORE TO DIE, please read on . . .

SHORE TO DIE
by Valerie Wolzien

She stood still, hoping that she had imagined it, knowing that she hadn't. She forced her reluctant legs to walk to the door, which she closed carefully before returning to the pile of rubble. Praying that she had been mistaken, she bent down and lifted the blue plastic.

It was a body, all right, and not so right, he was dead.

Josie took a deep breath, vaguely surprised that she hadn't fainted. She dropped to her knees, pushed her hair over her shoulders, and lifted the cover higher for a closer look. The man was lying on his side in a fetal position with his face turned away from Josie. The back of his head had been smashed in, but taking a deep breath, Josie peered across the mass of splintered skull, bloody hair, and tissue that she didn't care to identify to look at his face.

She didn't know the man. That fact didn't bring her much relief. She stared at him for minutes until she heard footsteps in the hallway. Then she gently lay the cover back over the body, tucking it in as well as she could without actually touching him, and she turned slowly and stood up.

"We've got it!" Chris announced, joyfully entering the room. "And he's getting a divorce!"

"Who is?" Josie's mind was still on the person lying on the floor behind her.

"Jason, damn it! Who else would I be talking about? He says his marriage was a mistake. This is going to be my day," Chris exulted. "Not only are we getting the crane early today, but Jason is going to take the afternoon off and operate it for us—for nothing!"

"For nothing?"

"I mean we're not going to have to pay him anything. He'll do it as a personal favor."

Josie couldn't think of anything to say. In fact, she was discovering that she couldn't think very well at all. "That's nice," she managed through clenched teeth.

But Chris apparently didn't require a more enthusiastic response. "I told him I'd call back with an exact time. Do you think we'll be ready by ten, or is eleven o'clock more realistic?"

Josie suddenly realized that she was going to have to tell Chris about her discovery or else move the body before they started work. But she couldn't seem to think beyond the immediate question. "Eleven o'clock," she muttered, only knowing that the choice gave her an extra hour to do . . . whatever she decided to do.

"Great! I'll call him back." Chris whipped a portable phone from her back pocket.

Josie didn't know what to do. She wanted to be alone. She needed to be alone.

"Damn!" Chris frowned at the phone. "What is wrong with this thing? First it works and then it doesn't. Where the hell is the nearest phone?"

"Probably the liquor store," Josie muttered.

"It wouldn't be open this early."

"Yes." Josie knew she'd spoken too loudly. "He . . . they are. I noticed as I was driving by this morning. There's a very nice man there who let me use the phone yesterday. Just knock on the door. He'll let you in, and the phone is hanging on the wall."

"Are you okay?"

"Fine. Just a little keyed up at the thought of all we need to get done this week."

"Then I'd better make that phone call right away."

Josie just nodded, waiting until she was alone again to lean against the wall for much-needed support.

Her mind was beginning to focus. She had to save Island Contracting. A man had been killed on Island Contracting's building site. The business couldn't possibly survive being connected with murder at this point. They might have to stop working on this project and they couldn't start another. How would they survive without working? The company was too vulnerable. The women on her crew were too vulnerable. She was too vulnerable. She didn't know what to do—except make sure that no one knew about this until she had time to think. She opened the door carefully and looked out into the hallway. She was alone.

She couldn't leave the man here. She and Chris would tear out the wall where the window was to go, but as soon as that was done, the pile of trash would be removed. She had to move the body before that happened.

Better yet, she should move the body now, this minute, she decided, taking a deep breath and tugging the tarpaulin back again. (He had been a big man, but years of hard work had put muscles underneath her layer of fat.) Still, it would be difficult to lift him by herself. Josie ran from the room, knowing that no one would check if she made noise. Theirs was noisy work. Silence only meant a break.

All the rooms had been stripped of their furniture as soon as Island Contracting arrived on the job a few weeks ago, but a pile of T-shirts and ragged beach towels found in an abandoned linen closet had been saved. Rags were always useful. Josie just hadn't realized then exactly what they were going to be useful for. She pulled the largest towels from the shelf and, stuffing a T-shirt printed with exotic leaves and the assertion IF YOU'RE NOT WASTED, THE DAY IS back in place, hurried to the bedroom.

It took her longer to overcome her fear of touching a dead body than it took to roll it over onto the towels and drag it from the room.

At the end of the hallway and under the stairs to the third floor was a small room lined with cedar planks that had begun growing mold in the damp ocean air. The future of the space was as yet undecided, but Josie thought it would make a fine temporary morgue. She shoved the body in and closed the door. There was no reason for anyone to go in there.

She ran back to the bedroom, her heart beating wildly. No one would notice the streaks in the dust on the hallway floor. There wouldn't be order in this mess for a couple of days—if then.

Then the working day began.

For the next three hours all five Island Contracting women were busy. Evelyn came upstairs to report that she and Melissa had completed their other jobs and were working together on the first-floor bathroom. Three deliveries of materials were inventoried and accepted, the trash company picked up the full Dumpster and left an identical one in its place. The women working upstairs had removed the wall where the new window was to be installed, cleared the space of all litter and trash, and nailed jack studs and headers in place.

"Crane's here," Chris announced, looking out the window. "I was hoping we'd be able to get some lunch first," she added, glancing at her watch.

"Aren't you going down to see Jason?" Josie asked. She had become more relaxed as the morning continued and she got into the routine of work. But now that they had paused, she felt her panic returning.

"Maybe Betty should," Chris answered, her back to the other two women.

"No, you should," Josie insisted, becoming irritated. "If you've decided that you're more interested in that man at the liquor store, you can just wait until we have this window in to let your former heartthrob know about it."

Chris had a scowl on her face as she left the room.

"Maybe you should offer to go pick up lunch for everyone," Josie suggested to Betty.

"You want me to go into that greasy spoon again?" Betty asked.

"It won't leach into your body. You have to eat it for it to kill you," Josie insisted. "Be sure to ask Jason or whatever his name is if you can pick up anything for him. Lunch is the very least that Island Contracting owes him."

"I—"

"Could you do it right now?"

"I—"

"Right now. Please," she added, knowing she was being uncharacteristically abrupt.

Betty also wore an angry expression as she left the room, but Josie didn't care about the feelings of her employees at that moment. She was almost sure she'd heard the squeaky latch on the hall-closet door immediately after Chris had departed. Josie ran to the hole in the wall and stared down at the ground. She watched the scene until Betty and Chris had joined the group and, once she was ensured some privacy, ran out into the hallway and pulled open the closet door.

The space was empty.

Josie took a deep breath, forced herself to move, and walked into the closet, yanking the door shut behind her. There was a light around here somewhere. . . .

She waved her arms around until she brushed against the soft string that hung from the naked bulb on the ceiling. She pulled and discovered that the light was only a few inches from her head.

She blinked her stunned eyes and peered around. No body. For a few seconds she doubted her own sanity. Was it possible that she had imagined the whole thing? Had the strain of owning her own company driven her crazy?

Josie shook her head and a bit of her old sanity returned. Of course she hadn't made up the whole thing. The man had been here and now he was gone. Just like he had been in the bedroom . . .

The answer was simple. Someone had moved him. Again.

Shore to Die
by Valerie Wolzien

Published by Fawcett Books.
Available in your local bookstore.

VALERIE WOLZIEN PRESENTS

Josie Pigeon—proud proprietor of the
all-women Island Contracting and
Susan Henshaw—America's favorite
domestic detective.

Published by Fawcett Books.
Available in your local bookstore.